The Cowboy Charm

The Cowboy Charm

A Coyote Cowboys of Montana Romance

Sinclair Jayne

TULE
PUBLISHING

The Cowboy Charm
Copyright© 2024 Sinclair Jayne
Tule Publishing First Printing, February 2024

The Tule Publishing, Inc.

ALL RIGHTS RESERVED

First Publication by Tule Publishing 2024

Cover design by Lee Hyat Designs

No part of this book may be used or reproduced in any manner whatsoever without written permission except in the case of brief quotations embodied in critical articles and reviews.

This is a work of fiction. Names, characters, places, and incidents are products of the author's imagination or are used fictitiously. Any resemblance to actual events, locales, organizations, or persons, living or dead, is entirely coincidental.

AI was not used to create any part of this book and no part of this book may be used for generative training.

ISBN: 978-1-961544-98-7

Dear Reader

My mother died in January 2023. We were very close, and she'd been in ill health for quite a few years, and yet she remained zesty about life up until the very end—literally the end. She was arguing with me about end-of-life care. It was devastating and yet hilarious and so *her* at the time, but there were no more medical interventions; and with good insurance and a strong pension plan and a love of life and a driving curiosity about everyone and everything, she had tried them all.

I had a writers' retreat in Canmore, Alberta Canada, scheduled for a couple of weeks after my mom's passing, and I had planned on canceling, and yet my husband and kids and Jane Porter, my longtime bestie, and Tule publisher, pushed for me to go. Jane, Megan Crane and Carla (CJ Carmichael) and I were going to plan out our 85th Copper Mountain Rodeo series for Tule Publishing. It was part of Tule's 10 Year Anniversary celebration (The 75th Copper Mountain Rodeo, was a multi-author series). During the retreat, everyone, including me, expected me to lose it at some point, and yet I was weirdly giddy—I think because the last few years had been so stressful with late-night phone calls when my mom was having a panic attack or had called 911. And then the multitude of doctor appointments and health scares and feeling on call all the time made me uncomfortable planning anything, and yet, I still tried to live my life, drop my kids off at college, run our small tasting room, write and edit and travel for work and pleasure even as I braced for all plans to be canceled or juggled at the last minute.

While Megan sweetly and doggedly tried to teach me how to knit—I am still an epic fail, but vow to learn someday soon—I was trying to explain my breathless excitement about being away, surrounded by such beauty and friendship and creativity. I thought I should feel guilty and sad, and yet I felt bursting out of my skin alive, taking picture after picture that I'd have to stop myself from texting to my mom as she loved to have the outside world brought to her when she was no longer as mobile. Jane advised to the effect, you should write about your feelings, capture the experience and use your conflicting emotions to create a story to explore your feelings.

The Cowboy's Charm is the fourth book in my Montana Coyote Cowboys series. The premise of the series is that former Special Forces soldiers go to Marietta, Montana, to fulfill a vow to their fallen team leader. I had brainstormed with Jane months earlier over scrambled eggs on the San Clemente Pier what sorts of amends or good deeds the soldiers, who had all grown up ranch and were determined to work on the land again, could do. We had a list of twelve things that I whittled down to six or seven that I thought would work well in books. Fulfilling community service hours was vague, but could provide a lot of conflict, tension and growth if set up right. And as I sat with these three talented women drinking tea—or it might have been wine with Carla—discussing our rodeo books, I decided that I would make the hero of my fourth book, Ryder Lea, a forced volunteer in Marietta's May Bell Center.

Years ago Carla invented the May Bell Center, and it had been used in a couple of books, so I asked permission to make some add-ons to the center so that it could be built out to serve my evolving premise so that my heroine, a physical therapist, and my hero cowboy and volunteer would be stuck together. This is where the magic of a book happens for me. Who are they, why are they there, how is this the worst place they could be (and yet the best), and why don't they get along, and what do they want and what's stopping them from achieving their goal, and how do they help the other person to learn what they need to learn?

For years my mom lived in a retirement facility down the hill from my house. First in a new, upscale, top-floor apartment with my dad, then a cottage because she wanted a patio so she could garden, then a different apartment she redecorated in the main building so she didn't have to drive to dinner or activities. It was interesting watching my parents age. They chose to enter 'Hillside.' And even with financial independence and health insurance and having my parents and then just my mom close, I felt like I couldn't breathe some days. I had to make hard decisions and try to find the best path forward and wow, did I have to juggle all the moving pieces of my life to help care for my mom. But as I watch other family members age and become infirm while their adult children struggle to help them while still parenting their own children or grandchildren and try to navigate a path forward, I realized how universal my emotional experience had been—different, but yet the psychic punch felt similar.

With *The Cowboy's Charm*, I wanted to explore the experience of two very different people, facing a similar situation, and how by working together, they can find the hope and the humor, and the humanity as well as forgiveness—and of course they fall crazy in love while they are attempting to remain impervious to that mischievous cupid hovering about with his quiver of arrows.

Dedication

I'd like to dedicate *The Cowboy's Charm* to Jane Porter, CJ Carmichael and Megan Crane, who listened and inspired. And also to two friends and assistants who helped my mom, befriended her, kept her entertained, and were always present and kind and respectful during the years and hours they worked with her—even on the days when she wasn't. Thank you Nicole Anderson and Ann-Marie Powell.

Prologue

THE DYING SIROCCO screeched and wailed at awkward intervals like a grieving mother. Ryder Lea winced. He rarely indulged in melodrama and never self-reflection, but today just might be the exception.

Warily he eyed his Coyote Cowboy Special Forces brothers. Were they waiting for him to crack a joke to ease the tension that clawed through them all? It was a role he'd adopted since childhood, but making light of this moment, this reality felt sacrilegious. All of them stood at attention waiting for the command to load the flag-draped coffin of their team leader, the best man Ryderhad ever known, on his final journey home.

He'd been proud to call Jace McBride friend, and had yearned to emulate him, but he couldn't indulge his grief. He was the light. Quick with a joke, a prank, or a throwaway line designed to recenter the team. Bond them.

He was the man who took nothing seriously.

Or so they thought.

But Ryder felt trapped alone in this new dark, and none of his brothers—waiting to pick up the remains of Jace's body—presented any better.

Cross looked like an old man about to puke out his large intestine and wrap it around his neck to hang himself.

Huck's eyes remained closed, perhaps in prayer that had gone unanswered.

Reluctant and temporary new team leader Wolf Conte looked more isolated than usual.

Rohan Telford was grim as the grim reaper shuffling home with his final soul of the night.

And Calhoun—the Big O Miller—looked like Duke, the Belgian Malinois he'd worked with for six years: focused, smelling trouble and poised to alert or attack. But the beautiful beast was not by his side. Maybe he never would be again. The loyal soldier had been injured in the firefight that had killed Jace. Calhoun had saved Duke's life long enough to get the warrior evacuated to medical care, but his career was over, and Calhoun looked like he'd had a limb amputated.

Shame rushed over Ryder. He hadn't been with his team. He'd been benched because he'd been stupid. And a beer over his limit on the unexpected night off when he'd finished his mission early. His easy success should have made him suspicious, not heady and definitely not relaxed. He couldn't remember a time when he'd loosed his control. He'd lived his life on the edge.

Wolf growled the first command, and all six of them grabbed a brass handle. Again, on Wolf's command, they lifted as one and walked Jace from the hangar to the conveyer belt that would carry him deep into the belly of the cargo plane. They all watched the slow progression of Jace's flag-draped coffin into the dark and then they ducked back into the safety of the hangar. There was a break in the storm—only hours before another would bellow heat, sand and doom down their necks, but no, Rohan had a six-pack of beer—ridiculous logo—a moose in a ski suit or something like that. It was tradition. When a team member mustered out, or transferred or died, they were saluted with their favorite beer. Moose Drool was Jace's although Jace, a master brewmeister as far as the Coyote Cowboys were concerned, had likely just been messing with them. One last laughing middle finger to his devoted team.

A moment like this was when Ryder would usually take a swig of beer and make a joke. He'd developed his jokester persona as a kid, hoping to dodge fists and kicks and protect his sisters from the stepdad of the moment. Sometimes it had even worked, and when he'd entered the service after struggling through his GED, he'd excelled at cutting tension.

Until today.

One more way he'd failed Jace and his team.

"It's time," Wolf intoned and pulled Jace's bloodied helmet out of his duffel. There were scraps of paper inside. They were to each pick one. A task. Or an amend. And complete it in Jace's honor. No matter what it was. No matter how long it took. No matter how impossible.

Dread pooled in his gut, but like everything hard, he

took a step forward, willing to go first.

No matter how much he wanted to rewind time, he couldn't save Jace, but he could have his death mean something. He could take Jace's advice. Make a goal. Live his life. Invest finally in himself. Let someone in. Trust someone.

Ryder picked the folded piece of paper and waited for his brothers. As one, they looked down and read.

Ryder pocketed his slip of paper unread. He'd intended to follow Jace to Marietta, Montana, in a few months after his last stint was up, but that was before Jace's brutal death. Jace had spoken about his hometown so reverently. He'd made the town sound magical, like it was frickin' Disneyland. Not that Ryder had ever been to the theme park. But Jace had implied miracles could happen in Marietta. Redemption. Resurrection. Like a man could become anyone he wanted.

And Ryder had always wanted to be someone else.

Jace was maybe the only person who'd seen through him and had welcomed him anyway. He'd made him promise to join him in Marietta, and Ryder always kept his promises.

"Hey," Calhoun busted up his glum thoughts. "Need a solid."

His voice was barely a whisper. They'd all trained to be as noticeable as wraiths, a whisp of candle smoke in a dark room, but Calhoun had been better at it than most.

"Anything."

Calhoun handed him something metal on a chain.

"Guard it for Jace 'til I'm stateside."

Ryder didn't even look at the object, just tucked it in a small, zippered pocket in his combat pants where he kept his extra Ka-bar 5020 Fixed Blade Knife.

"With my life," Ryland said, but didn't have the stomach to meet Big O's intense golden-brown gaze.

"I might need another solid."

"Anything."

Absolutely. Anything.

"I'm tapped for something with Wolf."

Ryder did look at Calhoun then, but he asked no questions. He may have miscalculated on his last assignment, but need-to-know was ingrained in their bones.

"I'm mustering out later than I thought due to a mission that might have more legs."

Ryder nodded. Sometimes missions went south. Other times they extended, and you only thought you saw the light at the end of the tunnel.

"I'm approved to keep Duke."

Ryder caught his breath, his heart leapt, and though he thought he'd never smile again, he did and gripped Calhoun's shoulder.

"Good news. The Duke pulled through." Best news in a long time. The dog was a soldier and part of their team, though Calhoun had been his handler.

They'd all felt sick when Duke had taken a hit alongside Jace and Huck. He was one of their own. It wasn't uncommon for a handler to get to adopt his dog after their service was completed, but it also wasn't guaranteed. The dog was considered a noncommissioned officer and property of the Department of Defense.

"A former soldier in Texas is rehabbing him, retraining him for civvy life. He'll keep him for me until I'm out and ready, but if and when Duke is healed up and graduates his program before I'm out or if I…"

Ryder suddenly didn't know where to look.

"I'd prefer him to be with you, with family."

His eyes burned. Family. The word just busted open the bottomless well in his empty heart. He'd always envied Calhoun having Duke. He and the soldier had had a mystical connection, and the soldier had saved them and hundreds of civilians over the years.

"If something happens…"

"Yes. Absolutely," Ryder interrupted, not giving his brain time to process the words or form an image of Calhoun on the ground, bloodied, never again rising up.

"Life's better with a dog," he quipped, something Calhoun always said. "Especially when we're the dogs."

Calhoun stared him down, and Ryder forced himself to face Calhoun, expecting to see blame. Anger. Resentment. He hadn't been at Jace's six.

Instead he saw trust and felt gutted.

'Let go of whatever happened and take the first step forward and then another,' was something Jace used to say.

Jace wasn't the only one needing to make amends.

Chapter One

EDISON MARTIN STARED at her reflection in her grandma's antique full-length cherry mirror. She'd loved this mirror as a child—watching her grandma adjust her slip under her home-sewn dress, braid her hair, tie her scarf and then she'd smile at her. 'What do you think? Am I ready to face the world?'

Edi frowned at her tan scrubs, long, angular body and hair slicked back into a low bun.

Was she ready to face the world?

Nope.

She wasn't even ready to face her new reality—her grandma's failing health, her new job in a new town, in what felt like a completely new field—something she'd avoided during her extensive training but had to learn to embrace or she and her grandma could lose everything.

Some days it felt like she already had.

Edi squared her shoulders. Her grandma has always been strong and there for her. She would not let her down.

"I got this."

She turned away from her reflection and flipped off the bedroom light, trying not to read any symbolism into being swallowed by the dark. She was strong. She was smart. She'd survived the worst thing life could shove in her path.

She shrugged into her parka, packed her tennis shoes and Dansko clogs into her tote, along with an apple and a bag of mini carrots, and checked that her charger and iPad were tucked into the protective cover. She stepped into her new, heavy winter boots and braced herself for the shock of breath and mind-stealing cold.

"And I thought Seattle winter weather sucked," she muttered, locking the door behind her though there was very little to steal. True this was a small town, not a hotbed of crime, but she couldn't afford to replace any of the worn, but once cherished furniture and knickknacks.

Edi would rather walk to work, but instead she drove the several blocks to the May Bell Center as the dark, heavy clouds promised more snow. Since she was salaried, she didn't have to clock in. Instead, she gathered her exercise equipment at the center's main gym and ran up the flight of stairs, taking them two at a time, the small, blue exercise balls in net sack bounced lightly against her butt.

She didn't want to be late her third day on the job. She had trained at one of the best PT programs in the country and no matter what life threw at her, she was a professional—even if no clients showed up to her group exercise class for the new residents of the assisted living wing. Today, she was going to hustle up a few clients before she lost her mind to boredom. Or worse, her job.

Geriatrics and indifference were not what she'd signed up for as she'd worked her way through her doctorate in physical therapy, but Edi had been trying to make lemonade out of very sour lemons her whole life. By thirty-six she thought she'd be better at it, but the last two years had thrown her into a tailspin, and she still felt wobbly.

"Excuse me, dear." A matter-of-fact voice startled her, halting her momentum and some of the balls in the bag twisted between her legs awkwardly. She staggered, and the frail elderly lady reached out a steady hand, which Edi dodged. She didn't want to take down a potential client and cause a hip fracture her first week. She was here, if not to heal, at least to slow the ravages of time.

Edi stepped over the balls and then lifted the bag over her shoulder again like an exercise-enthusiast Santa.

"Oh, Mrs. Johanson." Edi smiled in greeting. "Are you coming to exercise class? We'll be starting in five minutes." She smiled brightly.

Please come. Please come. Please come.

She just needed one. She could build from that. Edi had trained to work with one client at a time, and while she'd trained to work with clients of all ages, for the past nearly ten years in Seattle, she'd specialized on working with neurodivergent children.

Geriatrics would take some getting used to.

And I will become awesome in geriatrics.

She had to be. Her gran's well-being depended on it.

Mrs. Johanson blinked at her. Silent. Observing. And Edi felt a frisson of... She wasn't sure.

"Is that a dead body?"

"What? No. Of course not. It's ummmm..." Why was she so rattled? "Balls," she said, belatedly realizing she was staring at the older woman.

Two more slow blinks and Edi felt like she was eight again being dressed down by her mother for getting dirt on her tights.

"Surely that's not appropriate, dear."

Edi stifled a snort. Really? An off-color joke? Maybe her grandmother hadn't been teasing when she used to say she still felt twenty-five inside even though the mirror had said sixty, seventy, eighty, before her mind had slowly started abandoning her.

Edi didn't know too much about Mrs. Johanson yet, but perhaps she too was in the early stages of some form of cognitive decline. Edi's heart pinched in sympathy and fear.

Don't think about that.

"For group exercise class." She smiled brightly as if that would banish the fear of bad news. "I hope you're coming."

Mrs. Johanson's lip curled. "Exercise." She made it sound like a curse. She jabbed a finger toward Edi. "I want to know what happened to his body."

Whose body?

Her heart sped up in alarm, even though she knew she was being ridiculous. This was Marietta, Montana, not

Seattle. And Mrs. Johanson had a farming family who were helping to cover the cost of her assisted living apartment. She was not part of a big-city crime syndicate.

"Ummmm, Mrs. Johanson?" Edi felt her grip on the bag of balls loosen.

"How would you get rid of a body. Two of them maybe although I hope not. Surely not the boy."

Edi peered past Mrs. Johanson's frail form, almost too nervous to look inside her apartment, even though she knew, absolutely, her suspicions were absurd. Still, goose bumps pimpled the back of her neck.

"People bury bodies, but where?" Mrs. Johanson pointed at Edi again. "Is there a garden here where you could bury a body?"

Edi dropped the bag and the small-size yoga balls bounced and rolled joyously down the carpeted hallway.

RYDER LEA HAD never stood in front of a judge before. He probably should have. Definitely more than once. But he'd been lucky. And charming, often able to smile and twist himself out of trouble.

The judge's young clerk clicked around on her computer.

"I thought everything had been digitized by now," the judge said, rather fussily.

The clerk looked frazzled, and she kept sneaking nervous

looks at Ryder and blushing.

He smiled—the dazzling one he'd pull out on occasion in an off-base bar when he didn't have a place to stay for the night and didn't want to be alone with his own company. All bars were off base now. And after his last fiasco, which had left him grounded and not on Jace's six, Ryder had no intention of entering even a stateside bar until his promise to Jace was fulfilled.

He'd been in Marietta, Montana, for less than an hour, and in that time, he'd bought a coffee and bacon, egg and cheese sandwich at a place called the Java Café. He'd eaten in his truck, not liking all the suspicious side-eyes he received in the cutesy-cute café as locals tried to place 'the stranger.' Heck yeah, he was dressed like a cowboy—let lightning dare to strike him down. He had the boots that Wolf Conte had bought them from some boot-making outfit outside his hometown Whiskey River, Texas. Bit fancy for his taste, but why not? He'd grown three sizes in the service so his boots from his teen years working a dude ranch for spoiled rich families and their snotty offspring outside Ogallala, Nebraska, had long ago stopped fitting.

He'd bought a used truck in Bozeman and had gone to an outlet store and bought some western work wear geared for the harsh Montana winters, but he wasn't all that confident that he'd be able to swing a job on a ranch or with a stock contractor in January. His ranching résumé was pretty thin and pretty far in his rearview. But he'd find something.

He had to. He didn't have a huge savings or any family to fall back on, although until this month he regularly divided up most of his paycheck to deposit into the college accounts he'd set up for his two nieces and nephew though he'd never met them.

He'd headed directly to Marietta, determined to carry out Jace's request. He had three of his army Coyote Cowboys living and working near Jace's hometown. They might have a lead on employment though he was uncertain what his commitment to Jace entailed. Jace had said he was a 'wild one' in high school. No worries. He'd clear Jace's slate then build his new life. Maybe in Marietta like he'd promised—although working with Jace to get his family's ranch financially in the black again had been the original goal.

But he wanted ranch work—physical, long hours, outdoors, purposeful. If he could get a job with a stock contractor, he'd be dealing with animals more than people, and he'd be traveling half the year, and that appealed. He didn't have much experience with putting down roots. Nebraska didn't call to him, and he hadn't seen much of the United States he'd spent years protecting except army bases. Working with animals and seeing the country sounded like the perfect combination.

"Are old records kept in file boxes in the basement?" he asked only half facetiously.

The young clerk giggled and blushed more furiously. "They are. Maybe we should go look together."

And probably get arrested. How old was she anyway? She looked like a high school kid working on Christmas break, but by end of January students would be safely back in school—at least he thought so. He'd never been one of those regular kids.

"Cherise, hardly," the judge said repressively. "You are doing an internship in law and government this semester. You head to the basement, and I'll interview...ahhhh Master Ser..."

"Ryder's fine," Ryder interrupted, regretting that he'd showed the judge any papers from his service, but he thought it would help him to appear more legit, coming in without an appointment and asking about completing the eighteen-year-old community service hours of a dead man.

"So why again are you wanting to fulfill the community service hours of local hero Jace McBride?"

"It was a promise we all made, sir. Your Honor." That was what he was called, right?

Clearly the judge wanted more.

"Jace was due home, Your Honor, but he ran a mission that was his last, Your Honor. We found a list he'd made of things he wanted to settle when he came home to his ranch and started his new chapter of civilian life in Marietta, Your Honor."

Maybe he was laying it on a bit thick, but Ryder had been raised to be polite, at least he'd been terrorized into it and then later, coaxed before his nana couldn't remember his name much less a please or a thank you.

Had the judge known Jace? He certainly looked old enough. Jace had said he'd seen some trouble when he'd been a teen, but Ryder had only met the responsible, loyal get the job done and take care of his men Jace.

"Admirable but, son, you have served our country for twelve years. You don't need to take on another man's service debt."

"It will be my honor, Your Honor." The words sounded unbearably formal, yet true.

"Surely you must have family to see, a home to visit, news to catch up on, friends."

His heart squeezed, but he ignored it. "No family, no home, Your Honor. Got some friends in Marietta. Aim to honor my commitments. Make my own way and stay."

Ryder Lea was no one's burden.

The sympathy on the judge's face was as unexpected as it was unsettling. No one ever felt sorry for him, and Ryder had never had use for pity.

"What's a few more hours before I start my next adventure?" he asked cockily.

"I found it, Grandpa Neil," the clerk, make that intern, returned waving a piece of paper.

"Jace McBride fined two hundred fifty hours of community service. Looks like you'll be in town more than a few days, Mr. Officer. Soldier. Sir?" She blushed merrily.

"OH, NO." EDI scrambled for the balls, terrified an octogenarian would choose this time to shuffle down the corridor and stumble, but instead she tripped over another ball that rolled between her feet as she lurched forward straight into a wall of solid muscle.

"Good morning to you too."

The smile was as dazzling as the sun, and he knew it. Deeply tanned face meant he likely was a visitor from more tropical regions. Sparkling blue eyes like sapphires, and shaggy dark-honey-colored hair waving back from his face that looked more magazine rugged than real.

"Wha...?" Edi tried to form words as she stared at the apparition of masculine health and amusement. "Whooooo...?"

"Ryder Lea. Temporary stumbling-woman and ball catcher."

"Ahhhhh." Edi clung to his hewn forearms like she'd been tossed into a storm, even as her mind repeatedly yelled to let go of him.

"Steady?"

Hardly. She was a lurching disaster. Some physical therapist she was.

"Huh?" She couldn't get over his masculine beauty and the warm energy that radiated like the sun. She felt thawed out and almost expected to turn into a puddle of DNA goo on the floor.

"You good?" The smile was knowing, and his eyes appraised her, and she knew how lacking she was in the appeal to masculine fabulousness market.

"I'm staring, aren't I?"

"Yes." Again that beautiful smile.

This must happen to him all the time. Women stumbling over their feet as he sauntered by. Cars braking hard, driven into bushes rear-ending the car in front. There should be a warning siren before the man was let loose in public. His eyes creased in the corners, creating lines that skewered his Montana mountain top chiseled cheekbones.

"Sorry." She grabbed for some dignity but still didn't let go of him.

"I wasn't expecting anyone under eighty to be walking this hall." She strove to sound wry although her mother had repeatedly reminded her that humor, charm and grace eluded her as did most anything else femininely appealing.

"Yet here I am." He spread his arms wide. "Ryder Lea at your service."

Edi barely refrained from rolling her eyes. "Why?"

"I'm a helper," he answered with another grin that belonged on a cereal box. He took the net bag from her limp fingers and quickly gathered the balls—creatively spinning a few on his fingers or bouncing one back into the bag with his head. His hands were huge. He could palm the darn things like they were baseballs, making her feel petite by comparison, which rarely happened since she was five-eleven and too solid to ever be a model. He had a large, olive-green duffel bag swung over his shoulder like it weighed nothing.

"Young man." Mrs. Johanson stepped forward. "You got a dead body in that bag?" She got up from the seat on her walker with the help of her red cane with the glittery flower stickers Edi had purchased from an arts and craft store in Bozeman on her last supply run in hopes of engaging with her gran and some of the residents.

She waved the cane at the duffel bag.

"It is not, ma'am."

"How much would you charge for getting rid of a body?"

Edi swallowed her sigh and tried to ignore the wave of weirdness that rolled over her.

"Depends." Ryder scratched his cheek with his thumb.

Edi glared at him.

"On what?" Mrs. Johanson asked curiously while Edi wished for the gift of telepathy so she could tell the way too handsome and sexy stranger to shut up and not encourage this flight of crazy.

"Big body? Little body? Where is it? Where you want me to put it?" He listed possibilities as if he'd given this nonexistent—hopefully—body problem some thought.

It was cruel to mock the seniors, and Edi wondered if she could subtly kick him. Or stomp on his toe, but his boots looked shiny new in contrast to his worn Wranglers, and she didn't want to scuff them.

Oh, for the days when she could buy herself a new pair of new ankle boots with a chunky heel.

"If you had a body to hide, where would you hide it?" Mrs. Johanson set her stance, both hands on her cane. Clearly she planned to continue grilling Ryder Lea, unanticipated gift to octogenarians and lonely physical therapists.

Lonely? I'm not lonely.

She'd always enjoyed her own company.

"Depends on the terrain. I'm new in the area. You got a body you need me to take care of for you?"

Why was he raising one of those model-thick eyebrows beautifully one tone darker than his hair at her as if asking her opinion? Did he think this was a joke?

"No, she does not," Edi snapped, feeling like she had to reel Mrs. Johanson back to reality. "And it's not polite to play pretend with the clients."

"Who says I'm pretending?" He smiled, and the light in his eyes flipped a switch down low in her body that she'd thought permanently extinguished. "Man's got to eat."

The smile he delivered felt like a zap to her clit, and she nearly squeaked in prudish outrage because he didn't seem to be talking about food. Men didn't flirt with her, but she was disturbed that something inside her wished he would.

No. She was done with all that. Dead inside.

Edi pressed her thighs together.

"Do you like pretending?"

How did he make the question sound so dirty? Maybe it

was the unholy light in his eyes, his smile, his…his…his everything—the energy rolled off him like the waves of the Pacific crashing on the shores of Diamond Beach in Laguna where she'd once written absurdly broody, 'feel sorry for me' poetry in high school. Ugh, she wanted to snatch her bag of balls back, take a whack at him for being so sexy and beautiful and herself for being so dumb.

"No," she said. "Certainly not. I have a job to do."

"So do I."

What job could this off-the-charts sexy Romeo possibly have here? She pressed her lips together to keep from saying something rude or, worse, revealing. She didn't know who he was—maybe he owned the place, and she needed, absolutely needed this job. Wanting it was a different matter.

His smile hit her like a slap, dazing her senses. "You must be Edison Martin?"

"Edi," she corrected automatically.

"That's cute. Like Edie Brickell and the New Bohemians. My nana loved that song 'What I Am.' She used to sing it all the time when she was gardening, and cooking. Taught me how to harmonize."

He actually started singing the chorus and dancing a little, spinning one of the blue balls on the tip of his finger, which she didn't even know was possible. How could he be so unself-conscious? Although to be fair, he was staggeringly handsome, and charm wafted off him like a really expensive, pheromone-laden fragrance. Naturally he had a fantastic singing voice because life was inherently unfair, and the universe loved to mock her with her own shortcomings.

"How do you know my name?" she demanded and belatedly held out her hand for the bag of exercise balls. "What are you doing here, Mr.—" How could she have forgotten his last name already? Probably because his smile was so beautiful it had fried her brain.

"Ryder."

Yes, please.

Edi nearly slapped herself. What was wrong with her? She was like the anti-sex. She hadn't had a fantasy since…better not go there.

"I'm your assistant."

Edi stared at him in numb horror.

He smiled as if he knew he was catnip to her humiliating suddenly feral feline.

"You're welcome."

Chapter Two

"IT'S IMPOSSIBLE," EDI announced at the end of her shift, relieved that the center's director, Holly Castillo, was still in her office.

True, she was slouched at her desk, eyes closed and rubbing her temples.

"Headache?" Edi asked sympathetically. "You want me to help with some pressure points on your palm?"

"I'm fine." Holly jerked up like Edi had pulled a string. Holly's dark eyes were wide, and her gaze slid guiltily toward the wall, and Edi saw two black pumps tumbled into a corner.

Yikes those were high heels. She'd topple over if she tried those, and shoe designers probably made very few cute, sexy stilettos in size ten.

"Sorry, what's impossible?" Holly clutched her hands together as if worried Edi would grab them and start some vigorous, painful massage.

"He's impossible."

Holly blinked at her like she had come in on the tail end of a conversation instead of at the beginning.

"Like this." Edi splayed out her left hand and, with the

thumb and forefinger of her right hand, she gently pinched the webbing and slowly massaged. "It's called LI-4 or Hegu, and it can help with pain and headaches. I can demonstrate," she offered, but Holly looked defensive. "Sorry. I'm just so used to putting my hands on everyone." Edi tried to make light of the awkward moment that she'd unleashed like air in a balloon, and it was threatening to thrash around the room, taking up even more space.

"That's a good line to use in Grey's."

"I don't go into bars," Edi denied, horrified by the thought. She knew no one in town except her gran, and she was definitely not looking for a man. Her stomach went acid.

"Why not? Grey's has great music, a good selection of microbrews, wines and a bartender who can make any cocktail ever invented, when he's in the mood—which is never, but Jason Grey can make it with an exquisite scowl. And he's got a hot nephew named Reese."

TMI. Edi nearly put her hands up in a time-out, but she stopped. Holly was probably her age. Or younger. And she too was single in a small, nowhere western town that was cold enough to freeze bones, and if one more person told her winter had barely started, she was going to strangle them—not that she could with all the neck layers people had to wear.

"And the cowboy energy." Holly's smile went sly, and she closed her eyes again, this time looking more blissed than stressed. "And pool and darts and did I mention cowboys?

What's not to love? But who's impossible?"

"Him."

"Who?" Holly asked innocently.

"I don't want to say it. It's like Voldemort. I'll summon him or something worse."

"Worse?" Holly sat forward in her seat. "I'm sorry, Edi, you'll have to be more specific. Which client was specifically difficult?"

Edi's mouth dropped open. Client? She would never complain about a client—and today she'd seen plenty. "Not a client. Ryder. The volunteer," she said sourly. "He's impossible."

"How so?"

"He's…he's…" Hot. Distracting. Bossy. Arrogant. So many adjectives jumbled her mind, tumbling in an attempt to escape. "Pervasive."

"Pervasive?" Holly played with the word, thoughtfully.

"He totally took charge. We met in the hall, and he started banging on doors, shouting orders like some kind of drill sergeant, and soon he had nine of the twelve residents lining up behind us like ducks, and he barked questions about favorite ice creams, television shows and most intense movie villain and best Bond while they—no joke—marched to the exercise and therapy room. Well, it was sort of a shuffling march."

"That sounds sort of cute. Did you get pictures for marketing?"

"No," Edi said. "I was trying to get everything back under control. And he and his bossiness didn't stop there."

Edi frowned at the memories of how she'd started the gentle chair stretches while Ryder encouraged everyone and prowled the room, examining the equipment and scrolling through his phone like an overgrown, rangy and way too hopped up on hormones teenager.

"And then he switched activities like he was in charge of anything," Edi expostulated, fully in Holly's office now and pacing.

"He opened a box—unasked—and pulled out some exercise bands that he then slid over everyone's ankles—without consent or asking me for permission or instructions and then set up this sort of ricochet game. Then he swiped trash cans from a few rooms and set them up as targets in different positions around the room."

"Oh." Holly brightened. "The new exercise bands I ordered a few days ago?"

Edi frowned. That was Holly's takeaway about Ryder's impossibleness?

"Yeah. He just took over and started using them in weird ways and doing tricks like he was trying out to be in the next YouTube or TikTok exercise influencer."

She snapped her fingers. That's it. "I think he wants to be an influencer. He's using us. He could be posting videos about the center without permission. And he's way too young."

"He's almost thirty-one."

Edi gulped. Way. Too. Young.

"He was distracting."

"Really?" Holly drawled sitting forward in her chair, and her eyebrows raised, but her expression wasn't what Edi had expected.

"He treated the clients like they were there for his amusement or like they were preschoolers—playing music and singing and playing a name game and then games with letters as they tried to hook the ball back to him."

"I looked in a couple of times, and it seemed like everyone was having fun," Holly said.

Edi plopped down in a chair.

"The clients seemed challenged and engaged, and Ryder seemed like he was enjoying interacting with them," Holly added.

Edi gripped the chair on either side of her thighs. "He was," she said bitterly. "But…"

"You told me that you'd had trouble getting the clients to come to the group exercise class."

"Yes, but it's new and…"

"And today they came."

"Well yes," Edi admitted. "But I had a plan to market the class."

Sort of. She'd explored some online options for making flyers.

"But now you don't have to because you and Ryder had

a successful class, and you can build on that."

"But…" She stared at Holly, dismayed.

"And Ryder did take some pictures and a few videos, which he showed me, and I had him forward to the marketing department with permission—all the clients sign a photo release when they attend the May Bell's adult day care program and now the assisted living wing," Holly said, firmly. "There was even a picture of you smiling at him."

Edi felt the prickle of color wash across her face.

"I would say that his first volunteer shift was a success."

Edi could barely swallow. More Ryder with his beautiful smile, sunshine energy, teasing, flirting, jokes, genre-bending playlists and phone scrolling while she was trying to explain something. More Ryder stripping down to a short-sleeved T-shirt so she could see the cut musculature of his arms, with the sleeve of tats and the hint of washboard abs when he exhorted the class to lean back in the chair and stretch out their legs. And the way his thighs strained against his jeans when he moved and his tight ass that just might rival Michelangelo's *David*.

No. She couldn't notice a man's ass, especially Ryder's.

No more trips to Italy.

No more men.

"But he's temporary, right? Just a few service hours." She could deal. She'd had worse. "I can't build a program with a man who's only going to be here for a few days or so. If that."

Ryder was playful. Too hands-on and sexy. He wasn't serious about anything. He wouldn't stick around. He rolled in, took over, gave a wink and a nod and he was gone.

Sort of like my father.

No wonder she disliked him.

"Two hundred fifty hours," Holly said, and each word was a nail in Edi's coffin of hope. "And he'll need to spread them out, since he's going to need to find other employment, but who knows." Holly brightened. "He might love it here and want to stay. I'm counting on you, Edi. You know how short-staffed we are. We need an activity director and at least one more assistant in the day program. And I'm trying to get an intern for you from one of the college programs. I should be able to swing it as we can provide housing and meals. But once the assisted living wing fills out, we will need another physical therapist on staff and an assistant, ideally two. Ryder's finished with the military. Maybe he'll like it here and be willing to do some training so that he can stay," Holly enthused.

"You're joking," Edi breathed.

"He's perfect."

Edi's mouth dropped open at that wildly off assessment.

"And currently free, which helps our bottom line. I'm sure all his energy, his male energy, is infectious. Use it to build on."

She stared at Holly, horrified. The director practically smirked, although she made a stab at looking innocent and professional.

Wait, was Holly—the director, her boss—teasing her?

Something unexpected stirred in her heart, and Edi battled against it. This was too important. The job and success were too important. Her gran's well-being was on the line, and Holly was making Ryder sound like a stud at a horse-breeding facility.

"Edi, I know geriatrics is not your specialty."

Far from it. Edi had steered away from the specialty during her schooling and training. She'd always wanted to work with neurodivergent children. Always until pediatrics became too painful, reminding her of all she'd lost and would never have.

"But we need you. The clients need you, and their goals are different from the children you were working with in Seattle. Here you are trying to keep mobility, and emotional health and engagement is just as important, if not more so than the physical."

"I know." Edi had never felt smaller. "But I have training, and I..."

"I'm not worried about your training, Edi."

The sympathy in her voice and expression had Edi's eyes inappropriately prickling.

"I'm fine," she said instinctively. Hadn't she been insisting she was fine for the past two years through she kept stumbling back to teeter on the lip of the pit that continually beckoned her to fall back in?

A rap on the doorframe near her had her jumping just as Ryder peered into Holly's office.

"You wanted to see me?"

RYDER KNEW HE shouldn't eavesdrop. It had been a useful tool as a kid to try to avoid trouble or prepare a defense for it. And he'd acquired high-tech listening skills in the army, but as an adult and a volunteer and a man trying to become a civvy, he knew it wasn't cool. But he'd been so stunned by Edi's total rejection of how hard he'd tried this morning in the exercise class. He felt like a kid again where everything he'd done had been wrong and criticized and belittled.

He'd worked his ass off in the army to become a highly trained asset, and to utterly fail as a volunteer while trying to honor Jace had been a blow. It had taken him more than a few minutes to rally and assess Edi's opinion.

She didn't like him.

He could deal with that.

He'd taken over.

Maybe. But she'd been running the class like a tentative zombie inducting new trainees.

But perhaps he had fallen back too much on his training. Sure, as a soldier he'd been trained to follow, but he'd also had to improvise in the field when things went sideways, and Edi's half-hearted attempts to engage the seniors had seemed doomed to failure. They needed to buy in. Be energized. Seeing the seniors shuffling, not making eye contact and not paying much attention had nearly killed him. He kept seeing his nana's decline even when he'd thought of games and activities to engage her before and after his long days at work trying to earn enough to support them. And at the dude ranch, he'd tried to anticipate everyone's needs and be everything to everyone so he'd get more tips. As a teen, he barely earned enough to pay for the one-bedroom apartment, buy nutritious food and the occasional small luxury like yarn so that she could knit until she forgot how.

He shook off the memories that crowded close and the claustrophobic feeling of inadequacy.

Edi's fair, freckled complexion flushed a furious pink when he rapped on the door.

Yeah. She was worried he'd overheard her litany of complaints. She should be ashamed for not even giving him a chance.

He smiled at her discomfort, and the pink cheeks went red, even blotching down her long neck to her prominent clavicles before disappearing in the color of the tan scrubs. She couldn't have picked a worse color for her complexion, but maybe it was a uniform provided by the May Bell Center. What color would suit her pale, freckled complexion and curiously colorless hair?

Oops he was staring.

"You asked me to stop by after I spoke with Mike in

maintenance?"

"Yes, Ryder, thank you." Holly cast a worried look at her shoes she'd kicked off and then smiled at Ryder. "How did it go?"

"With Mike? Fine." He shifted his attention to Edi, wondering if he'd really heard her sigh in relief or had just imagined it.

Edi blew out another breath and plucked at her top as if she was hot. The center was pretty warm. He'd had to strip down to a T-shirt during the group exercise class and then again later after clearing out ceiling vents in the assisted living wing and dining hall under Mike's supervision.

"He'll have the odd job for me since he's down to one part-time assistant. He called me Cowboy. Has a brother-in-law named Ryder and guess they don't get along too well." Ryder smiled at the memory. "I'm hoping to line up a job interview this week," he revealed, wondering if that announcement would send another whoosh of relief through the judgey Edi.

"I'm looking for part-time until I finish my volunteer hours—hopefully on a ranch." Rohan had texted him today telling him to meet him this evening along with Cross and Huck at some bar in a hotel called the Graff. He was hoping one of his brothers might have a line on a job or a suggestion of where he could look. Part-time was fine this winter, but he'd need full-time by spring for sure.

He'd be fine as a ranch hand, but becoming a stock handler sounded more appealing. He tried not to feel the frisson of nerves that shot through him because while all the Coyote Cowboys had grown up ranch and knew the drill, Ryder hadn't exactly been truthful. He hadn't lied, but he hadn't fully explained that the ranch wasn't a family ranch. He hadn't lived on it. It had been a dude ranch for tourists, and Ryder had been an underage teen employed under the table to work in the stable caring for the trail horses, and helping out with groups and cookouts.

He'd never worked with cattle.

And Montana was all about cattle and rodeos.

He sucked in a deep breath through his smile. His lack of skills and experience was a problem he'd solve later. He'd been googling and watching YouTube videos to get a feel for the work and the terms. He wouldn't lie in any interview, but he could fudge the past a bit, and he was a quick learner.

"Well, until you land a job, we feel lucky to have you here, Ryder. Edi was just commenting on your energy and creative ideas for the exercise class."

Edi froze, and Ryder nearly barked out a laugh that likely would have had her all kinds of red again.

"And the few times I looked in, everyone seemed to be having a ball."

"There were a lot of balls rolling around," Ryder said gravely as Edi seemed to choke on her spit.

She placed her hands on her face, as if to cool her flaming cheeks, and he tried not to stare. She had beautiful hands. Pale. Soft. Elegant. Smooth with short, rounded nails. And yet she was strong. He'd seen her helping the different patients with getting in and out of wheelchairs or their walkers when they were working with some of the equipment or when she'd been helping them back to their apartments.

"When I get my new work schedule," he said—manifesting the reality he wanted, something Jace had instilled as a team leader, "we can set up regular hours for my volunteering at the May Bell Center, where you think I can best be of use." He drilled Holly with a stare, ignoring the way Edi flapped her hands and then tried to cover the movement up by fiddling with her severe bun.

"I'll let you two talk." Edi suddenly seemed to realize this was an optimal time to escape.

Not so fast, Edison Martin.

He wasn't going to let her dislike of him fester. He'd swallowed enough burning anger and anxiety as a kid. The army had taught him how to talk crap out.

"Hold up, Edi." Holly halted Edi's flight. "I'd like you to give Ryder a tour of the facility."

"I thought Mike…"

"I've seen the maintenance office and the ceiling air filters." Ryder smiled at her dismay, mentally saluting Holly for making this so much easier.

"I'd like Ryder to see the activity room for the day clients, the dining room, the gym, and the new activity and therapy rooms in the new wing. And of course the physical therapy room in the skilled nursing wing," Holly listed.

"But he's not…"

"You are going to need the help, Edi. No one can do everything for everyone alone."

With a quick bob of her head, Edi strode out the door and down the hallway. She wasn't running exactly, but with those long sexy legs of hers… He jerked his mind to a stop. No. He would not think about Edi's legs. Or other body parts. And he'd stop wanting to make her blush so he could imagine how far below her collar the cute pink would extend. And he wouldn't speculate if the freckles on her face were everywhere and how many and how long it would take to taste them all.

Men are beasts.

And he was feeling particularly feral since he'd stayed away from women after the debacle that had benched him separating him from his team when they'd headed out on a mission based on faulty intel that had become an ambush.

"Is this a race?"

"Do you have to make everything a joke?"

"Wow."

Edi stopped. "Sorry," she said. "Sorry, I'm not usually such a bitch."

He had not been expecting Edi's mea culpa and had to hollow in his cheeks so he wouldn't gut-respond that it was fine. It should be fine, and he was dismayed that her dismissal and criticism had hit so hard.

"Since I aim to fulfill my commitment to Jace, and the judge assigned me here, and Holly's assigning me to you for the bulk of my hours, we should figure out how you can best use me, and I can least irritate you."

She looked up at him, her gaze troubled.

"I overstepped this morning in the exercise class."

She looked away. "Yes. No."

"That's helpful."

"You don't…" She worried her lip, and Ryder tried hard not to stare. "I don't want to talk about this now."

"If we're going to work together—with me as your volunteer assistant…" he forced himself to qualify in case she was all about the hierarchy—he had little idea how regular businesses functioned "…then I am going to need direction. Specific tasks. And you'll need to train me to be an asset, not a burr in your ass."

"I…um…" She blushed again. "You're right." Her worried gaze met his, and he felt like he was falling into her unusual eyes. They were a grayish green with some black and yellow and seemed to always be changing.

Fascinating.

"Are your eyes hazel?"

"My what?" Her lips parted, and he tried not to notice how kissable they were because he would most definitely not be kissing the uptight, play-by-the-rules Edi Martin. She'd toss him out, and he would have failed Jace on the first day, and that was unacceptable.

"Sorry. I've just never…" He broke off not wanting to dig himself deeper.

The alarm on her watch went off.

Edi jumped. "I have to go." She shifted nervously and kept looking at her smartwatch like it just might bite her.

"When should we do the tour then? Tomorrow?"

"You're here every day?"

"Plan to be."

"Aaaahhhh, let me look at my schedule."

Edi fumbled the ever-present tablet she carried everywhere, and she slapped at it like an errant volleyball to keep it aloft.

Ryder caught the tablet and handed it to her without looking and she clutched it to her chest. A pulse beat in her slender neck like a runaway horse, and he had to force himself not to smooth his hands down neck and help her to square-breathe to calm her down, soothe her. If he touched her, he'd probably give her a heart attack.

"I'm sorry," she whispered. "I'm so bad at this."

"Bad at what?" He prompted, totally out of his depth but compelled to make this tension bordering on panic right.

"Just…" She sighed, looked at the ground, kicked her clogs on the boring tan and blue carpet that screamed institutional, safe and bargain price. "Bad."

"You're doing fine."

She moistened her lips. "I'm not," she said, but then she

drew in a deep breath and looked up at him—her wide, clear gaze hitting him like a punch.

"If you give me your number, I can text you…"

"You want my phone number?" She squeaked, looking outraged.

"I was going to text you my availability in case I get an interview set up, not a dick pic."

Again her cheeks flared red. She pressed her lips together and pulled her phone out of her back pocket.

Ryder thought of all the women who tried to give him their numbers over the years. Two had tried this morning as he'd stood in line for a breakfast sandwich and coffee. Maybe he should play that game and meet them for a drink some night. It might cut through some of this awful tension that clawed through him. But no. He had to focus on fulfilling his obligation to Jace. His last sexual foray had partially if not fully set this whole ugly and depressing drama in motion.

They exchanged numbers. Edi gasped in surprise when he took a photo of her.

"For the contact," he said, unable to resist needling her again.

She hesitated and then surprised him by holding her phone up. He flashed what he imagined was a smoldering cowboy look straight out of Hollywood.

She gasped. Okay maybe too over the top even for him.

"Do you take anything seriously?"

"Edison Martin…"

"It's actually Dr. Martin," she interrupted and then flinched and colored again as if he'd interrupted her.

"Dr. Edison Martin." He grinned and winked. "I take everything seriously."

EDI LET HERSELF into her gran's small, one-bedroom apartment. The studio would have been better financially, but after making the decision that she couldn't safely take care of her gran's mounting health issues and also work, the one-bedroom apartment in the May Bell's new assisted living wing wouldn't be as much of a shocking change. Her gran had been able to bring some of her furniture and artwork. But she still was unhappy.

And Edi was racked with guilt—one more stain on her soul when her gran had taken her in when she'd been a young teen so that her mom could have more freedom to pursue acting roles and men. Edi had finally felt safe, cared for and not nearly as judged—at least at home. School had still been a nightmare, but by burying her nose in books and her studies, she'd managed to screen most of it out, and her height had finally been a blessing in high school as coaches drafted her for basketball and volleyball.

"Hi, Gran," Edi, still so flustered with her unsettling reaction to Ryder, dug deep for enthusiasm.

Her stomach dropped when there was no answer. Cautiously she walked into the small bedroom that only fit the antique double bed, a chair and a nightstand. The bed was empty and so was the bathroom. The clothes she'd helped her gran choose and put on this morning because since moving to the May Bell her gran hadn't wanted to get out of her pajamas and robe, were in a pile on the floor.

Edi stared at them uncomprehendingly, feeling frozen, even though her brain was screaming at her to run.

Her gran was missing. Her gran was maybe naked. Edi rushed out her gran's door and not seeing her in the hallway near the lobby, she headed right toward the large activity and exercise rooms.

She kicked off her clogs and was in a full sprint by the time she rounded a corner only to pull up short like a cartoon character when she saw Ryder, arm in arm with her gran ambling toward her. Relief clutched her heart, even as confusion and dread trickled through her.

Her gran wore a bathing suit and a flowered shower cap. She had a towel over one shoulder and she chatted happily to Ryder about how to woo women—'listen to them.'

Ryder must be in full wooing mode because he was hanging on her gran's every word.

"Gran!"

Her gran frowned. "Edi, where are your shoes and why are you panting like a dog?"

Relief made her woozy. Her gran sounded like her gran. She recognized her.

Of course she does.

"Edi, is there a swimming pool here?" Ryder asked like it was normal to find an octogenarian walking the halls in a swimsuit. "Lydia's a new resident and is looking for the pool. Because we didn't have time for the tour, I don't know where the pool is. This is my first day volunteering," Ryder said chattily, and Edi nearly groaned.

"A therapy pool," she said stiffly. She'd loved swimming with some of her young clients, who'd had severe sensory disorders, but she'd yet to jump into a pool with any of her geriatric clients—she hadn't worked out the logistics yet, and she'd need assistance—something Ryder probably would offer, but no way would she strip down to a swimsuit with Mr. Hottie Soldier who probably had a physique rivaling Chris Hemsworth's Thor—and not the depressed chubby one.

He waited, maybe expecting more information.

"It's not for free swimming."

"I don't want to go to the pool with all the old people complaining about everything." Her gran made a face. "I want to go to Miracle Lake. I know you don't like me driving anymore, but this young man can take me."

"It's January. In Montana."

Her gran stared at her, brows crinkled, and Edi could see the moment when her gran understood her lapse.

"Oh. Oh. Of course. I..." She looked around, and slowly pulled away from Ryder's gentle hold. "How silly. For a moment I thought. Oh. And I didn't have a cover-up. How bold you must think me." She put a trembling hand over her mouth. "How silly. I was thinking about…"

"It's okay," Edi swallowed her fear. "It's okay." She pulled her gran into her arms, but her gran pulled away and wouldn't look at her. She tried to wrap the towel around her gran, but she swatted at her, and both she and her gran faced off trembling like frightened squirrels.

"I got this," Ryder said, his hands gentle as he wrapped the towel around her gran like a sarong. "That color matches your suit." Ryder tucked the end in. "Edi, maybe you could offer a water aerobics exercise class. Is the pool big enough?"

Ryder looked so sincere and kind and gorgeous when Edi felt filleted—exposed to Ryder so he could see her on the brink of falling part. She hurt, and Ryder looked like he hurt for her, and the fact that he was being so nice when she just felt so…so…angry and vulnerable and…

"No," she snapped and was immediately ashamed. "Thank you, Ryder. I can take my gran back to her apartment," she said stiffly.

Please don't say anything. Please don't say one more thing.

"See you tomorrow," she said quickly. "Have fun tonight."

"Big date?" Lydia asked chirpily.

"Friends from the when I served in the military."

"A soldier." Lydia looked him over like she was assessing a prime cut at the butcher's. "I once dated a Marine," she said slyly. "He was very charming and romantic and had a lot of staying…"

"Okay, Gran." Edi felt like she was on fire. "Let's get back for our tea and the scones we made this morning. You promised that you'd keep our game night date tonight, and I'm holding you to it."

Edi firmly steered her gran away, but her gran balked and turned back to Ryder. "What branch?"

"Army." He winked at Lydia. "The best at everything that matters."

"Really?" Her gran looked at Edi as she choked on her spit. "Interesting."

Chapter Three

"RYDER, WHAT IT is." Remington Cross, one of his former teammates reeled him in for a hard hug and a massive hand slap on his shoulder before Ryder could get more than two steps into the elegant lobby of a historic-looking hotel.

Why the heck had his brothers wanted to meet here? The grand lobby with warm lighting, gleaming floors and rich, dark colors was not their scene. And then he saw the bar that looked like an Irish pub, although he'd never been near Ireland. The long, highly polished slab of wood looked like it had stories to tell, and the blonde bartender behind the bar was so stunning, Ryder's eyes hurt. She probably got hit on so hard and so often she'd have a hard time pulling pints.

"Eyes back in your head," Cross murmured in his ear. "She's taken."

Duh. No cowboy town in America would let a gorgeous woman free-range for long. But then Huck was there, chest-bumping him and then pulling him in for another hard hug. Rohan waited until Huck released him before doing the elaborate bro-handshake that Jace had come up with years ago. Usually, it would end with them throwing back their heads and howling like coyotes. Calhoun—the Big O because he hated his first name of Otis had added a yodel and yip at the end, but even Ryder knew a howl wouldn't go over well in an elegant hotel.

He looked at his three brothers. Four were now home safe. But not Jace.

His chest burned.

Keep Calhoun safe. And Wolf.

Who was he praying to? Who'd ever listened to one of his prayers?

"When'd you get out?"

"When'd you hit town?"

"Where are you staying?"

Ryder's shoulder's relaxed as the three Coyotes peppered him with questions. Cross led them to a booth. It was pretty quiet in the bar. A few groups of people drinking cocktails and wine, wearing business casual, and then two women in suits talking rather intensely, a laptop between them.

They'd barely sat when the bartender sauntered over carrying a tray with four pints of beer.

"Local IPA. Welcome home, Soldier. First one's on the house—after that, Cross has you covered."

Her eyes were the most unusual blue he'd ever seen—like some European sea in travel magazines, but he couldn't forget all the expressions and colors that had danced in Edi's eyes today—especially how they'd darkened in fear when she'd run up to him after he'd discovered Lydia, wandering the exercise room. He'd been inventorying the equipment, so he knew what he and Edi had to work with. She'd soften up and let him help, eventually. He'd learned to get his way most of the time with honey, not bullying, and no way was he going to just follow her around like a lost puppy hoping for a pat on the head and a cooed 'good boy.'

Jace's memory deserved his best, and he intended to give it.

"You're staring again," Cross murmured.

"What?" Ryder tried to focus on Cross, but his afternoon with Edi kept interrupting.

"*Now*, you don't value your life?" Huck murmured.

"Lots of changes to get caught up on." Rohan took a sip of his beer and kicked Ryder under the table.

"Huh?"

He looked at his brothers, finally seeing them, not the storms brewing in Edi's eyes that she'd barely bothered to suppress when he'd been trying to help infuse some life into the exercise class this morning.

"How are you all doing?" He roused himself—that was why he was here—to reconnect with his brothers, see if they had any leads on jobs and if anyone had a couch he could crash on.

"How are *you* doing?" Cross demanded giving him a once, twice, three times over piercing stare. "Where you crashing?"

"I was going to ask…"

"I got you."

"I got you."

"I got you."

No hesitation. All three of his brothers offered at once, and Ryder felt overwhelmed by the support. He'd expected help, but hearing the words, seeing his brothers' sincerity, feeling it brought an unaccustomed prick at the backs of his eyes that he blinked back.

He looked at each of his brothers—so familiar and yet different. They smiled back, the picture of health and something new—a lightness, something almost indefinable.

"What's up with all of you?" he asked. "You got an apartment? Jobs? Did you complete your mission for Jace?"

Cross leaned back and folded his arms. Defensive? Not a usual pose for him. Cross was more of an attack and then get names and apologize later if necessary. And then as Cross stared him down, Ryder's attention was snagged by a thick band of gold on Cross's tanned third finger.

"What the…?"

"Language," Cross counseled. "Hey, baby, come meet Ryder Lea—the latest Coyote Cowboy to climb out of the army's jowls."

The beautiful bartender now brought them a heaping plate of nachos, pretzel bites with mustard and cheese and boneless chicken wings dripping with what looked like barbecue sauce. Ryder's stomach rumbled. Cross jumped up to help her with the plates while Rohan grabbed linen napkins wrapped around silverware and some small plates from a service center near the bar. Huck distributed the plates, silverware and napkins. It was like they'd done this more than a few times, and Ryder felt like he'd just been shoved outside the circle. Othered.

Cross's arm was around the woman's waist, and he kissed the top of her head before beaming at Ryder—actually beaming. Ryder felt like he was staring at a stranger.

"Good thing you're sitting down." Cross smiled. "Ryder, this is Shane Knight-Cross, my wife."

"Your wife? You're married?" He'd seen Cross's ring, knew what it meant, but couldn't absorb the enormity of his statement. "What? Why? How? When?"

He stared at the couple, mouth open, probably rude AF.

"Married," Cross confirmed. "Best decision I ever made. You writing a news article or what?" he challenged.

Ryder knew there was something he should say. Congratulations? But his brain and mouth wouldn't connect. Never once had he anticipated that not only would Cross leave the army, but that he'd also get married. What was next, a kid?

"Shane's the most brilliant and beautiful woman in the world. I fell boots over butt in love within days. Backyard wedding at Shane's parents' house in Tennessee. September."

Cross answered each question, sporting a smirk. Shane laughed, and then with her knuckles she gently traced one of Cross's cheekbones, her expression tender.

"Welcome home, Ryder," she said. "Enjoy catching up, cowboys." She included all of them in her radiant smile, and then before returning to the bar, she walked over to what looked like a glassed-in gift shop across the lobby, briefly chatted to a young girl with a short dark bob haircut sitting at a small table that looked full of arts and crafts. She had a small, scruffy dog on her lap and was bent over her computer typing quickly.

"Got a daughter too," Cross said. "And a creature she insists is a dog."

Ryder stared.

"I'm married too," Huck said, holding up a hand with a wide silver and gold ring with an unusual stone set in it. "Baby on board, due in two months."

The hits kept coming.

"How is that even physically possible?" He gaped at Huck, who as far as he knew, had mustered out on medical leave soon after Jace's body was sent home in early July. "Super sperm or something?" Mentally he counted the months that Huck had been in Marietta.

"Oh something." Huck clapped him on the back and stole the chicken wing he hadn't gotten around to eating because of the shocking news. "Good to see you, Ry."

"I'm engaged to my high school sweetheart," Rohan added. "I'll be a stepfather to her twelve-year-old son, Lucas, come spring break. You're invited and can stand up with me and the other Coyotes."

How was this—any of this—possible? Ryder stared at each of his brothers, who seemed like different men. Once again, he was on the outside looking in. They'd been out mere months. Rohan less than two, and yet they'd found homes, jobs maybe, but definitely women.

"Damn." He finally found his voice as a longing he'd never imagined contained in his body cracked open and seeped up through what was left of his soul. He had to make light of the situation. He was the tension-breaker. He brought the light, the fun. Only now he was the only vessel containing tension. "I feel like I'm in another dimension. You brothers got game."

"Time to catch up, Ry." Cross grinned and it had a wicked tilt.

EDI WAS EXHAUSTED—STILL freaked out that her gran had left the apartment looking for a pool. So far Edi hadn't been able to get her to leave her new assisted living apartment—not for the dining hall or for exercise or any activities including the knitting circle.

"I told you to call or text me when you wanted to leave your apartment."

She'd said this before while she'd made tea, and her gran had ignored her, arms crossed.

"I'm not a prisoner. I won't leave the facility. There's

guards watching."

"They are not guards. There's a nursing station and a lobby with receptionists." And cameras at every entrance and a buzzer and light when every door that opened to the outside automatically locked except the lobby, which was manned twenty-four seven.

Maybe it did feel like prison.

"I want you to be safe." Edi felt chilled to the bone. She was on her second cup of tea, even though she preferred coffee. This was her first Montana winter and though the state was wide open and breath-stealingly beautiful, it was also colder than she imagined possible. Seattle definitely had gray days and more rain than she liked, but it had never been this cold, and it was only January.

"I want you to be happy," her gran retorted. "It's time to start living again. You're still young. What about the young man I met—Ride 'Em All Night?"

"Gran," Edi yipped, mortified. Now her gran was totally lucid and bawdy. Maybe going to the Monday game night at the Graff Hotel wasn't such a good idea.

But then she looked over at her gran who smiled impishly. "I think you like what you saw, Edi."

"I miss your smile," Edi said without thinking.

"And I miss yours," her gran said and then she looked around the small apartment that Edi had painted light blue to match the walls of the bungalow that her gran had lived in for the past fifteen years.

On a visit nine months ago, she'd realized her gran's health was slipping. Edi's divorce had been finalized. Her workplace and Seattle had felt depressing and toxic, being around so many children had reduced her to tears at the end of each day, so she'd made her leave from her job permanent and left everyone and everything in Seattle behind to move in with her gran and take care of her. But as her gran's health and mind slipped faster than she'd anticipated and the good days were fewer, Edi quickly realized her savings wouldn't last. She hadn't asked Derek for anything in the divorce—she'd wanting nothing from their brief life together.

She could sell her gran's house, but they'd still have living expenses. She could earn good money, but she couldn't leave her gran home alone for hours.

The May Bell was a compromise neither of them had wanted to make, and Edi wondered when she'd stop feeling so dang guilty about so much.

"So…" Her gran was smiling still. "Game night?"

It was the one social routine she and her gran had and the last thing Edi felt up for, but she reached out and covered her gran's hand. "I heard they have a group of old-time ranchers who never miss a Monday," she teased.

"Then I'd better change and touch up my lipstick and add a splash of Chanel No. 5—you know where I keep it."

Her gran was still reasonably spry when motivated, and it only took fifteen minutes until they were in her gran's Subaru and driving across the railroad tracks and into the

Graff Hotel's circular drive.

"We're here," Edi sang, hoping her body would reenergize if she just kept pushing her perky. "Wait for me. I'll help you inside," Edi cautioned, and suppressed her sigh when she saw her gran's sour expression. She'd always had a zest for life. But now her moods were quicksilver. The current grumpiness had been caused because Edi couldn't find the perfume. Edi had even resorted to looking in the fridge and oven, which had had her gran snapping at her.

"Do you think I'm crazy?"

That was what her life had become. A series of befores and afters. Good moments and then worrying ones. And the normal moments were almost heartbreaking because Edi kept anticipating the bad ones.

"I wonder what games Shane will have arranged tonight."

Her gran's lips puckered more. "You hate games. I don't know why you bring me."

"Because I love you."

Her gran's features softened. Edi no longer wanted to go out at night. Give her a book and a glass of wine and a chair by the fire, and that was her idea of perfect. But her gran needed stimulation. She'd played bridge for decades in a group, and she'd had bunco nights, gin rummy and of course she'd headed a book group and a cooking and craft group.

But now…?

Edi tried to shake off her heavy mood, but it clung to her

like a bad odor.

"You ready?" She shoved the car in park and hopped out and hurried around to the other side, afraid her very independent gran would try to get out on her own.

She hated the expense of valet parking, but she couldn't leave her gran alone long enough to get her settled at a table and then self-park, and then repeat the process when her gran was tired.

"You should be having an evening out with a young man," her gran said as soon as Edi opened the door. Her gran's hazel eyes, so much like her own only greener and prettier, were no longer sharp with intelligence or shining with humor, and every time Edi looked at her, she wanted to cry. But she wouldn't.

"A strong man who is kind. Not that cold fish doctor whose name I'm happy I can't remember. But you should choose a warm man who's fun and helpful and who will give you the babies you want." Her gran's smile was so sad, so sweet, so full of longing, and her fingers in the bright red mittens reached out to brush across Edi's abdomen, covered by in her puffy parka.

"Aaaah, Gran." Edi furiously blinked back tears. Why was her loss and her sorrow the one thing her gran never seemed to forget? She rarely remembered baking pumpkin chocolate chip muffins, feeding the ducks on Lake Washington or kayaking around the arboretum or roasting s'mores on the patio of what Edi had hoped would be her forever home when her gran had visited her in Seattle. She didn't recall teaching Edi to knit or spending dozens of hours walking through museums and art galleries. All those fun memories seemed to have evaporated for her gran.

Just the other evening when Edi had gone to make dinner with her gran she'd found her watching *Wheel of Fortune* with the sound off and crying because she thought she'd gone deaf.

"I'm done with all that now," she said brightly. It was too late. "I'm focused on our new life in Marietta."

"Some life," her gran said acerbically, struggling to her feet to get out of the car as Edi held on to her, under her armpit.

"I can walk. You do know that, don't you, Doctor?"

The irritation, the sarcasm was new—maybe yet another sign of her decline. Edi recognized and catalogued every one of them.

"We both need to find joy in the small moments like tonight," Edi said, seeing the van from the May Bell Center pull up with a few of the more active members in the small, assisted living wing. The May Bell was in the process of expanding. The demand for senior housing near medical facilities was sadly growing exponentially.

Her gran could still ride the shuttle on her good days, but Edi wanted to spend as much time with her as she could while her gran still remembered her.

"Your friends are here," she said brightly.

"Stop trying so hard," her gran snapped.

Edi helped her gran up the stairs, with the older woman making disapproving noises. "I'm losing my mind, not my mobility."

Edi had an inappropriate urge to laugh and cry. "Maybe I'm the one who needs the support," Edi said.

A doorman opened the fancy doors wide, and Edi's gran shook off her hold.

"That's the only reason I agreed to come. There's a bar, and I want a Beefeater's on the rocks with four olives." Her gran turned her back to Joseph, who now worked as a bellman, so that he could help her slide out of her coat. "Good evening, Joseph," her gran said with great dignity. "I've brought my granddaughter so she doesn't become a shut-in."

"Nice to see you both." Joseph grinned cheekily.

Edi tucked her gran's mittens in her parka before hanging it up on the large coat hanger and looped the scarf collection over the hanger before dealing with her own winter wear.

"You need to get out of that old-lady bungalow," her gran said. "It's filled with old-lady crap. Next thing I know you'll have five cats."

Edi's too-sensitive heart lurched. The 'old-lady crap' was her gran's. Edi had left Seattle with little more than her clothes, a quilt her gran had made for her when she had come to live with her at thirteen and art supplies she still hadn't unpacked, three boxes of books that were her favorites and a small painted wood box of framed pictures and treasures. She slept in the guest room.

Why did she continue to wallow? Loads of people had it worse. Edi dug for a smile that physically hurt when she tried to arrange her face.

"I wonder what mocktail Shane is making tonight," she mused, determined to keep trying even if she choked on her fake cheer.

"Mocktail. I want the real thing. Make it a double. Bring on the olives," her gran called out. "Do you remember the time I…" Her gran trailed off, her soft face crinkling in confusion. "You should probably have a drink." Her gran smiled craftily. "I can drive."

"You're not on the insurance."

"You're no fun, and it's only a four-block walk."

"In temps in the low twenties."

"You sound like an old woman." Her gran tried to shake off her arm. "Leave me. I see some definite possibilities tonight."

Edi ignored the hurt crashing through her. She was too sensitive. Derek had told her that over and over at the end. And she was acting old and boring and used up, but she couldn't gather the energy to care all that much.

"Got your eye on one of the silver fox ranchers, huh?" she asked only to realize her gran was determinedly making her way toward a table full of young and rather large and potent men.

Oh, dear. "Gran." She tossed her coat on a hook, and for once didn't stay to help the others from the May Bell Center as she took off after her gran.

"Good evening, gentlemen." Her gran drew herself up to her full height of five feet nothing. "Are any of you single?"

Four large men in the booth rose up politely, and Edi skidded to a stop to see Ryder standing next to three men she'd never seen before, but they all radiated masculine charisma that pulsed throughout the bar.

This scene could be in a movie or an ad selling…anything.

Two years ago, she would have bought whatever they were selling and bathed in it. Greedily.

"Did you need a single man for something tonight, ma'am?" one of the men—the largest in a group of large, handsome, rugged men; and that was saying something—asked.

Edi stared at Ryder, who smiled at her, before shifting his attention to her gran.

"Yes, I have a granddaughter who needs to poop or get off the pot. Excuse my crude expression."

Four sets of amused eyes met Edi's, while her gran glared at her.

"Good to see you again, Lydia," Ryder said into the silence. Edi's cheeks burned.

"Gran." She tugged gently on the thin wrist. "Let's go find a table and…"

"Hello, Ride 'Em All Night. Maybe you can help my Edi. She's wasting prime time grieving over a son-of-a-bitch doctor who didn't deserve her, and she's not getting any younger, and she's already lost one..."

"Gran." The humiliating agony of her gran spilling the pain of her past, of her life, into a circle of strangers and Ryder who already thought she was a stuck-up rhymes with itch, nearly had her clapping her hand over her gran's mouth.

"Well ma'am." The tall man with black hair that fell to his shoulders, who had the mysterious-looking grayish-silver eyes, smoothly interrupted what Edi felt must be the most awkward scene in the Graff's history—history that went back over a hundred years at least. "You are in luck. Ryder Lea here is single and new in town and looking to make connections, and it seems as if you are already acquainted. He's my brother in arms, and I can vouch for him."

"You are pimping him out rather aggressively, young man. Edi deserves a choice in men."

One of the men mouthed 'pimping,' eyes wide with wonder and amusement, and how the four men didn't dissolve into laughter was utterly beyond Edi's comprehension. She'd never been so humiliated in her life.

"Oh, my God," Edi breathed out. "Gran."

"You know better than to take His name in vain," her gran, who'd never been to church to Edi's knowledge, snapped and then her steely gaze assessed Ryder. "He doesn't look like a cowboy. And I know he likes a hard, long swim. Good," she said to the three cowboys standing with Ryder as if something had been decided.

The three men glanced briefly at Ryder and then back at her gran. They practically stood at attention. Were they all soldiers? These must be the friends Ryder was hoping to get a job lead from, and she and her gran were interrupting their evening out.

Edi mouthed *sorry*, but none of them looked put out even though she wanted to sink through the floor and go a long way from here, hopefully someplace tropical.

All four men looked like most of the cowboys in town, and not in the touristy way she'd seen couples and families dress up who were visiting the dude ranches. But there was an air about them—something that whispered and growled danger.

"You have a job?" her gran demanded.

Ryder opened his mouth to speak, but the tallest of the group interceded smoothly.

"We were just speaking about that, ma'am. Ryder here has just been honorably discharged from Special Forces where we all served together, and he's come to Marietta to settle down with his brothers. We work at different ranches and are planning to open a business together but are just in the hashing-out stage. He has money saved and good prospects."

"But we can talk about it later if you'd like to quiz Ryder

about his prospects," a dark-haired man with a wicked-looking scar on his neck nudged Ryder toward Edi.

"Ryder does have a commitment before he can settle down, but nothing of a romantic nature," a man with green eyes that practically danced in amusement slotted in.

"But we have his back, ma'am. We all served together," the tallest man spoke again. "I'm Remington Cross, this is Huck Jones and Rohan Telford. Rohan's family owns a spread up north of town. Ryder will be living and working there part-time this winter, while he finishes a commitment for a friend of ours."

Despite her mortification, Edi's ears perked up. Ryder got a job. He must be so relieved. Maybe it would be more than part-time so that he wouldn't have time to volunteer, and she wouldn't have to be shoved at him like the last white elephant gift at a sad company Christmas party.

"So you really are cowboying up?"

Ugh, why was she becoming as snarky as the middle school girls who'd tormented her? She needed to keep her big mouth shut. Ryder's grin was positively sinful. And Edi tried hard and failed to not think of the hundred-plus cowboy romances she'd read starting college. It was a romance hook that had always been one of her favorites.

"Ryder lives to serve." Rohan who just might be Ryder's boss was no longer trying to hold back his smile while the others looked like they were about to have a fit of giggles or coughing.

"I'm just bummed, Miss Lydia," Rohan continued, "that I never thought to call Ryder Ride 'Em All Night. We were lame just sticking with Ry."

Edi could see Ryder flip off his friend behind his back.

It would have been funny if it had been happening to someone else, but Edi found it horrifying. Her gran was treating her like a 4-H calf on the auction block at the fair. And she'd learned that her so-called volunteer was newly released from the army. Special Forces, his friend had said, which made sense considering how fit and hot he was and the masculine swagger he exuded. And now he really was a cowboy? Total romance fantasy package. Hook and Hook, her first-year dorm roommate Annie would have said.

But she had to stop staring and wondering. She was done with fantasies. She hadn't even opened any of her romances, not even in the bubble baths she luxuriated in in her gran's claw-foot tub on Friday nights—bubble bath, candles, music and a glass of sauvignon blanc—no romances. She was done with that. But the heat stirring between her thighs teased that maybe she wasn't quite as much done with that as she promised herself.

"Would you ladies like to join us." Ryder smiled and pulled out two chairs while Rohan grabbed two more. "We've demolished the nachos and pretzel bites, but Cross ordered jalapeño poppers."

"Do you play gin rummy?" Gran eyed Ryder speculatively.

Ryder's smile was slow, but sweet, and Edi hated noticing that he had crinkles on the corners of his eyes that creased down his cheeks and made him just look so edible.

"I could be persuaded to play a game," he said looking directly into Edi's eyes.

If he'd pictured his first night in Marietta, playing cards with three octogenarians who grilled him on his family history, plans and prospects had not once featured.

He'd initially agreed to play cards just to twig Edi because she'd tried to get rid of him earlier today. But then his oversized compassion had reared its needy head. How he would have loved some help with his nana—someone kind who took an interest, who talked to her, who had ideas for help. Edi had looked so panic-stricken this afternoon, and tonight she looked to be about to dangle on the end of her rope as she shifted her weight from foot to foot and flushed a pretty pink and then bright red at her grandmother's unfiltered mouth. But as usual, his playfulness had come back to bite him. He hadn't played cards with Edi but instead with her gran and two other women from the May Bell Center. And they'd all speculated about his stamina, size and if he'd look as good naked as Chris Hemsworth in *Thor*.

Edi had sidled to the left, looking like she'd choke on both her embarrassment and laughter. She also looked guilty

AF, and that had him all kinds of curious. But Edi stayed close, carefully watching her gran. His buddies had deserted him to join several other groups of seniors, leaving Ry with Lydia and several other May Bell residents.

"I almost saw Edi's young man naked," Lydia told the other two women—one was Mrs. Johanson who'd been curious about how to get rid of a body. He should dismiss it as an age issue, but something niggled at him. Surely the logistical challenges of disposing of a body wasn't something that a mind beginning to unspool would kick out.

The sound Edi made was more animal than human, and he wondered what she'd sound like when she came.

Not gonna happen, pal. She's no one-and-done.

"He was taking me swimming."

"There's a pool?" Mrs. Johanson asked.

"There's no pool," Edi stated.

"There's a therapy pool. I haven't seen it yet, but Edi is taking me on a tour tomorrow. I'm going to research water aerobics."

"Jump in and swim," Edi's gran said.

"We could have a swim league. Races," Ryder speculated.

The look Edi gave him was pure flame shot out of her beautiful, narrowed eyes and hot enough to burn.

"And you haven't seen Chris Hemsworth naked, Lydia," he objected. "I've seen all the Marvel movies, and he always has some clothes on."

"Strip poker." Edi's gran eyed him speculatively.

"Very funny ha, ha, Gran," Edi said.

"Fun, dear, not funny." She waved her cards up and down his body, giving him a full view of her hand. "And it's past time you got back on the horse, Edi."

More mortified pink flushed across Edi's freckled cheeks.

"Giddy up," Ryder teased.

"Yeehaw. Not."

"Don't be like that," he said softly, testing her, but focusing on his hand.

Even though his brothers were on their second beer and engaged in playing checkers while Huck played speed chess with an older man whom he seemed to know well enough to flip verbal barbs back and forth with, Ryder felt he'd been done dirty.

He'd wanted to drink a beer, catch up with his brothers and get a bead on a place to live and even better, info on potential ranches that might be hiring. Did Rohan's folks really have a position open on their ranch? He didn't want charity. He paid his way, always. The questions and worries spun around and around in his mind, even as he focused on the card game and worked to engage all of the women in banter so they'd have a fun evening.

But his mind returned to the dangled part-time ranch job. Would it lead to stock contracting? He'd been googling that. The Telford Family Ranch worked with another local ranch—Wilder Dreams—breeding bucking bulls and broncs and stock contracting both for local rodeos and at the national level. He blew out a breath. No pressure there. Telford Family Ranch was big time. Ryder had taken care of horses as a teen, but never cattle, and he'd never had to load and unload them in a trailer—the vet had come to the dude ranch. He'd be loading up potentially a dozen animals and driving them from rodeo to rodeo—he'd already signed up for a commercial trucking course.

And then there was the chute work. He'd need to learn that. He'd been watching YouTube videos, but it was focused more on the cowboy than the stock handlers. But he learned quickly. He could fake it until he made it. No way would he let Rohan or his family or his other Coyote Cowboys down.

"I'm exactly like that."

Edi's voice held a warning and dragged him away from his anxious thoughts. He needed to focus on the now. The future would come soon enough. He heard the hurt in her voice, and he wondered about the idiot who'd caused it. Childhood? Dumb ex?

Not my business.

He wasn't in the market for anything beyond a hookup. That was how it had always been for him—the only thing that made sense for a man whose career meant that one phone call or text could send him thousands of miles away for days, weeks or months, and he couldn't share anything about the mission.

You could be different.

The thought was so unexpected, astonishing in its ballsiness, that he choked on his spit and looked up at Edi. She quickly looked away. Satisfaction tricked through him. So, she was noticing him as he was noticing her.

Don't notice.

She had complicated stamped all over her, and he didn't do complicated. He was complicated enough.

He noticed the lull in the play and caught all three of the octogenarians watching him. Edi's gran's gaze was particularly sharp and withering. Ryder had no idea what the story was behind their relationship, but he could tell that Edi loved her gran fiercely even though she'd felt on the spot and humiliated. Seeing their relationship had him missing his nana with an ache that felt as sharp now as it had when she'd passed just before he'd turned seventeen.

"This doesn't count as a first date." Lydia pointed a finger at him. "And if you hurt her like that other jerk with too many four letter epi...epi...what word do I want? The one in the Greek myths you used to love so much." For a moment the mask of fierceness slipped, and a frightened child peered through.

"Epithets," he and Edi said at the same time. He dredged up the word with an air of triumph as it had been a long time since he'd thought about the Greek myths he'd been introduced to in sixth grade.

"Yes. Ep-i-thetssss." Lydia sounded out the syllables, stumbling a little. "I'm tired."

"Okay, Gran." Edi stood up. "We can go home. It's almost time."

"Not until after the game." Her gran waved her hand at Edi, again exposing her cards. "I'm old, but if you hurt her, I will come after you and—" She made a sawing motion and pointed at his lap.

Seriously?

"Ouch." Shane—Cross's wife—appeared, smiling, collecting the glasses. "Now, Lydia, you know you're supposed to play nice here. Ryder is a friend of my husband's, and he's just come home."

"He's dating Edison," Lydia invented.

"You move fast, Soldier," Shane said cheekily, laughing a little, probably at his WTF expression.

"We're not dating," Edi interrupted. "And we're done here." Edi made a sawing motion at her neck.

"What's with you and your gran threatening to saw off body parts?" Ryder laughed at the pair of them. "Is there a cut-rate medical school in Marietta I'm not aware of? Or do you both secretly work in the medical examiner's office?"

"Maybe," Lydia said saucily. "I've done a lot of things in my life."

"Dish," Ryder invited. "Tell me something about Edi from when she was little."

"C'mon, Gran, it's late and the games are wrapping up. Thanks, Shane."

"We have to finish the game," Lydia insisted, her voice

getting more querulous. "I'm not leaving until someone wins. And…and…what's his name…"

"Ride Her," Mrs. Johanson supplied.

"Yes, that's it…asks you out."

The expression on Edi's face was hilarious. Who knew the drop-dead serious physical therapist, who looked so stony at work, had such a mobile face that couldn't hold back the hundreds of emotions bombarding her after hours.

"Ryder." He repeated his name to Lydia for about the tenth time that night. Poor Edi and poor Edi's gran. The ghost of his nana lay heavy on his soul tonight.

"Gin." Ryder laid his hand on the table, fanned out like he was in Vegas, and he stood up, looking at Edi. "Coffee tomorrow before work. Java Café. What time?"

"That's not how you ask a beautiful woman out," Edi's gran grumbled. "Did your mom teach you any manners at all, young man?"

He heard Edi make an irritated sound at the back of her throat.

"Nope." Ryland shrugged like an aw-shucks cowboy.

"Why not?"

"Long story."

"I got nothing but time," Lydia suggested, even though Edi was helping her gran up from the table.

"Gran, it's time to go." Edi's voice was soft but held a worried edge.

"What time works for you tomorrow?" he asked Edi,

wanting to make it clear he would not be shoved off on various May Bell departments. He was doing right by Jace, end of story. "We need to talk about the job, and expectations, hours that you need."

"That doesn't sound like a date."

"It's not a date," Edi said, her voice going a little sharp. "Gran, please." She was gathering up the cardigan her gran had shed, embroidered vest and long, knitted pink and lavender scarf.

"Let me help." Ryder laid his hand on her arm, and Edi dropped her gaze as a live current shot between them.

Yeah, he'd been feeling the strange pull all night. Wondering about it. Why her? He and *Dr.* Edison Martin had nothing in common, and she was all wrong for what he wanted—a few hours of sexy and generous indulgence. He was sure Edi's gran would not approve of his short-term aspirations.

Neither would his nana.

If only his nana could still be around to comment on his behavior. The deep hole he'd barely patched together after her death split open a little wider.

"She only wants the best for you," he said.

Glistening eyes and barely banked misery was not the response he'd expected.

"I know my grandmother." Edi jerked away from his touch. She took a step back, bumping into her gran, who staggered.

Edi dropped the outer winter clothing in an effort to catch her grandmother, but Ryder had the better angle. He gently righted Lydia with an arm around her waist. He was careful of her ribs.

"Sorry." Edi's fingers trembled and covered her mouth. "Sorry."

"I'm not made of crystal," her gran snapped, but Ryder felt the exhausted droop of Lydia's frail body. "Stop treating me like a child or an old woman."

"No harm done." He smiled, picked up the parka and scarves and handed them to Edi, and, giving her space, he helped the other women out of their chairs and with their coats, and in one case retrieving a walker.

Cross, Huck and Rohan helped the bus drivers get the seniors on the bus back to the assisted and independent living facility, while a few of what Ryder suspected were older ranchers pushed in chairs and helped put the games away.

Ryder hesitated on the stairs of the bus headed to the senior center. Edi was helping her gran to a bench near the lobby door, clearly instructing her to sit, while her grandmother glared and pushed at her. She waved her skinny arms around like she was chasing crows. The scene was piercingly familiar though over a decade and a half old.

He hopped down the last steps and strode back into the lobby. He still hadn't sorted out who, if any of his brothers he could crash with for a couple of days until he found a place to live and work, but learning they were all married or engaged kiboshed the idea of crashing on one of their couches. Playing third wheel was not his style. And a woman didn't need her new man's past showing up on her doorstep hoping to be housed and fed like a foster shelter dog.

There must be a cheap hotel around. And he had his truck. He'd definitely slept rougher, but not usually in the dead of winter.

"Thought I'd get some dating advice," he interrupted Lydia's tirade that she didn't want to wait and that she could walk to the car and drive herself to Edi's condo in Seattle.

Edi looked like she'd been punched in the stomach.

She stared at him mutely.

"You get your car." He smiled. "Lydia can set me straight with dating tips. I'm desperately out of practice."

Edi gaped. No snappy comeback this time, and he missed her hint of snark.

"That I doubt," Lydia said sourly. "But I do have advice, young man."

"Let's hear it." He rubbed his palms together. "Lydia's Top Ten Tips." He winked at Edi and pulled out his cell phone. "I'll take notes. I'm behind in the game of love."

"Love is not a game," Edi pointed out, a hint of fire in her eyes and pink in her cheeks.

"Yes, it is," he and Lydia said at the same time.

Chapter Four

"I DEFINITELY SHOULD not be doing this," Edi muttered and pulled open the door of the Java Café.

She'd walked the two blocks from the May Bell Center as the sidewalks were fairly clear. The last snow dump had been late last week, giving residents of the cute neighborhood on Church Street time to clear their driveways and sidewalks. She'd hoped the temperature in the high teens would freeze some sense into her brain but no luck—she was still meeting Ryder for coffee.

And she knew she was being unfair. Ryder had handled the weirdness last night with charm and aplomb. He'd been a pro, and she'd been a stressed, snippy, defensive mess.

I will do better.

"Good morning, Edison." Ryder rose from a table in the corner and greeted her. His eyes appraised her warmly, and his smile nearly knocked her sideways.

He barely knew her. She hadn't been charming. She'd all but told Holly she didn't want to work with him. And yet he was smiling like he was pleased to see her. She couldn't remember Derek ever seeming so happy to see her.

Edi's heart skittered in her chest, and her lips tried to

move but nothing came out. She actively tried not to think about Derek or that dark time anymore. She'd barely climbed out of the black hole, and her gran needed her.

It's the cold.

It wasn't the cold. It was him. He snapped with electric energy and seemed like a man who could and would make things happen.

Edi felt the ground shift just a little. She had to get herself under control. She'd never been the kind of woman bowled over by a man. And she wouldn't hand over any of her agency now, even if he had a smile that reminded her of summer sun, and his dark honey-brown hair with streaks of gold was brushed back from his high forehead and curled appealing around his ears and the nape of his neck. It was thick like a mane, and she forgot utterly that she had always admired cropped, tidy hair on men, not thick and unruly.

For a moment, she nearly swayed with longing, wanting to feel his hair between her fingers. It had been so long since she'd been touched.

"Coffee." She pointed at him like lack of caffeine was to blame for her overcharged hormones.

"Got your favorite." Again with the smile.

"How do you know my favorite?" She sounded defensive and cranky. Hardly a good start to anyone's morning. Shame sat heavy on her shoulders.

His sly smile slid over his features, crinkling his eyes and divoting his cheeks.

"I have my ways."

"Lydia's top ten tips?" she asked drily, but even as she spoke, stupid hope hopped in her heart. Had he asked her gran about her coffee preferences and her gran had remembered?

He laughed, turned away and headed back to a table in the corner by the small gas fireplace. Edi followed, sucking in a deep breath and forcing her features to relax. She didn't want to become bitter or cold or isolated. She wanted to be her again.

What had happened had happened and was no one's fault. Fate. God's will. Edi didn't know. She'd had no control over losing her baby eighteen hours and twenty-seven minutes after birth. And she'd had no power over Derek's reactions and choices. She couldn't control the course of her gran's disease. Her grief counselor had said that repeatedly. Maybe one day it would finally stick. She did know that after two years of feeling stuck and battered by hit after hit, she had to live again. She'd always imagined herself to be strong—she'd had to be considering what her childhood had thrown at her. To be this weak and wallowing was humiliating.

"It doesn't matter how many times you fall," she whispered under her breath. "It only matters that each time you get up and move forward."

And she was. Maybe not with a hop, skip and a jump, but she was taking steps. Except this man who'd appeared yesterday, like a conscience taunting her, made her feel like she was stuck in mud and gunk and goo.

She looked at the cup and the plate of several of her favorite pastries that she rarely allowed herself to indulge in. There was a box on the shelf of the window near where Ryder sat with the weak winter sun haloing him. Even as his prime butt hit the chair, he shifted positions, so he was facing the room, and now the beginnings of the sunrise were pink-golding the side of his face.

She looked at the cup, almost afraid to ask. Maybe her gran hadn't remembered her favorite latte.

"I haven't poisoned anyone…yet." Ryder smiled. "But it's still early. Lots of daylight left to rampage."

She picked up the cup and tried to sniff unobtrusively.

"Hazelnut latte. Nonfat milk."

"Thank you." She breathed in the aroma. "About last night…" This was not where she'd intended to begin, but perhaps if she could…clear the air between them, she'd be able to function as his…whatever she was, volunteer hours coordinator. Leader or boss sounded absurd. She couldn't imagine Ryder following anyone, and yet in the military, she'd always imagined that there was a strong chain of command.

"Yes?" He raised a brow as if inviting a confidence that felt sexual in nature, and she definitely shouldn't let her thoughts skew in that direction.

"My gran. She's…not doing so well."

A server brought a breakfast sandwich to Ryder—a bagel with an egg, spread of some kind, ham and a bunch of what looked like arugula poking out.

"Do you want to share the breakfast special? I asked them to cut it in half," he asked, holding out half.

"No," she said quickly, feeling disarmed. Derek had never shared, not even a bite of anything. "Thank you."

Not thinking about Derek.

And she and Ryder weren't friends.

But maybe…

That little voice of hope still popped up after so many years of being shot down, Edi marveled, not sure whether to roll her eyes at herself or cheer or cry. After all the criticism and disappointments lobbed at her by her mother, coupled with her parents' casual indifference mixed in with the jeering taunts by classmates throughout her childhood over her freckles, her height, her skinniness, she'd found most of her friends in books.

College had been a little better. She'd felt almost normal in her graduate program, and yet so much damage had been done that she still often felt like an imposter playing a part navigating social situations. Her gran had been her safe haven.

And now I'm hers.

"Are you sure?" Ryder pushed like a fallen angel on her left shoulder. "It's delicious. I had it yesterday. Hit the spot."

What spot was that?

Stop it.

"I'm not a big breakfast eater," she said, shocked by her pervy thoughts—all the more reason she couldn't work with Ryder. "And then by midafternoon if my gran doesn't eat the lunch I prepared, I often don't eat either because I'm so worried."

"Since I volunteer afternoons, I'll bring you a snack to avoid any hangry moments."

She risked a glance at him, already speculating which parts would be tastiest to snack on. *Stand down,* she ordered her libido and searched for a safer topic than snacking.

"You mentioned you might have a job," she led more than half hoping he'd be too busy to volunteer with her, and she wanted to kick herself for the pang of disappointment.

Ryder kicked out his long legs and again she noticed the flex of his thigh muscles. Her throat dried. She took a quick sip of her latte. Delicious.

"I'm aiming to be a cowboy again."

"Again?"

"I worked on a ranch as a teen," he said carelessly, taking another bite of his sandwich and not meeting her curious gaze. "A dude ranch for rich folks, but still." His gaze was wistful. "I took care of the horses. Helped on the trail rides and did the grunt work for the picnics and campfire dinners. Loved working with the horses and riding. I felt free. Necessary."

The last comment was swallowed with his food, and his gaze skittered past hers again to sweep the room. He leaned back in the chair, balancing perilously, in Edi's opinion, on two legs.

"You want to be a..." she searched for the right word "...ranch hand?"

He took another bite, chewed, and she wondered if he'd answer. Had she sounded judgey? She hadn't meant to. He was just so out of her realm.

"Yes, I want to be a ranch hand." He lowered to all four chair legs on the floor. "Lydia Dating Tip Three. Sharing my thoughts, small as they are." He took a deep swallow of his massive coffee.

He seemed momentarily vulnerable or embarrassed, which seemed out of character though she barely knew him.

"We're not dating."

"We are according to Lydia. I asked you to meet me. You agreed. You showed. I bought breakfast. I shared something of my past. One. Two. Three."

Edi stared at him. He wasn't serious, was he?

"Those aren't really dating tips," she said. "And this is not a date." That second fact she was certain of.

"What is it then?" he challenged.

She made a face. It wasn't like he wanted to date her. She wasn't fun anymore, although she doubted she would have been his type before. She wasn't sexy. She wasn't spontaneous. Those two adjectives had been hurled by Derek like a javelin of accusation and had hit the mark and lodged deep.

"No idea. We're not really colleagues, but if you are set

on volunteering we should talk about the clients and their needs and what would be safe for you to do."

"I'm all about safety first."

She nearly choked on her quick sip of latte. For some reason his flip comment made her think of condoms. He probably had a couple in his wallet right now. Edi squirmed a little, racking her brain for something, anything mundane to say.

She realized her mistake. Instead of avoiding Ryder, she should have typed up something that looked official detailing his duties for his volunteer hours. A plan would have been good. And she needed to refocus herself so that she too had a plan for her clients instead of dragging herself through each day, scattered, guilty and swamped by fear—and emotionally distant last night—but she'd been too exhausted from the workday and the stress of watching out for her gran last night at the games evening. Time to own up to her responsibilities.

She gulped in a breath. "About yesterday, what I said to Holly."

That blue gaze lasered on her, and her confession and apology fell apart like a house of cards. They stared at each other—breakfast sandwich, coffee and latte forgotten. Edi could swear she could hear her heartbeat.

"We need a plan," he said softly.

Desperately.

As a physical therapist she was accustomed to being in

charge—somewhat. She often worked collaboratively on a client's health program with doctors, other health care providers and family members.

She needed to give Ryder a plan.

"I…" She sighed. It was time to come clean, at least a little. "I'm sorry about what you overheard in Holly's office. It wasn't personal."

Good thing he didn't have a lie detector, but by the way his eyes narrowed a little, and his expression was just that much more inscrutable, maybe he did.

"I was overwhelmed. My gran's health. New town. This is a new job for me."

His expression softened a little and that encouraged her to continue.

"I've worked primarily with kids who are neurodivergent. That was my specialty. I moved to Marietta to take care of my gran, but my savings weren't going to last because she's in good physical health, but I could see that she was mentally declining, and…" She sucked in a deep breath and played with her coffee lid.

Ryder leaned forward and she could smell him. Fresh hay, citrus, a touch of spice and something earthy—maybe the horses he would be working with. And leather. She wanted to close her eyes and just breathe him in. Center herself.

"I couldn't get a job as a PT in a pediatric clinic in Bozeman because…" she wasn't ready to tell him everything so she settled on the partial story, "it would have been too far away from Gran in an emergency, and we already had a few scares like yesterday. The May Bell seemed like a good alternative. I'd be on site. It's easy to check on her and more secure than her alone at home."

"That's tough. Scary," he admitted. "I watched my nana decline."

Tears washed through Edi's eyes, and she gulped in a breath and dabbed at her eyes with a napkin. 'Scary' was the perfect word.

"Do you think memory care…" He stopped.

She pressed her trembling lips together. She didn't want to go there. And she didn't want to talk finances with Ryder. The break she got on her gran's monthly costs from being an employee made her situation manageable. The increased costs of memory care that was more than double would force her to sell her gran's house, and it felt like she'd be letting go of her last piece of her gran. And what if that money didn't last?

Ryder's hand covered hers, warm and strong, and even though worry clamored through her brain and her veins, she relaxed just a little.

"Not yet," she whispered. "I hope. She still has good days."

"That's good."

She had an odd impulse to bring his hand to her cheek. Breathe him in, imprint his hand on her bones. A man's hands had always been one of her turn-ons, and Ryder's were strong and gorgeous and big and rough, and she shivered thinking about how they would feel on her body, how his tanned hands would contrast with her pale, freckled softness.

"It's admirable that you are completing community service hours for someone who can't," she said, swallowing her want. "And I don't want to make it uncomfortable for you."

He shifted in his chair, his blue gaze drilling through her.

"I'll give you a tour of the facility sometime today and work up a plan of duties—things you can help me and the clients with—and you can let me know what hours you can volunteer," she whispered softly, but when he leaned forward, and his breath brushed her ear, her train of thought scattered like birdseed.

"Careful, Dr. Martin, this looks suspiciously like a date."

Something inside her threatened to come loose. To pop one brick from her wall and then another—letting something in or out, she wasn't sure. But she knew she had to hold him at arm's length. Safer. She couldn't build Humpty-Dumpty back by herself.

Not that you did a supreme job of it last time.

"Please." She realized her eyes were scrunched shut, and she opened them and turned her head slightly and found herself caught in the superb brilliant blue of his eyes and rather dramatic sweep of his long lashes, combined with the hard planes of his face offset by his disturbingly sensual mouth. "Ryder," she whispered. "Stop."

His reaction was instant. He removed his hand and leaned back into his space. She felt the distance like the composition of the air between them changed. "I won't tease you." His face was a mask of seriousness.

Disappointment hit hard. But necessary.

EDI WAS WOUND tight and complicated. He didn't do complicated so why did he find himself so drawn to her? He was taking the first steps to build a life outside of the army, and it wasn't fair to drag her along with him just because he was curious.

And lonely.

That thought made him wince. He was fine on his own. He had his hours to serve for Jace, and hopefully later this afternoon after he met with Rohan, his brother Boone and their father, Taryn Telford, he might have a part-time job for the next few months and a shot at a full-time one come spring.

He knew his service for the past twelve years and connection to Rohan would likely be the deciding factor, but the three ranchers assumed he had a deep background in ranching, when in reality it was pretty thin and not what they were expecting.

Solve one problem at a time.

He didn't have much schooling or ranch experience, but he worked hard and learned quickly. He wouldn't let Rohan down.

"Ryder." Edi interrupted his musings. "Do you really want to volunteer with the seniors exercise and activity program?"

"It's what the judge ordered for Jace's hours. Fulfilling Jace's hours is my task."

"At ease, Soldier," she muttered. "I get it. But do you want to do?" she pushed.

He laughed. "Baby, if I only did what I wanted to, I'd have starved a couple of decades ago."

He didn't mean for that to come out so harshly, and he jammed the last bite of the sandwich in his mouth to shut himself up and give him time to think. His nana had taught him think before he spoke. Too bad she hadn't lived long enough to know that her lessons and her care had stuck—for the most part.

"There are other ways you could fulfill your community service," she suggested.

Edi was still trying to get rid of him, and perversely, it made him more determined to stay whereas, initially, volunteering with geriatric patients had sounded terrifying. He'd been afraid he'd hurt them. Or the memories of his nana would haunt him. Instead, he felt settled, like he was exactly where he was supposed to be.

Jace's spirit?

Maybe.

But he wasn't going to fight it. He chewed and swallowed. Fate in the form of a judge had decided for him. A way to make amends. Who was he to question? One more cog in the wheel. One more soldier following orders. One more soul stumbling home.

"I'm good," he said, wondering if she was intending to give him an out, or herself.

But then he remembered what Rohan and his father had said to him last night when he'd followed Rohan home. He'd placed his duffel on a bed in an empty room in one of the two bunkhouses that had four rooms each, with Jack-and-Jill-style bathrooms between them. He'd wondered how he'd sleep with all that quiet before he had rejoined Rohan and his father at the entrance to the bunkhouse.

"We'll talk about the job tomorrow after your meeting at the May Bell Center," Taryn Telford had said, and Ryder had tried to swallow his unaccustomed bout of nerves.

He'd felt like he should confess then and there about the true nature of his ranch experience.

Rohan had looked at him a long time. "Ry, there's no shame in asking questions or for help when you need it."

"Yeah." He'd kept his mouth shut.

Rohan had leaned against the wall after his father had left. "Don't keep everything locked too tight," Rohan had added. "I made that mistake. Let people in, little by little, and it can become a habit."

It should have been laughable. Rohan Telford, badass Special Forces sniper, who could go hours, days without speaking telling him to let people in. But Rohan hadn't been laughing, and Ryder hadn't either.

He dragged his mind back to the present and the woman perched on the edge of her chair in a coffee shop that seemed such a long way away from where he'd been even a week ago.

"I won't lie and say working with elderly folks is a career goal," he said carefully, taking another sip of coffee, gauging her reaction. He didn't want to be negative because he owed his best to Jace. "But I have some experience." His voice caught in his throat, but he forced the rest out to reassure Edi that he wasn't going to take her patients' needs lightly. "I told you I lived with my nana. I was her primary…caretaker."

He felt a little like he had when he'd taken his first jump out of a plane—the ground rushing up—and he took a huge gulp of the scalding coffee to control his voice. "I have experience with frailty and fear and confusion," he said, keeping his voice low and level when it wanted to short out on him. "But I'll be honest, I'm not used to spending so much time inside. It feels claustrophobic, and I get a little antsy and need to move."

"Oh," Edi breathed, her beautiful gaze like leaves and dirt in a mountain stream, met his. "I hadn't thought of that—how different your life has been."

"And the beige walls are madness-inducing," he added, knowing he should zip it.

"There's a courtyard off the therapy and activity rooms,"

Edi said. "It's not pretty in winter, but there is a covered area, heaters, fire pit. You could step outside for a break."

She meant it. No shame. Just kindness, respect and problem-solving. The wary Edi was gone. The compassionate Edi, who had entered a field of healing, whereas he had jumped into a career of protection, was back.

"If there's a covered area and heaters, maybe we could do some outdoor exercises or games one afternoon," he said, testing her a little.

The look she shot him should not have been hot, but it did make him want to put a very different look on her face.

Not on the menu, pal.

"I want to be a help, Edi, not a hindrance," he admitted, wanting to hold on to this bit of warmth blossoming between them. "I can learn quickly. It's what I do. I know I pushed too hard yesterday trying to be…helpful, keep things moving, but yesterday the memories were too close." He stretched out his legs, a little dismayed that he was still talking, but thanks to Rohan's late-night reminder and Lydia's sly dating tip number four—'share a little of yourself even if it scares you'—Ryder knew he had to operate differently as a civvy if he wanted to build a life with meaning after the army.

"I lived with my nana growing up off and on and always on from age eleven. She got ill when I was fourteen, COPD and congestive heart failure, and she started forgetting things, and I took care of her…as best I could."

"Oh." Edi's hand was on his. Warm, soft. So alive. And something unexpectedly shivered through him. "Ryder. That's so hard. You must have been so frightened."

Terrified.

A host of memories slammed through him, and he held himself still, stacking the memories, like boxes, unopened, in the corner of his mind. He was good at this part. Holding memories, feelings back. Even when the packing tape on the boxes flapped in the wind threatening to spill the contents like a modern Pandora's box.

"I dealt."

"You were a child."

"Almost a man," he said defensively, but he didn't jerk his hand away.

"Fourteen is a child."

They'd have to agree to disagree on that one.

"Did you have help? Family? Social services?"

How to explain that time? Who he'd been. How he'd thought. It didn't make sense to him now, and back then, he'd been in survival mode.

"She was my family. She'd done right by me, and I did right by her." He swallowed away. He felt itchy, and his hair was in his eyes, but he didn't want to lose Edi's touch. He flipped his palm around so their fingers were linked. "Well, the best I could do, but it wasn't enough," he admitted still shamed. "I wasn't enough."

"Ryder," Edi whispered, holding his fingers so tightly,

and the pressure grounded him.

"There wasn't money for much medical care and social services would have taken me away."

Not that he'd explored that avenue. Too much risk, and his nana had been so scared.

"It must have been so difficult." Edi's eyes were huge, soft with emotion, and glistening a little. "You had school, friends, sports though?"

There'd been no money or time for any of that either, but he wasn't about to add to the pity party.

"Yeah, well, I managed as best I could," he said, pulling his hand away from hers. He didn't deserve her comfort. His best hadn't been nearly good enough.

"Ryder." Her eyes searched his like he was a book she could read. She reached out to maybe brush her fingers along his cheek, and he braced himself, not because he didn't want her touch, but because he wanted it too much.

"I'm sorry about your nana. We have that in common. I feel like nothing I do for my gran is enough." She looked down at her lap. "I wanted to take care of her in her home, but..." She nervously moistened her lips, and he had no right to fixate on that. "I get a break on her apartment by working there," she admitted, "but you're right. I'll have to move her to memory care sooner than..." Edi's voice trailed off and now he was the one giving her fingers a quick squeeze.

Who would have guessed he'd spill his guts in a fancy

coffee shop in a Montana winter?

Edi dragged in a shaky breath, while he reminded himself at least three times not to pull her into his arms for a hug. She wouldn't want that. She didn't trust him. They weren't friends, and they weren't even colleagues, not really.

He was temporary.

"Sorry." She looked up at him. "I didn't mean to get so heavy and lay my troubles on you. That's not why we were meeting, and now I've got to get to work."

He checked his watch. He should head back to the ranch and learn the details of the job opportunity. He'd been researching what a stock contractor employee did as he'd thought the job would suit him. But he didn't know what winter chores would entail other than feeding and cleaning out the stalls—were bulls even kept in stalls? His fingers itched to start inputting questions into his phone.

"I'm heading back to the Telford Family Ranch to talk about part-time work. Hope to have a job and schedule so I can give you a schedule for my hours," he said. They both stood up at the same time, and he was pleasantly reminded about how much he liked her height.

She was only a couple inches shorter than he was so he could look into her expressive eyes, map the myriad of freckles on her pale skin. He wouldn't have to bend down to kiss her. And if he did kiss her, he'd feel her body imprint with her breasts to his chest, hips aligned, thighs pressed.

Not your rodeo, Cowboy.

Still when their breath mingled, he felt a charge, and it reminded him that he was a man and alive and getting another shot at life, which Jace wasn't so he shouldn't waste a moment.

"I mean it, Edi." He dragged out the words. "I want to be a help, an asset. It's important to me so put me to work. I work hard. I learn fast. You can count on me."

She pressed her trembling lips together and tears swam in her eyes. She jerked her head in a nod. "That's kind of what I'm afraid of," she said cryptically. "Thank you for the coffee."

"Anytime."

She hurried toward the door then stopped and turned around. She didn't say anything but held her fingers up, crossed again like yesterday, and it was so sweet and so cute that Ryder, for a moment, was too choked up to move.

"You got this," she said.

And Ryder wasn't sure that he did, but he was determined to squash any concerns and prove Edi and Rohan and Jace—who'd always said a man could succeed on his own terms if he put his heart and soul and will into it and just kept trying—right.

"See you this afternoon," he promised as her hand was on the door. He swung his arms wide, channeling that cocky kid he'd once been. "I'll be all yours to train and command."

Edi's mouth dropped open, and he nearly laughed at her shocked expression. A few women who'd been chatting together at a table, one of whom had a baby in a stroller next to her that she was gently pushing back and forth, looked at him speculatively, but he kept his gaze pinned to the blushing Edi.

"Careful, Soldier." She recovered her poise. "That might go to my head."

"Cowboy." He strode toward her, full of purpose. He expected her to scurry out the door, but she held her place, and he crowded her a little. The sexual tension that had hummed between them cranked higher, and he breathed it in, reveling in how alive he felt. "And, Edi…" he dropped his voice low so only she could hear "…I certainly hope so."

Chapter Five

RYDER WAS LATE.
Not that she had been counting the minutes since this morning's coffee that still had her unsettled. She'd thought when they'd stood in the doorway of the Java Café that he was about to kiss her. She'd even swayed toward him like she was in a Lifetime channel movie.

As if.

But even after his reveal about his nana and how he was all in on the volunteer position because he'd made a vow, he was late.

And it wasn't because he got caught up at work because Ryder had texted that he would be working mornings on the ranch, leaving the afternoon free to work at the May Bell Center. Then he'd said he was on his way to her.

'To her,' had jump-started her silly heart, but that was nearly an hour ago.

Not that she was looking at her Apple Watch again.

Edi sprayed down the equipment she'd used during the last client's session and prepared the room for her next client. She was not listening for Ryder's footsteps. That would be stupid. He'd just sauntered into her life yesterday, and he could and would swagger back out when his time was served.

"Ugh." She gave an extra-hard swipe to the railing. "He's not a criminal."

But she had to stop thinking about him. She was giddily aware of the clock and the fact that she'd been holding her breath, attuned to the footsteps in the hall, proved she was not ready for anything with a man.

Not that Ryder was offering.

Or that it would be appropriate.

He was a volunteer where she worked.

He was younger than her, by more than five years.

He was a soldier. A cowboy. He didn't have to beat his chest or posture. He just was a man. Innate masculinity. Utterly tummy-flipping, blood-pumping, heart-skipping physical.

What am I doing?

She picked up the set of one- and three-pound hand weights and scrubbed at them with the antibacterial wipes as if the weights were muddy. Was she trying to talk herself into or out of fantasizing about Ryder?

Out.

She'd never dated a lot. She'd been too self-conscious of her freckles and long, skinny body as a teen to even look at boys. But she and Ryder had tight bonds with a grandparent in common, though he'd lost his nana when he'd been quite young.

Had her gran really given him dating tips? A man as

masculine, handsome and oozing with a sense of fun, charm and adventure didn't need any dating tips. The idea was ludicrous. She needed them, no doubt, but since she had no intention of dating again, especially a man as masculine and sexy as Ryder, any tips would be wasted. Her gran had had many adventures in love. She'd regaled Edi with stories that had made Edi laugh and blush and marvel at her gran's fearlessness.

Edi had always felt too self-conscious. Her mom's shocked disappointment that her daughter was so physically plain had shamed her so she hadn't ever tried to improve her appearance with makeup, hairstyle or clothing. She'd buried herself in books and schoolwork and in high school sports too. She'd been deep into college before she'd explored dating and her choices had been quiet, academic, professionally ambitious men—not a man who could wield an assault rifle one day and rock whatever cowboy or rodeo fantasy she had the next.

And look how dating the safe, quiet nerd turned out.

Scowling at her thoughts, Edi put the weights away and spritzed the harness that hung near the stairs of the therapy bridge she often used to help clients with balance issues. She'd always had a disciplined mind, not one that detoured into speculating about eye-candy men, but today she kept remembering the light in Ryder's eyes, the slant of his smile, the energy zipping through his body.

"I'm doing it again," she accused.

"Doing what?"

Ryder's cheerful voice startled her, and she yipped like an excited coyote and jumped, stumbling over the chair and clinging to the harness to stand upright.

Ryder stood several feet in the room with her next client. He had the therapy belt looped around Rebekah Silver's skinny waist with just the right amount of tension. Mrs. Silver clutched her red walker with pug stickers on it and stared up at Ryder instead of at her pink-slippered feet.

"Now that's giving me ideas." Ryder grinned, looking at the harness and then into Edi's eyes, inviting her to share whatever inappropriate fantasy his mind had dredged up.

"Whaaat?" She gaped at him even as her inner voice tried to save her by yelling about keeping her cool. He'd just made a sexual innuendo and in front of a client. Or was she so hyperaware of him that she was reading things that weren't there?

Younger. Hotter. Not serious.

Mrs. Silver twittered and slapped at Ryder's arm. "You are a naughty one."

Edi dropped the harness, and it swung a little drunkenly around her. She brushed her palms on her scrubs, digging for dignity. "What are you doing here?"

"I am bringing Mrs. Silver to her physical therapy appointment. She tried to charm her way out of it by offering me tea and lemon scones her granddaughters brought to her this morning. Oh, and they brought her pug Pugsley for a visit."

"You weren't supposed to tell."

Ryder smiled. "I have to tell Edi; she's my boss."

"I bet you know how to keep a secret from a woman, young man, and Edi is a young, single woman. She's a catch."

"Edi's all that and more, ma'am," Ryder said cheerfully. "Let's see what fun activities she has in store for you today."

Ryder's grin was infectious, and Edi had to bite her cheek to keep from smiling back like a giddy teen. She had to take control of this situation and set some ground rules. She hadn't even worked a full week at the May Bell Center and her clients and volunteers couldn't be calling her Edi.

"It's Dr. Martin," she reminded them softly, but she still sounded like a pretentious ass.

Like Derek.

But she had to remind Ryder to remain professional because he was so…so…unnerving. Her body felt like it had an electrical current that he'd flipped on just by walking in the room and smiling at her. She didn't want her body to wake up. Crave things. She didn't want to feel. She couldn't hold any more hurt inside.

Anger and despair flared, and she didn't know what to do with either of them.

Ryder's smile was gone. Mrs. Silver frowned.

"You're late. And…and you shouldn't use equipment you're not trained on." Edi hurried forward to ensure that Mrs. Silver was stable, which she should have done immediately.

"I'm fine." Mrs. Silver's mouth set in mutinous lines, not unlike the neurodivergent toddlers and young children Edi used to work with. Mrs. Silver pushed her walker at her.

"I only came because he showed up at my door." She rammed Edi again. "I bet no one says no to him ever."

"Hey now." Ryder's voice was low and smooth, and he kept the tension on the belt with one hand while he held the walker still with the other.

To have that strength, coordination and reach... Edi shut down that observation. Men were not better physical therapists. She was highly trained. Had been in the profession for years. Just because she'd changed...well just about everything, didn't mean she was starting all over—although most days it felt like she was.

"Dr. Martin is here to help you maintain your strength and agility," Ryder reasoned. "You don't want to be trapped in a body that no longer works so you can't enjoy tea and scones with your granddaughters and friends. Your granddaughters said your goal is to get out of skilled nursing care and into one of the assisted living apartments. They have a deposit down on one."

Mrs. Silver bowed her head.

"But you need to regain some strength and mobility so that Pugsley can join you."

Mrs. Silver pursed her lips. "But it hurts."

"I bet," Ryder said. "But Dr. Martin's here to help, and by showing up and trying each session, you'll achieve your goal, and you and Pugsley will be in your new home."

Mrs. Silver smiled tremulously and blinked as tears fell.

Edi tried not to notice the shaft of winter sun that pierced the mostly gray clouds and highlighted Ryder's face and cheekbones through the window. The light cast sexy hollows, planes and shadows, making him look both beautiful and broody like a god alone on a distant planet preparing for war. Or seduction. And then there was his tone. What would it be like to lie in bed in the dark and listen to him talk?

She could barely swallow at the audaciousness of that random and inappropriate thought.

"Can I work with you?" Mrs. Silver asked, almost childlike.

"I'll be here." Ryder smiled. "I'll assist Dr. Martin and provide the comic relief."

Edi opened her mouth that comedy was the last, absolute *last* thing they needed, but there was something in his tone that stopped her. She shot him a look, but his face was devoid of expression, suspiciously so.

"And Dr. Martin has a few tricks up her sleeve so I'm sure you'll have a good time and once you stop resisting her, your strength and mobility will return, and you can move into your new apartment. Maybe one day after one of your sessions, we should look at some decorations online—get some inspiration for your new digs."

"I have a phone with unlimited data," Mrs. Silver said.

"My granddaughters bought it for me, and they give me lessons. Maybe you can help me find some decorating sites."

"I probably could. Depends on how you take to your therapy," Ryder said seriously, and Mrs. Silver glared at him suspiciously and then she smiled.

"Think you're so clever, young man."

He quirked a brow, and Mrs. Silver's body tension relaxed a little. "Okay, you win," she said. "I'll do it for Pugsley."

Guilt slithered through Edi.

She used to try to make therapy fun for her young and adolescent clients.

Why was she being so judgey, practically militant now? No wonder none of her new clients seemed happy to see her. And she was taking her feelings of failure and rejection out on Ryder. It wasn't Ryder's fault that she felt like an imposter because she'd never wanted to work in geriatrics. It wasn't Ryder's fault that her life had fallen apart, and she'd lost everything, and now was facing losing her gran. It wasn't Ryder's fault that he was so appealing and hot that she couldn't swallow her own spit.

Pull yourself together and do your job and focus on other people's feelings, not your own.

"It's nice to see you, Mrs. Silver." Edi kept her voice warm. She knew she'd have to have a talk with Ryder. He meant well, but he couldn't show up late, and he definitely couldn't transfer clients and bring them to the therapy room on his own without training. Her clients were frail.

Mrs. Silver snorted her disagreement and looked at Edi suspiciously. "I don't abide by tricks."

"What? Oh. No. Ryder was joking. I don't have any tricks up my sleeve." She waved her arms in the air feeling ridiculous.

"I'm a little disappointed, Dr. Martin," Ryder said. "Coming in here and seeing you testing out that harness I was hoping for something special today. Aerial acrobatics. Swooping around the therapy room like Supergirl. Maybe we should put some P!nk music on the Sonos speakers. I know all the words to 'Get the Party Started' and 'Blow Me.'" He winked. "'(One Last Kiss).'"

Edi choked on an inappropriate laugh that threatened escape, but Mrs. Silver's pinched face broke into a smile and then she laughed.

"Young man, you might be the death of me, but what a way to go." Still smiling she pushed herself farther in the room, Ryder still partially supporting her weight with the strap.

"Let's get this party started," Mrs. Silver said. "And I do want to work out to that song," she said imperiously.

RYDER SAT ON a bench down across the hall from the staff lounge and between the arts and craft studio and the woodworking studio. The woodworking studio was dark, the door closed, but the craft room door was ajar, and several women were knitting in there and talking in happy tones.

He closed his eyes and leaned back against the wall. He wasn't tired, not physically. But he felt empty. Cold. Disconnected in a way he didn't understand. He remembered holding yarn for his nana, when she still knitted. He'd hold, and she'd quiz him about his school assignments or upcoming tests. He allowed the emptiness to wash over and through him. It was a testament to how much he'd loved her. And she'd been the only one to love him.

He had to get up and get back on the road to drive back to the Telford Ranch to meet with Rohan's father and his brother, Boone. They'd texted that he should swing by to see the more of the ranch including all the barns, and equipment sheds. They'd also invited him to look at the training arena for the bucking broncs and the bulls and to discuss his experience and what he was looking for. Boone had also said that since he was bunking on the ranch, he could take over some of the evening chores. The extra money would be welcome.

The doubt crept in even though he was almost thirty-one, and had been a highly decorated soldier. He might not have grown up ranch, but his nana had. She'd told stories about her family's small ranch. And he'd worked on the dude ranch for a few years before joining the service. He could learn, handle himself. It wasn't like he hadn't been googling working cattle ranches and bull and bronc stock contracting operations, since Jace had talked to him about mustering out, but he couldn't shake the fear of letting Rohan down. He didn't want to disappoint or be exposed as a fraud, or worse, get someone or an animal injured due to his inexperience.

'It's a matter of will. Working hard enough to achieve your goals.'

Jace's words floated back to him, and he forced himself to sit up straight just in case Jace's spirit was checking on him.

He could do this. Winter was slow. He'd have time to learn and gain the Telfords' trust. Others might have many advantages, but no one could outwork him. No one. In another month or so calving would start and by the spring, he'd either be working long, ranching hours, or transporting bucking broncs or bulls to the different rodeo circuits. He hoped he earned enough trust to get that job. Life on the road would be easier to adjust to after twelve years in the army. And he'd finally see some of this great, vast country.

But first he had to finish Jace's community service. And stop pissing off Edi—Dr. Martin. Maybe if he thought of her as Dr. Martin it would be easier to slip her pull. He wasn't sure why he was so attracted. She wasn't his usual type. Somehow, she'd reached inside of him. Made a place there. But why? She wasn't a woman out for an easy good time. Edi was serious, sweet, more than a little sad, and so smart he could smell it on her. What would she want with a man like him?

And yet, stupid idiotic him, he wanted to make her smile. Notice him. And that had him showing off a little, wanting to make her laugh, relax, trust him.

Great. I'm back to the emotional maturity of a fifth-grade boy.

"Hey, I thought you'd left."

Edi. He popped to his feet. "Working on it."

"Takes a lot out of you," she said, her voice warm with sympathy that he didn't deserve.

She went into the staff lounge and returned with two cups of coffee and a frosted sugar cookie.

"Last one." She split the cookie in half and handed it to him along with a cup of coffee and a small napkin. "Calories don't count at work. Not that you need to worry about that from what I can see."

She looked a little shocked by her comment, and her cheeks pinkened. A million juvenile male thoughts flitted through his head, but he kept his mouth shut. He also felt unbearably touched. Edi had split the cookie with him. No one had shared food with him since it was just him and his nana. His throat tightened.

"What's wrong?" Edi sat down next to him.

Her presence was surprisingly soothing. Earlier this afternoon, he'd sensed her tension layered with more than a spoonful of judgment—not that he hadn't faced more than huge helpings of that during his life, but it was the sexual tension that had zinged through the room when they'd accidently touch or one of them or one of the clients would say something that triggered their shared sense of humor.

"You okay?" she tried again.

He didn't know how to answer that. When he'd been with his unit, he had to be okay. They relied on him. He kept the team's spirits up, used humor to keep the tension and fear at bay.

"Yeah." He took a bite of the cookie, and chewed but felt like he couldn't swallow.

"Tough guy," she muttered taking a sip of coffee just as he said: "Delicious."

Edi clapped her hand over her mouth and made a weird sound and hunched over, her shoulders shaking.

"Hey." His hand stroked down her back. "Are you okay?" She wasn't choking was she? Edi coughed into her napkin, and he splayed his hand between her shoulder blades, wondering if he should pound on her back or do the Heimlich, but she was so slim he'd probably rupture her spleen.

"Fine," she choked out. She coughed some more. Cleared her throat and sat up, her eyes watering.

"Typically unsmooth move," she said derisively, smiling a little. "Edi Martin's in the house. I was always uncool and ungraceful, and my…a friend always said it was a force of irony that I became a physical therapist."

"You move just fine," he said and cringed. That wasn't sexual was it? He'd spent the whole afternoon trying not to think of her sexually, but his runaway brain and mouth had made that challenging, so of course he'd teased and flirted.

"I'm glad I caught you," she said. "I wanted..." She sipped her coffee. "I don't want to seem ungrateful, but..." She paused searching for words.

Ryder sat up, trying to think of what he possibly could have done wrong when he'd been so focused on taking care of the patients and trying to anticipate every need and every danger. He'd imagined each one could have been his precious nana if only he'd been older, better able to care for her, work harder.

She sat up straight, sucked in a breath and looked him in the eye, angling so that her knees brushed his.

"If you're going to complete your community service here with me, you need to be on time and keep to the schedule."

"Copy that."

She'd already opened her mouth to continue so there must be a list of flaws she'd noticed. Fantastic. Just like his mother, who'd back up every 'stepfather' over him. And his sisters had always found something to nitpick to the point they'd dumped him on his nana's doorstep while she'd been at work and left him like a stray dog.

"And you need...but you weren't on time," she interrupted herself.

"There was an accident on the highway. I stopped to help right the truck out of the ditch, but a livestock fence had gone down so cows were wandering everywhere, and I had to call for help. I texted you and left a message at the front desk that I'd be late."

"Oh, I don't look at my phone during work. Something else you should adhere to," she said repressively.

He opened his mouth to tell her he'd been looking at videos on how to transfer geriatric patients out of bed and walkers and wheelchairs and physical therapy exercises and games, but figured she didn't want to hear excuses.

"And no one notified me," she said into his silence. "Were the cows okay?"

"Not the driver?" Ryder smiled, charmed by her faint blush.

"Him too," she added, clearly an afterthought.

"He was fine. Embarrassed. Black ice. And I only use my phone at work when I'm looking for tips on how to help the pa…clients with transfers or equipment or exercise technique." He'd learned never to defend himself as a child—he'd get slapped, kicked or walloped, but as an adult, he wasn't going to get pushed around.

Edi sucked in a deep breath, and he braced for another criticism. "You did a good job today," she surprised him by saying. "I know you are trying your best, and want to be helpful, but you're not trained, and so I think it's best to leave the transfers and the…"

"What do you want me to do, just sit and watch and hand things to you or your patients?"

"Clients. Yes."

"I can do the basic things. I googled techniques last night."

She blushed even pinker, and then drew herself up like a ballerina about to go on stage.

"I have a doctorate in physical therapy, and all of that can't be achieved in one Google search."

"I know, but…"

"So let me do my job. I'm licensed. You aren't. We have to protect the clients and the center from a lawsuit."

He nodded, a quick jerk of his head, and stood up. She was right. He wasn't needed. He definitely wasn't educated. This was for Jace. Temporary. He and Edi weren't really colleagues, and they certainly weren't going to be friends.

"Hey." Her fingers brushed his, and her touch, although brief, rooted him. "I'm not trying to be a bitch," she said softly. "I'm just protective of my clients, and of the center and of you."

"Me?" he asked in disbelief. He didn't need anyone watching out for him.

"Yeah, you are trying to help, to do good in the world, and I don't want something bad to happen to a client or to you that we could avoid."

He hadn't thought about it that way.

"You have other goals. Dreams. You're building a new

life for yourself. Working on a ranch. Your volunteering at the May Bell Center is admirable. You're trying to do more good in the world to honor your friend. I don't want anything to mess that up for you."

"Train me," he said.

"What?"

"Show me at least how I can help with the transfers and walk with the clients back to their rooms. Teach me to do some basic things so I'm a help, not a pain in your ass. And not a risk to anyone."

For a moment she stared at him, and he wondered if he'd overstepped. Again.

'Always wanting more,' something his mother had said and later his sisters had parroted before they left him with his ailing nana when all he'd wanted was to belong and to have a purpose in the family.

"Please." He forced out the last word that tasted like ashes in his mouth. "I don't want to be a burden or useless. I am here to help, to honor Jace. Let me help."

What else did he have to offer the world other than his strong arms, strong back and willingness to serve?

"Are you interested in a career in health care?" The doubt in her voice was tangible, and he didn't blame her. His GED was a hell of a long road away from her doctorate.

"No," he admitted, knowing he needed to get out of the facility so he could breathe and see a horizon and reset. "But like I told you, I was the primary caretaker for my nana for a few years so helping elderly patients…clients," he corrected, "is not totally new, and I can't help but think that if I'd had training or help my nana would have lived longer."

He blew out a breath into the stark silence that greeted that unexpected and unwelcome confession thirteen years too late. He was an idiot. 'Always wanting more' than the crumbs.

"See you tomorrow afternoon." He practically launched off the bench like he'd seen bull riders dismount after hitting eight seconds and quickly strode down the hallway. He took the stairs two at a time to the main level and shoved the glass door open and stepped into the pale sun and sharp cold that cut into his lungs and would hopefully clear his head before he met with the Telfords to discuss what might be the first full step into his new life.

Chapter Six

"Hey, Cowboy."

Ryder hung up the keys to the snowmobile when he heard Rohan's deep growl of a voice. Ryder had just waved off his potential stock contracting partner, Garrett Hayes, who had toured him around the lower pastures—covered in snow—where the cattle wintered. They'd checked the water and added to the feed before heading back to the barn. Garrett had said he still had a couple of hours of work in the arena but had declined his offer of help, saying Rohan wanted to meet with him.

"Want to have some fun?" Rohan asked.

"By that you mean...?" Ryder trailed off, pulling his work gloves off his hands to tuck into his back pocket.

"You're going to want to keep those. Glove up. Protection first." Rohan practically smirked.

"Oh, that kind of fun," Ryder dead-panned, doubting Rohan, Mr. Engaged Coyote Cowboy, was inviting him out for a beer again.

"Better than." Rohan smiled. "You didn't think we just fed and groomed these beasts, did you?" Rohan walked out of the barn and headed toward his truck. "We train them.

And we invite some cowboys for training if they got the balls. You can ride with me."

"Is that a challenge?" Ryder had ridden a lot of horses as a teen, but never a bucking bronc. His heart kicked up.

"In the truck." Rohan laughed at his no doubt stupid male bravado. "After twelve years in the field, I prefer to keep you in one piece stateside." Rohan started the truck and put it in drive before Ryder was halfway inside.

"I can see that." He plunked down on his ass, slammed his door and buckled up just as the annoying beeper sounded. "So definitely a challenge?"

Rohan's green eyes glinted in the light of the cab that slowly faded out, and his face had a mysterious red-green tinge from the dashboard lights. Rohan's ranch truck was top of the line, and Ryder stuffed down the ping of envy. He was lucky to be alive with everything functioning. He had wheels—so what if his truck was six years old. He knew how to keep an engine running. And he had a job and a bed and three squares if he wanted to go to the bunkhouse kitchen.

"You ever ridden a bull?"

Shame filtered through Ryder, even as he kicked it aside. He'd been accepted into the Coyote Cowboys because he'd told them he'd worked on a ranch in Nebraska. That hadn't been a lie, but he hadn't told them it was a high-end dude ranch. And he hadn't told them he'd been a teenager and responsible for caring for the horses because the guests weren't expecting to get dirty. He'd saddled up, brought up the rear on the trail rides and schlepped gear for picnics and cookouts, and was mostly there to assist or rescue if a guest or horse had problems.

"No." He shrugged. "Horses."

And he hadn't been on a horse in over twelve years.

"You do rodeo when you were a kid, junior circuit?"

Ryder forced his body not to tense. "This the second part of the job interview?"

"You got the job."

Ryder waited for the rest. No use handing a man the rope he might use to hang him.

"We got cameras on the livestock when they're in the barns and pastures close in."

"Yeah." Ryder had noticed. "High-end. Figured you had something to do with that."

He also figured that where there were cameras, someone was watching. He didn't like it, but some of these bucking bulls could bring in six figures, and that was before the stud fees.

"My dad and Colt Wilder rigged up a good system. When I came home at Christmas, I made it better."

"You came home at Christmas, and you're already engaged?"

Rohan laughed. "That's your takeaway?"

Ryder silently cursed his reaction. A couple of days off base and he was going soft, and his mouth was too big.

"Wonder why women get the reputation for gossip,"

Rohan teased.

Ryder stared out the windshield. It was starting to snow again. Good. It was going to be his job to get up before daylight whispered and rev up the tractor with the plow to keep the main access roads on the ranch accessible. But there were also the snowmobiles when bigger storms hit. Still, he was glad he'd been assigned a job that was clear-cut and mattered. He'd driven the tractor without having to pepper Garrett with questions. And while the evening feeding had gone smoothly last night, when Garrett had talked about some of the tasks awaiting them as stock contractors in late March, some of it had sounded like a whole new language.

One I will master.

"Ginny," Rohan said. "And Lucas."

"Huh?" He looked at Rohan, and now it was his former teammate's turn to stare straight ahead like the road might suddenly switch directions if he didn't keep vigil, even though Rohan was the fourth generation on the ranch.

"Ginny was my high school girl. We...split first year of college. I walked out after my first semester of college, joined up, and pretty much stayed away until I came home for good late November. Wasn't sure I could stay. Lot of water under that bridge, but it feels right."

Ryder nodded. Kept his mouth shut, not willing to ask Rohan what he'd been thinking walking away from his family, from his home, from his legacy, from his shot at college, from his girl who loved him.

Unfathomable.

But what did he know of Rohan's life before?

Ryder's childhood had been a series of increasingly squalid apartments until he'd landed with his nana. He might have had to sleep on the couch, but she kept the apartment clean, stocked with food and had even sewn curtains for the windows and had flowers in a few pots by the front door.

"I had some tough moments adjusting when I came home," Rohan said.

"I'm fine." Ryder didn't want one of those talks. He could lock everything down tight. He was a vault.

"I know you will be." Rohan looked at him, a smile ghosting across his face.

"Because if you need something, you ask." His voice got stern, and though Rohan had outranked him, Ryder didn't think he'd use it as a civvy, but he was technically his boss or maybe his younger brother Boone was. He should probably get clear on the chain of command.

"You got me. Huck. Cross. A former ranger named Colt Wilder has a nonprofit that helps vets adjust. Cross's wife is a former army psychologist, and she's running a couple of groups and taking individual appointments starting this spring when she gets her license in Montana. You met Shane at the Graff."

"The bartender's a shrink," he stated. Come to think of it, that wasn't that much of a jump. "Don't need her. I'm fine."

"If we could will ourselves fine, we'd all be fine so don't be an arrogant jerk."

Ryder shot him a look.

"Need you to download the security app for the ranch so you can see what's going on in all the barns with the bucking bulls and the broncs, although we won't separate all of them for the circuit this year until late March, early April, but we've peeled some off for practice to get a feel for their temperament and skills."

Ryder downloaded the app following Rohan's terse directions. He quickly scrolled through the feeds.

What's going on in building 5, the arena?" Ryder asked. He saw Garrett laughing, chatting, looking way more at ease than when he'd been showing Ryder around.

"It's showtime. Boys to men." Rohan stopped the truck alongside another Telford Family Ranch truck. "Although today it's only dummies."

"Nice way to talk about your brother."

"I'll tell Boone you said that. He's got some bull-riding and bucking-bronc buckles, but he still holds the Copper Mountain Rodeo fastest time in steer wrestling so trash-talk at your peril."

The second stab of envy poked sharp and unwanted. Life was what it was, and Ryder dealt with what came, didn't wish for a different lot, but it was hitting home how little he belonged here. How far he was from a true cowboy.

But he could become whatever he wanted. Make a place

for himself through hard work and loyalty. He'd achieved that in the army, and he'd succeed here. Rohan had thrown him a lifeline, and Ryder wouldn't let go.

As they walked toward the barn, he was shocked when Rohan threw his arm around his shoulder, and pulled him in for a tight, side hug.

"My father watched you with the bulls this morning and out in pastures A and B with the horses. You got a gift, a gentleness and comfort he wasn't anticipating."

The unexpected praise washed over Ryder hot and fast, leaving him wordless with embarrassment. He'd enjoyed meeting the bulls, taking their measure, eyeballing them for health. Freshening their water, weighing out their food. The tasks had been mundane, and yet magnificent.

"You did every task with care, focused on detail, and you greeted each animal. That's important to my dad. The bulls and broncs that compete are family to him. The animals are important to all of us."

Ryder paused in front of the small door to the right of the massive roll-up door.

"It's important to me too," Ryder said. "I want this job, Rohan. I want to work on a ranch. I want to take care of the animals. I want to travel the west. I want to…"

He barely broke off in time. God, he'd nearly said he wanted to matter. What was next? I want to have a home? Would he and Rohan pop popcorn, unwrap Hershey's Kisses and watch Hallmark movies? Sign him up on a dating app?

Hard no.

Rohan waited for the rest. He could wait all night.

"You can belong here if you want, Ryder. It's up to you."

He could barely swallow so he bobbed his head and tried not to say or do something stupid like shout the F-word and run back down the slope they'd just driven up. He'd already run out on Edi today. He'd never done the feels. Usually, he just made a joke. But this was too important, and he didn't want Rohan to think that he'd take his family's business and their animals lightly, ever.

Rohan's searching eyes lightened, and he nodded as if he understood what was happening. Good, because Ryder felt out of his depth.

"But before we get you out on the road, you have a lot to learn."

"Bring it," Ryder said and opened the door to the arena, not sure what he'd find, but ready to take it all on.

"YOU GOING TO try to knit something this afternoon, Gran?" Edi asked, noting that she only had ten more minutes of her lunch hour. She'd made her gran spaghetti Bolognese, but her gran had mostly pushed the pasta and sauce and the grilled peppers around on her plate. She'd only taken a bite of the garlic toast.

"Knit?" Her gran looked at her blankly. "Why would I

knit?"

"You used to love it," Edi said, feeling the all too common urge to cry. "You would knit little beanies for the newborns at the children's hospital."

"I did?"

Edi smiled. "Yes." Then she focused on putting her gran's lunch that would maybe become her dinner in Tupperware. She'd hoped that her gran would start enjoying having lunch with others in the adult day program, and join some of the activities with the other seniors in her wing or in the adult day care program, but so far she'd refused.

Edi tried not to get discouraged. Moving was an adjustment, and her gran hadn't wanted to leave her small family home. Edi had thought that if they ate lunch and dinner together, her gran would have more of an appetite and Edi could better monitor her nutrition. Most days that was a distant dream. She made a note in her phone to make an appointment with her gran's doctor to see if there were ways to boost her appetite. Edi made a second note to research a few more recipes that might tempt her gran.

She tucked her phone back in her pocket. She needed to leave to prepare for her group exercise class. And have her calm on when Ryder arrived.

"You taught me how to knit, embroider, crochet. We used to have fun. You volunteered at the knitting store, taught classes to beginners and had an open knitting circle."

Her gran stared at her, and a chill ran through Edi. It

was like talking to a stranger. How could she leave her like this?

But she couldn't stay. Her clients were counting on her.

Maybe I should have put her in memory care straight away.

But she hadn't been ready for that huge of a transition. And the cost. Edi swallowed her fear. The memory care had felt too much like giving up.

But her gran would have been safe. Yet she still had good moments where she was sharp. Funny. Curious and wanting to do things. She'd rallied at the Graff games night on Monday. The justifications piled up, leaving Edi even more confused and anxious.

She promised herself that she'd spruce up her gran's house and put it on the market in the spring so that she'd have the money for the memory care wing.

What if it's not enough?

She'd work extra shifts, maybe work at the hospital on the weekends, rent a room in someone's house to keep her expenses low. She'd make it work. Her gran had loved her. Accepted her. She'd never found her lacking or felt the need to list her faults as if they were on a scroll. Her gran deserved her best, and she'd get it.

"Were the hats any good?"

"Adorable," Edi enthused. "I have pictures." She pulled out her phone, happy she'd always taken pictures—sometimes the visual prompt helped her gran, but today she turned away from the phone.

"You loved to collect yarn. Look." Edi pulled out her gran's familiar knitting bag and showed the colorful balls of yarn and several sizes of knitting needles. "There's a knitting group that meets Tuesday and Thursday afternoons. Maybe one day we could go together. You taught me how to knit, but it's been a hot minute."

"Why would we go there?"

"It would be fun."

"Would it?"

"Gran, what would you like to do?"

Her gran turned away. "You're always working."

The role reversal felt like Karma nibbling on her ass.

"During the day, yes," she said carefully, but her gran looked out the window at the denuded small trees planted in the garden. The one closest to the window still held one of the birdfeeders she had brought from the small house so her gran could watch the birds when they returned.

"But I always have lunch and dinner with you, and then we watch a show before I head home."

"That's no way to live. You should be going out. Having fun." Her gran crossed her arms and glared out the window, seemingly smug at the no-win situation she'd created. Edi worked too much and wasn't available. Edi spent too much time shut in her gran's apartment. She should go out and have fun—with men probably.

Not.

Before she could dredge up a reply, her alert went off on

her Apple Watch.

"Time to go," her gran said softly in an eerie imitation of Edi. "Bye. Bye."

Edi felt sick, but she kissed her gran and let herself out of the small apartment and brushed back a few hot and inconvenient tears. More gathered and she closed her eyes and lightly hit her head against the wall a couple of times to stave off the gathering storm of emotion. She had to pull it together. She had to. She needed this job. Her clients needed her best.

Edi grimaced and practiced her smile. She had to be stronger than this. She had to get on for her next two clients and then the exercise class. And she needed to build some walls against Ryder's charm.

"I can do this. I will do this."

Pasting on a smile she rounded the corner to go to room 34, only to pull up short when she saw Ryder already there reading something on his phone. He was early.

"Good afternoon." He smiled, pocketed his phone and earbuds once he had them in a case.

"No escaped cows this morning?"

"Not a one," Ryder said. "Berry smoothie with cacao and protein powder, your afternoon pick-up according to Lydia and Sally Driscol at the Java Café."

Ryder handed her the drink, and was she awful for letting her fingers brush his as she took the unexpected offering? When was the last time Derek…no, she wouldn't think of him anymore. He was the past, and she needed to stay in the present.

"You don't have anything to atone for," she said feeling like her eyes were oddly prickly. Oh. God. Please don't let her tear up because someone was nice to her.

"Good." He smiled, and she felt knocked sideways.

"But why…is this one of Lydia's highly suspect dating tips because I can't remember the last date she was on, and you and I aren't.…"

"Not a tip," he said. "Well, kind of a tip, but not a needed one. She said I should be kind to you, and so I called her and…"

"You called my gran?" Edi stared at him astonished. "And she answered?"

"That's usually how it works." He grinned.

"I told her I wanted to get you a treat and did she know what you liked?"

Edi felt flushed. And naked. She looked down at her body as if her scrub pants could have fallen down without her noticing.

"Have you been crying?"

"No," she said as a fresh spurt of tears leaked. "It's your cologne," she accused although he smelled fabulous fresh and piney, and of sawdust and a hint of something spicy that stirred up her tummy like she was hungry, and his scent was probably just him.

"Pure pheromones." Ryder inhaled deeply. "Masculine

energy with a hint of cowboy and barn in a bottle," he teased. "Rohan and I are going to produce and sell it. Make our fortune."

She choked on a laugh but then more tears fell in earnest.

"Hey." His voice was soft, and he used a bandana to gently wipe her tears away.

A bandana? Seriously? Who had a bandana in their back pocket? It was like cosplaying a cowboy, and yet his actions were so sweet, so natural and the bandana smelled like sun and grass and laundry detergent, and what good would one of Derek's silk pocket squares have done her anyway?

"In case you're a mind reader, we aren't really going to call the cologne dung," he said softly, a hint of laughter in his voice, and the way his hand splayed on her back had all the tension leaking out of her.

She put her palm on his chest, thinking maybe she should take charge and keep her distance, but instead she just left her palm on his chest, absorbing his warmth and the steady beat of his heart.

"Your gran?"

She wanted to deny it, but his sympathy tongue-tied the lie.

"I made her lunch, and she didn't eat it." And when her gran didn't eat, neither did she.

She expected him to interrupt. Diagnose the problem. Dismiss it. But Ryder waited, his blue eyes steady on hers.

"She doesn't want to eat. She doesn't take enjoyment

from anything anymore, and some days she's there, and other days she's not her. And I hate what's happening, and I hate that I'm scared. I hate that I can't be there for her all the time, but if I don't work there's no…" She barely managed to stem the flow of information.

She didn't need to tell Ryder that almost all her salary and savings were going toward her gran's care and soon it wouldn't be enough, even with the discount she received for working here.

She barely knew Ryder. And he had his own struggles. But he'd brought her a smoothie when she'd been a stuck-up rhymes with itch yesterday, telling him that he needed to call her Dr. Martin.

She needed to stop trying to climb on her high horse. She'd fallen off and was in the dirt, and she needed to stand up, but stay off the proverbial horse.

She took a desperate sip of the smoothie, hoping the chill would calm her so that she could pull herself into a semblance of a competent professional. The flavors burst on her tongue, and she wanted to close her eyes and savor them, but Ryder was so close that she could see his hair follicles and the way his thick dark chestnut hair with the gold streaks that women would pay hundreds for grew back from his forehead.

The need to touch him was primal, and her fingers itched to try.

"It's hard to be strong for yourself and for them every

day. It feels impossible to watch them slip away," he whispered.

He'd watched his nana's decline. He knew what she was going through, and for a moment, she didn't feel so alone. She nodded.

"I feel like she needs more from me, more than I can give, but I owe it to her to…to…help her. Stave off the decline. Help her find things to engage her."

"Like exercise and activities? Recreate the zest for life?"

"Zest—I like that," Edi said. There was a spice at most grocery stores promising zest. If only it were so easy, sprinkle a little from a bottle. "I definitely do need to shake things up," she said ruefully.

"Consider me your shaker," Ryder said.

She smiled, something that had felt impossible moments ago. "This isn't your burden."

"I am here for two hundred forty-two more hours, but who's counting? I'm happy to shake, shake, shake."

He moved his hips to the beat of his words, and Edi thought of the Taylor Swift song that exhorted listeners to just shake off the bad juju life brought and move on with their days. Good advice that she hadn't taken.

"I would not have figured you for a Taylor fan," she said. "Maybe Luke Combs or Blake Shelton or Kane Brown."

"Yes, yes, yes and yes. Shall we?"

"What?" What was he asking her to do—dance? Here in the hallway of the May Bell Center? With no music?

"You were going to teach me how to safety escort your clients to and from the therapy room," he prompted.

Edi slapped both hands on her head. Of course. That was why he was waiting here, not in the therapy room. And she'd been falling apart and having weird, inappropriate thoughts. Good thing Ryder wasn't a mind reader.

"Yes. Yes, I was," Edi said firmly and drew her spine up straight and angled her shoulders back like she was in a beginning ballet class she'd taken as part of her therapy program when she'd been studying core exercises. Ballet and yoga and Tai Chi had been helpful and now she just needed to remember why they were both there and avoid all flights of fantasy.

She knocked on the door. "Mrs. Bigginger, it's Edi and Ryder." Forget the Dr. Martin for a hot minute until she pulled herself together better. "Can we come in?" She checked the door, and it swung open to reveal Mrs. Bigginger, dressed and standing with her walker.

"Took you two long enough." She looked between them. "I hope there were shenanigans."

"Of course not," Edi said primly.

"I was working on gathering my courage, ma'am," Ryder said seriously.

Mrs. Bigginger cackled. "It takes courage, young man, and ingenuity and impulsiveness."

"Edi's grandmother is giving me her top ten dating tips. We're up to four. Perhaps five is to get in a brave frame of mind." Ryder moved to Mrs. Bigginger's left side. "Perhaps you'd like to add to the list," he said solemnly.

Edi shot him a look, and he just grinned at her before turning his attention back to Mrs. Bigginger.

"You'd better speed that list up," she said. "I was married sixty-seven years, and it still didn't feel like enough time. Life's short, young man. You need to live."

"I'VE BEEN THINKING," Ryder said slowly as he helped Edi clean off all the equipment after the second individual client.

Edi pumped air into some of the small exercise balls, and he took a moment to admire the efficient way she moved, all long-legged, business-like grace. What did she do to unwind after work? What did she do for fun?

Then he realized she'd stopped moving and was staring at him. He'd been lost in watching her and speculating.

"Planning out a new exercise to hijack my class?"

Her eyes glinted—amusement or challenge he couldn't tell, but the corners of her delicate mouth tipped up in a slight smile so maybe she wasn't as irritated as he'd imagined she might be.

"I have been googling physical therapy exercises for seniors."

"Really?" Now she was laughing at him.

"I'm growing on you," he said, pleased, wondering if he

just might be working up to asking her out to dinner or…or…what did she do on her off-time? Did she allow herself to have time to relax? Refill her spirit? Jace had understood how finding moments to relax or play was critical for their mental health and teamwork.

But he had Edi's attention, and he didn't want to lose it.

"I was thinking about what you said about engagement."

She nodded.

"Well, a couple of things." He hesitated. Was he overstepping again? She'd gone to school. She knew what she was doing.

"Spit it out, Ry," she encouraged.

He liked that she used his nickname. His teammates had called him that.

"Not like you were shy with your ideas the first class." She finished pumping the last ball.

"Well, I was thinking first about the exercise class—the chairs. If we built the exercises around them all sitting, then we wouldn't have to worry about anyone taking a spill, and the clients who really need the chairs might feel more on equal foot—ha." He laughed at the irony. "They wouldn't feel like they were at such a disadvantage, and I still think we could make it aerobic."

"Clearly you know a lot about exercise." Edi looked him over, and he had to fight to not do something juvenile like flex or kiss his bicep, but he kept himself still, sensing this moment was important. He was building a new life, and if he wanted to be taken seriously, maybe he'd need to dial back on the irreverence, or choose his moments instead of swinging at everything.

At the Telford Ranch last evening, he'd watched everyone and everything, trying to anticipate what would be needed next and how he could be an asset. And then he'd googled bucking-bull and bronc training. And this morning he'd asked a lot of questions. Rohan's brother Boone had been much chattier than anyone else. He'd been open and eager to show him his rodeo school for teens that he had as a side hustle. He'd also shown him his woodworking studio.

"I have been looking at senior-focused programs online," Ryder started, "but I thought we could make it more interactive—you and I could tag-team on exercises, improvise a little, and then encourage the…the clients to take turns coming up with something that we—you and I and the others follow, so the participants feel more invested."

She stared at him. "That's really putting a client on the spot and could screech everything to a halt."

"Maybe." He shrugged. "But we'd be there to bring the energy back up, and we could work up to it. Encourage someone to think of a move—give them time to think and then call on them to demonstrate," he said. "I bet when they were younger many of them exercised. Participating more, having a say, more control might help them to accept this stage, but also to enjoy it."

Edi nodded, and Ryder felt a bloom of confidence.

"I noticed the assisted living clients don't seem to go down to the day client activity room or dining room."

"They don't," Edi said and chewed adorably on her lower lip. Then she sighed heavily as if shaking off the last of her inner Eeyore. "And you're right. We need to try something new—keep trying to engage them."

We. Ryder felt like the word was a sunrise in his chest.

"Great. Yes, *we* do," Ryder said and slapped his hands together, making her jump.

He rubbed his palms together, something he'd seen Jace do when the team had made a decision, and he was generating heat to light a fire under their collective asses.

"And we need better music. I'm in charge of that."

She opened her mouth to object, and without thinking, he tucked his forefinger under her chin and tipped it up and then pressed his forefinger against her lips.

It was the first time he'd touched her face, and it felt incredibly intimate, and out of place in the glaring fluorescent lights of the therapy room.

"Careful." She looked up at him. "I might bite."

"Careful," he responded. "I might like it."

Chapter Seven

RYDER SET UP the chairs in one long line, facing the mirror and leaving plenty of space between the chairs, and then instead of inspecting his work, he again looked at the tower of yoga balls she'd placed in the netted enclosure. She'd purchased them for the center both for her clients but also for the adult day care program for games or exercise. She hadn't had the motivation to use them yet.

Edi frowned at the line of chairs as she'd never tried this configuration and wondered if the clients would feel less pressure than if they were looking at her and Ryder facing them, or more because they'd see themselves in the mirror.

And just as Ryder's attention continued to stray to the large yoga balls, hers kept snagging on him like she was back in high school.

She tried to ignore the flex of muscle across his chest as he stood, hands on his hips, and the sleeve of tats on his right arm. Did he have tats on his chest? She felt weak at the thought. What was the story behind the images? She didn't have the courage to ask. And would his tatted skin feel different from untatted skin?

"We should discuss the exercises first." She tried to drag

her mind out of the gutter.

"Okay." Ryder turned away from his yoga ball perusal. "Do you want to have a set list?"

"Of course. I don't want to wing it."

"Of course not," he murmured. "But if we do get some takers to grab the spotlight, we will have an organic, spontaneous moment."

Was he laughing at her or was this one of those laughing-with-her moments she could appreciate if she weren't so uptight? A perfectionist, even though she'd learned long ago as a child that she could never hit anywhere near perfect. Her father always left, and her mom always wanted a different, prettier, less broody daughter.

Bitterness coated her mouth, and she clenched her hands together. She'd vowed to be different for her own child. Loving. Not only accepting but embracing. When she'd seen those two lines on the pregnancy test she'd been thrilled. Determined to be the kind of mother she'd always craved. Should she give up that goal to be kind and encouraging to others just because she was only allowed to be a mother for a handful of hours?

No.

"You might need to hold my hand. I'll be in such a panic if that happens." In the darkness of winter, she dug for humor. Even as her gran slipped away, and Edi was in a town where she had no friends yet, she needed to find some joy in the small moments. That was another promise she'd made to the spirit of her daughter. She would hold her spirit safe within her and remember her every day and show her the beauty the world offered, savor the experiences Aria had missed.

I've been doing a lousy job of it so far.

Montana was beautiful. Cold. But beautiful. And her gran still had good days or good moments. The staff at the May Bell had been friendly. And Ryder was disconcerting, but she was beginning to think in a good way. He jolted her awake. Not just her slumbering libido, but all of her. If anyone could remind her how to seize a moment, it was Ryder.

"I've been focusing on the wrong things," she said softly, her mouth spitting out the words before her brain had fully formed them.

She had Ryder's full attention now. God, he was spectacular. He listened with his full body, and she almost asked him out. Terror shot through her. What kind of a date would a man like Ryder want to go on? Ziplining through the icy forest? She knew there was a place to do that but probably not in winter. Skiing? He was so physical. She loved hiking and kayaking, but even walking outside in the winter still felt like she was in survival mode and about to Popsicle.

"I've been thinking about what the clients can't do instead of what they can." Edi stuck to a safer, but still true, topic.

"And maybe not just with the clients."

The tenor of his voice soaked into her body, feeling like warmed honey, and longing enveloped her until she wanted to cry. She just felt so damn empty.

I've been so cold.

And Ryder was the sun.

He'd shed his coat and vest when he'd come into the therapy room, and probably in prep for the exercise class, he'd peeled off his flannel button-down, leaving him only in a light blue Henley that matched his eyes. It was open, and she could see the sexy hollow at this throat. He was still fully clothed, but the Henley hugged his torso, hinting at the power underneath, and she should so not be lusting after her exercise assistant.

"Whatever are you thinking, Edi?" he asked softly.

"That I shouldn't be thinking it," she whispered, feeling like she was on a precipice.

He walked toward her, and her heart rate zoomed, and her mouth dried. His eyes were warm sapphire. "Maybe you should," he invited softly.

Think. Think. Think.

She had to save herself from falling...no jumping over the edge and doing or saying something that she'd later regret like touching him. Kissing him. Asking him out. Heck she'd even go on a winter walk with him. Too bad the Christmas-themed light show in Crawford Park and along the river had closed after the holiday. They could have purchased hot chocolates at Copper Mountain Chocolate Shop and walked along the lit path. Ryder radiated enough heat that she probably would have been wanting to strip off her parka instead of bundle up.

"Why...why do you keep looking at the yoga balls?" She hunted desperately for something safe to say.

She saw his smile in his eyes first. "Playing it safe, Edi."

"Always."

The corner of his mouth twitched up. "I wonder."

"Don't."

"I do."

The tension built and stretched and snapped between them until Edi felt like she was going to combust. Or would it be more of an explosion?

"I'll go easy on you..." he paused "...this time."

Edi nearly moaned and swayed toward him, but she cracked down on her misbehaving, longing, needy body, and locked down her rigid posture, mentally swallowing the key.

"Is there a music store in town? And a dollar store?"

Confusion filtered through her, and Ryder laughed. "You asked for it. What is the saying: don't avoid trouble because another kind will find you?"

"That's not a saying," she objected.

"I just said it."

"So you're announcing you're trouble," she challenged.

"Definitely." His eyes crinkled as he smiled, and Edi felt like he'd switched a light on inside her body. She felt warm and fizzling, and she'd made big, bad Special Forces soldier now cowboy Ryder Lea smile.

"But, Edi, there are many types of trouble for us to explore."

EDI FINISHED HER shift and hurried to her gran's apartment, still fizzing from her exchanges with Ryder, both before and during the exercise class.

"I had fun," she murmured, holding on to the glow and avoiding the creeping anxiety she always felt before she saw her gran.

The exercise program had been a bigger hit than she'd imagined, and Ryder's enthusiasm and uninhibited shout-outs, teasing and commentary along with the sexy rap music had been infectious, and she'd even found herself loosening up and teasing him back.

Flirting.

And for the first time in over two years, she'd felt like her again, maybe even a better, more confident, throw caution to the wind version of her.

And it was as terrifying as it was addictive.

She needed to keep herself and her clients and Gran safe, and yet, she'd never seen so many smiles. She'd nearly fallen off her chair when her gran, who'd attended at Ryder's sweet prodding, had laughed and suggested they exercise their facial muscles by making weird expressions.

Later Holly, who'd watched part of the class, had asked Ryder to help in the adult day care activity room, and when Edi had checked on him after her appointments with individual clients in skilled nursing, she'd found Ryder, at the head of the table, wearing his Stetson and calling out bingo numbers in a warm, western drawl. The usually sleepy game had been enlivened by his musical selections after each bingo win and 'stretch and booty shake' breaks.

He'd even exhorted her to join in the fun, and after hesitating, worrying about her image, and mentally cataloging the charts she needed to fill out and the plans she had to make for the next day, Edi had helped run one bingo game. Ryder had waved his bandana at her like a dare, and uncharacteristically, and lightly blushing bright red, she'd tied it around her head. Her gran, sitting next to Ryder said she looked like a pirate.

Ryder had snapped a picture with his phone and murmured that 'this is going to make the May Bell social media pages.'

Edi had forgotten that Holly had suggested they try to take pictures both for social media and also for the community board to 'liven the activity room up and show engagement.' She got so busy thinking about what she needed to do and then doing it that she forgot the fun and capturing the special moments.

Not Ryder, he'd created an impromptu air hockey game

using a long dining table. Books lined the sides and then two seniors used oven mitts and a red checker disk to pass it back and forth. And for a couple more clients, he'd retrieved some canes from the medical supply, wadded up newspaper and had them sit and used the two canes like a claw to spear the paper and raise it enough to drop it in a recycling bin. When Edi separated two tables and tapped a piece of poster board between them, and cutting out a hole so that clients could sit at both ends of the table and try to roll a ball between, she'd been embarrassingly proud at how much the clients had enjoyed the game, but Ryder's quiet 'well done,' and knuckle bump complete with an exploding sound, made her prouder than she could remember feeling in a long time. She'd already thought of a modification for tomorrow.

Still holding on to her glow, she quickly rapped at her gran's door and opened it.

"Oh. Hey," she said, surprised to see Ryder sitting with her gran, pouring out three cups of tea. "I thought you'd left."

"I would have said goodbye," he said, blue eyes steady on hers, and she mentally chanted to herself not to read anything into his look or tone. "When some of the day residents were getting picked up, and a couple of them asked about field trips, it got me thinking."

"Me too," Edi admitted. "All my ideas have been more summer or late spring oriented—outdoors—but I was wondering about maybe a chocolate-making demonstration at Sage Carrigan's chocolate shop or a cooking class or a mocktail-making class at the Graff," she started.

"Why not cocktails?" Her gran frowned at her.

"Every idea should be heard." Ryder smiled at her gran, who had a sly smile of her own. "I like those ideas. I wanted to run an idea by you and Lydia to see if she thinks it might work for an outing."

"I'd rather have dinner at Rocco's with a stiff Beefeater's on the rocks, but I suppose I'll have to save that for you two as a date and read about it on social media," her gran grumped.

"Is that dating tip five?" Ryder asked lightly. "Dinner at a nice restaurant and a stiff drink."

"Couldn't hurt. Edi could use something stiff in her life." Her gran crossed her arms and slouched in her chair, glaring at Edi as if she was the party pooper.

Light pink stained Ryder's cheeks, and Edi guessed she was once again lobster red.

"What was your idea?" She tried to switch the conversation.

"The outfit where I work, the Telford Ranch, is not too far out of town. On Tuesdays and Wednesdays in the winter, they have the bulls and a few of the broncs they anticipate using in their rodeo stock contractor business practice going in and out of the chutes."

That sounded dangerous, and cold, and she wasn't sure where he was going with this.

"Like a mini rodeo?"

"More like a dress rehearsal. Yesterday was the first practice of the season. But there are staff members, and they strap dummies onto the bulls' back to see how they buck. It trains the bulls and broncs but also the staff for handling the animals in the chutes. It's pretty cool-looking but also pretty technical. But I thought it could be a good outing for some of the clients who want to come. I'd talked to my boss yesterday about bringing some of the clients. It's in a large barn—more like an arena. They have some space heaters, some bleachers, and of course the arena is fenced so no bulls or broncs can break out."

Edi had heard that the May Bell clients did get a special section reserved to watch the rodeo each September.

"If we brought some of the clients for an outing, I could get a couple of the staff to do a roping demonstration, maybe a few would be practicing on bulls and broncs as they do have practice sessions for cowboys wanting to hone their skills before the season starts."

Edi listened, her usual caution flagging because Ryder seemed like he'd really thought this out, and it sounded fun. A lot of work and prep, but they did have some helpers for the day program who could maybe assist. Many of the staff were young and considering the gossip she heard in the staffroom when she'd breeze in and out for a coffee pick-me-up, single. They might welcome the chance to see some working cowboys up close and personal.

"There are facilities on site, and after about a half hour or more of analyzing the different bulls and practice moving them in and out of the chute, the Telfords fire up the grill and feed everyone. Tonight is pizza in a wood-burning pizza oven. Wednesday's burgers. I thought we could go."

"Tonight? We?" she parroted and stared at him, surprised by the invitation.

"Well, you need to see the setup to judge if it would be safe and manageable for the clients. We can troubleshoot any hazards ahead of time. You'll assess the access better than I would," he said soberly. "And we'd bring your gran as our test subject. See if Lydia finds it interesting." He slow-winked at her gran. "Lots of cowboys wearing chaps."

Her gran stared at him, her eyes narrowed. "Will you be wearing chaps?"

"Absolutely."

"Who doesn't like pizza?" her gran asked. "And leather."

For a moment, Edi could barely swallow.

He was not only thinking of the May Bell clients, but also her gran. And he was teasing her like she was a normally functioning woman, not in the early stages of dementia. Edi had expressed her worries about her gran being bored, shut in too much, not enough stimulation, not eating, and he was trying to troubleshoot.

Had Derek ever listened to her concerns? Had he ever tried to help? No. When their life had fallen apart, he'd bailed. Washed his hands of her. Told her to sign on the line and that was it—marriage over.

"Did you check with your boss?" she asked faintly. "We can go tonight?"

"Yeah. I asked about it last night—it was my first time seeing the training. I'll be working, well…" He looked momentarily shy. "Training. Learning the ropes, so to speak. But they were cool with me bringing guests, and my army buddy's dad and brother, Boone, liked the idea of community outreach. Boone works with teens in the spring, summer and fall with the rodeo skills. He has a nonprofit, so he liked the idea of offering a chance for Marietta citizens on the opposite end of the age spectrum getting to come out on the ranch and see what they do."

"That's…that's great," Edi said, surprised at how much she wanted to go.

"What do you think, Gran?"

"I'm dressed aren't I?"

EDI SAT NEXT to her gran. They each had a cushion and a Pendleton blanket to share. They held thermos mugs of tea, and her gran was nibbling on a bag of popcorn. Edi barely managed to tear her gaze off of Ryder who stood on a high rung of a fence that enclosed something called a chute.

"What do you think of this as a field trip for you and your friends?"

"I don't have friends." Her gran plucked more popcorn from the bag that she clutched like Edi was going to take it away. "Not anymore. I'm in old lady jail."

"You are living in a place that is safe. You could try to make friends with the other women on your wing." She thought about bringing up the knitting group again but didn't.

"So could you." Her gran ate the popcorn and reached for more.

Edi heard some yelling, a couple of curses and then masculine laughter and some teasing. Ryder stood high, conferring with another man. She thought that might be his buddy from the army but couldn't see his face. She'd never guess that's how they knew each other now. They both looked like total cowboys—boots, worn Wranglers, chaps as promised, Henleys, plaid, flannel shirts hanging open, Stetsons—born and bred Montana cowboys. They also wore thick leather vests when up on the chute that Ryder had said were protective vests, and Edi didn't have to use her imagination as to what Ryder needed protecting from. She'd seen the horns and imagined the hooves were just as lethal.

Ryder listened with his whole body while two men talked to him, one at least a couple of decades older, but still agile, climbing up and down the metal railing. A second bull barreled down the wide alleyway, a gate went up and Ryder slammed it down with his foot. Then she saw the men coordinating a floppy dummy with some straps.

Ryder was so close to the bull, Edi's heart thumped in her throat.

"Pretty wild, huh Gran? I've never seen anything like it." Ryder had probably seen a lot of scary action in his army years. Maybe this was mild.

"Cowboys are a special breed." Her gran's gaze never left the action, and Edi wondered if her gran was speaking about a personal and special memory or just in general. She'd grown up in Marietta but had left at age sixteen to blaze her own trail in Los Angeles first, and many other cities later.

"I think you like what you see, Edison Martin," Gran said.

Edi didn't answer but smiled.

It had been a good idea to come tonight. She hadn't seen her gran so focused on anything in a long time.

The door rolled up and another woman with long strawberry-blonde hair pulled back in a high ponytail walked in holding the hand of a toddler. She pulled a large, wheeled cooler behind her. Another woman with dark, curly hair walked with her, and a small, skinny boy followed, a few steps behind, and a mixed-breed dog followed the boy devotedly.

Edi's attention shifted a little to the little girl, and she braced herself for the familiar punch of pain though it was over two years and seven hundred miles away. It hit but not with full impact. Breath-stealing but more manageable. She breathed out in relief, and then noticed that her gran was watching her.

"Are you having an okay time?" she asked her gran, waving back at the strawberry blonde who waved and headed her way.

"Is okay your standard, now?"

Well, her gran was following the conversation and responding so she'd take the win even if her gran was behaving more like a middle school girl than the loving, nonjudgmental gran of her youth.

But then again, I've changed.

The thought was an epiphany. Perhaps she was more of the problem than she realized. She was still grieving both the loss of her baby, and the loss of the life she thought she would have. Before she'd begun to process, the pretty strawberry blonde with the toddler joined her.

"Hi, I'm Piper Telford. Boone's wife. This is our daughter Reid." She sat on the other side of Edi and held out her hand to Edi's gran to shake. "I'm Piper," she repeated to Lydia, her smile warm and lighting up her face like she was in a toothpaste commercial. "Welcome to the Telford Family Ranch and pizza night."

"Thank you for letting us crash your party." Edi wondered how much she should explain. "I'm Edison Martin—Edi, and this is my gran, Lydia Martin."

"That's Ginny, my almost sister-in-law and her son Lucas. So you're with Ryder?" Piper looked expectantly over at the group of men straddling the chute.

"That looks dangerous," Edi yelped at the new position Ryder was in.

"It is," Piper agreed, rather cheerfully. "You get used to it, sort of." Piper touched Edi's knee and smiled. "When I first met Boone I'd never even been to a rodeo, and we traveled together over the summer while he competed, and it took me a while to calm down and not have my phone out ready to call 911 every other moment. But yeah, it does take skill. That's why they train and practice, so that the crew and the bulls and the rodeo cowboys are as safe as can be. I haven't met Ryder yet. I was working when Rohan introduced him around to the crew. Is that your man in the blue and white shirt?"

"He's not mine," Edi said quickly.

"She'd like him to be," her gran inserted, and Piper smiled.

"Can't blame you. Once you go cowboy there's no way back. When I met Boone, I was a goner the first afternoon we spent together."

Edi heard the slide of metal and a bull with a dummy strapped to its back raced out of the gate, kicking its back legs up and out so it balanced briefly on two tiny hooves, and then the massive body twisted sideways as it jumped and thrashed around the arena in a tight circle.

Several people filmed the bull, and there was a cowboy on a horse, wielding a lasso, who galloped toward the bull, but the bull shied away, snorted and trotted through the gate that Ryder opened.

"That's Wrecking Ball. Boone and his dad have high hopes for him," Piper said as Rohan's fiancée stood up on tiptoes and kissed him. She and her son soon joined them on the bleachers.

"Who's the new guy?" she asked. "Is that Ryder? Is he yours? Whoot. Rohan's been waiting for him to arrive. I'm Gin Lane. About to be Gin Telford in a few months once the ground begins to thaw and we get a spring break. This is my son Lucas."

She sat beside them, and an easy companionship stole over Edi for a moment before she reminded herself that Piper and Gin belonged. She and her gran were visitors, and Ryder was a temporary volunteer at the May Bell Center. In a few months he'd be on the ranch full-time.

The four of them watched a few more bulls come and go. After each bull was released and bucked in a tight circle in the arena, there was a lot of conversation and reviewing the videos between the crew. Ryder didn't talk much, which was not how he acted at the May Bell Center.

Maybe he's still finding his way.

They had that in common.

She started guiltily, realizing she'd been enjoying the conversation with the two women but hadn't been including her gran. But when she looked over, Gin's son Lucas was sitting with her gran and showing her something on his tablet and chatting without seeming to need to breathe, and her gran's smile held a hint of wistful.

I'm glad we came.

And for the first time in over two years, Edi had a spurt of hope that she could be happy again. She could rebuild her life, help her gran, have meaningful work. Friends.

Chapter Eight

Other than almost becoming the dummy clinging to the back of a bucking bull once when his hand became entangled with the flank strap, and he'd nearly off-balanced over the chute fence, Ryder felt that the second training session had gone well. He'd googled and watched rodeo chute crew YouTube videos last night and this morning after chores as he waited for his truck to warm up. But more importantly, he'd watched and kept his mouth shut to the point that Rohan had asked him if he was feeling okay.

"Seriously, you don't have to do this," Rohan had taken him aside and whispered the promise. "There's plenty of work on the ranch in spring, summer and fall and so much maintenance during the winter that there's plenty of other areas you can be assigned to."

"I want to be on the stock crew," Ryder had reiterated. "I loved working with animals on the ranch as a kid, and I want to travel."

And because Rohan's green gaze was laser sharp and searching, Ryder had forced a lazy smile. "Without being shot at."

Rohan had laughed like Ryder hoped he would and let it

go. Once the chute work was completed, Ryder had finally allowed himself to drink in the sight of Edi, relaxed and smiling as she chatted with two other women. A young boy was playing some kind of computer game with Lydia and talking to her earnestly. A little blonde girl sat beside Edi, plucking at the messy ends of her hair sticking out of her bun. Edi didn't seem to mind, but when she looked at the child, her expression was both adoring and sad.

Edi would be a good mom. Conscientious. She wouldn't run through different men looking for *The One* and leaving her kids to fend for themselves. He wondered why she didn't have a couple of kids and an attentive husband already.

Not your rodeo, he mocked while he ensured all the stock that had been used for training tonight were settled in, fed and watered. Edi's love life and family life weren't his business. She was the house, mini-van, vegetable garden, hanging flower baskets and proverbial white picket fence woman. He was…hell if he knew, but he intended to find out before he jumped into a relationship like Cross, Huck and Rohan had done. They'd maybe had normal families—at least Rohan had. The other Coyotes except Jace hadn't talked about their families much.

His eyes lingered on Edi listening attentively to Boone's daughter, who stroked her little plush horse against her cheek. It was sweet and normal. So why did his chest feel constricted? Was he that badly damaged from his childhood? Was he that lonely? Was that why Rohan, Cross and Huck had jumped in feet first into a relationship? Maybe he should find out more, but then they'd harass him something fierce.

Again, he stole another glace at Edi.

She wouldn't want a man like him.

He continued to puzzle how his three Coyote Cowboy brothers had found love so quickly, and how they made it look so easy. He'd had success hooking up in bars over the years but had never once imagined having more.

Did he have 'more' to offer?

Ryder cringed away from that question and instead focused on taking care of the animals—spending a moment with each one, settling them in for the night before washing up to help with the dinner, whatever was required.

When he returned to the arena, the crowd had swelled. One of the side doors had been rolled open revealing a large, covered area with picnic-style tables. The inside of the wood-fire pizza oven was already glowing hot. Several heat lamps scattered around the arena and the covered outdoor area blasted out heat.

He took it all in, feeling almost weak with how much it looked like something out of a book he should have read, curled up somewhere in his classroom during D.E.A.R—Drop Everything And Read. He searched for Edi, hoping her gran was holding up.

He found her standing next to her gran and a petite blonde woman who was rolling out pizza dough like a pro and chatting like she had a lot to say.

"Isn't this fantastic?" Edi's eyes shone in the light of the fire, and her smile kicked him sideways.

"You like it?" He felt dazzled by Edi—creamy skin, hundreds of freckles, shining eyes, and that smile that made him feel special—as if somehow any of this—the homemade pizzas, the people, the companionship, the warmth in the dead of winter—was any of his doing.

"I love it," she said. "It's like something out of *Sunset Magazine*. I feel like I've stepped into someone else's life."

"Me too," he admitted. "Yesterday I felt like I was in a scene from a book I should have read instead of goofing off."

She laughed. "You goofing off? I can't imagine."

He smiled. Her happiness felt contagious.

"This is really spectacular. What a fantastic idea of the Telfords to host a pizza party after a practice session with their livestock. Seeing the bulls rush out of the chute and jump around like that was wild."

"It's called bucking," he said with mock seriousness. "Much more masculine."

"Oh." She made a face. "Of course. Were you tempted to get on the back of a bull?"

"Not even a little bit," he admitted. "Although a lot of the hands on the ranch are former or current rodeo riders. Rohan rode the junior rodeo circuit as a teen and was talented enough to get a full scholarship to college." Ryder shook his head, still not believing that Rohan would have given up college and family to join the army. "I've only been working here two days," Ryder admitted. "And I can't believe anyone would walk away from this."

Edi's gaze was searching. "Grass is greener," she said.

"It's not."

His voice came out harsher than he meant it to. It felt strange to be enjoying himself, but to be fighting off unpleasant memories and long-buried wishes at the same time.

"I need to focus on staying in the moment," he blurted.

"Me too." Edi touched his hand. "This place, this night, this event…I feel like I belong only I don't know anyone here but you and gran. You brought us here, Ryder. Thank you. This is the perfect way to hold winter isolation at bay for a night, and I think a lot of the clients would enjoy themselves if the Telfords are still willing to host a group."

"They are." Ryder looked around. "You're right—this is light in the dark."

A few of the hands had cracked open beers, but he was driving Edi and her gran home later, and he'd never developed much of a taste for beer or whiskey due to the overindulgence of the random men who'd crashed in and out of his mother's life. All of them had drunk six or twelve-packs or more of cheap beer, starting in the afternoon until they'd passed out. He never could figure out why his mom put up with any of them. He'd rejoiced each time she'd thrown one out until it became clear that another would soon arrive.

"There's a party-like thing here next Friday," he admitted. "It's annual, and a few of the crews and families from neighboring ranches come. It's sort of a solstice meets new season of work."

When did he become so awkward?

"Party-like thing." Edi laughed. "So specific. Hold out your hands. We need to talk and work, or you'll go hungry."

He held out his hands, liking the sweep of her sandy eyelashes along her freckled cheeks. He'd never dated a woman with freckles.

We're not dating.

You could. Maybe.

Did the freckles go lower on her body? Were they everywhere? He stared at her as she first used a wipe to clean off his hands and then she dabbed a little oil on his palms. Something strange moved in him at her care.

"Rub them together."

"What's that smell?"

"Rosemary. Isn't it gorgeous. Riley, Rohan's sister, has started infusing olive oils and making essential oils with your friend's wife, Shane."

"I met her my first night in town," he admitted. "It was weird to see Cross so…so…in love." He still couldn't believe it. "But I'm happy for him. It was just so…" He couldn't begin to explain all the thoughts rolling around inside of him like one of those bingo cages this afternoon that he'd cranked around until it spit out a number.

Edi sprinkled a little flour on his hands and then handed

him a ball of dough.

"There must be a lot of adjustments for you this week, Ryder. I didn't think about that and I'm sorry." She patted her dough flat, and he did the same. "I've been selfish, just focused on my own drama and insecurities about the May Bell Center. The job is new to me, and it's been an adjustment—bigger than I thought working with seniors. And I desperately need the job, so I need to do better. You've showed me how badly I've stumbled."

He didn't know what to say to that.

"Here are some rolling pins." The petite blonde with the heart-shaped face and bright blue eyes interrupted their moment. "No serious conversations when making pizza." She waggled a rolling pin in his face. "Hi. I'm Riley, Rohan's most favorite sister."

"And my least favorite since you're my only sister." Rohan joined them, holding his fiancée Gin's hand. Rohan called her Ginny, but no one else did, Ryder made a mental note as he always geared toward nicknames. He looked around for her son—Rohan had pointed him out proudly when they'd been working on top of the chute—and saw him still standing next to Lydia, discussing what toppings to put on their pizzas. It was so sweet, and for a moment, memories of him and his nana hurt.

Riley stuck her tongue out at her brother, snapping Ryder out of his funk.

"You have Miranda and Piper now as sisters so I can be

and still am your favorite."

"Or my least favorite." Rohan laughed at her. "Hand over the rolling pin, squirt."

Riley stood on her tiptoes. "I think of myself as very tall," she told Edi. "It's just that my three brothers stole all the height genes. Witt is ridiculously tall—good thing he never harbored rodeo cowboy fantasies. It's all about the center of gravity." She rolled her hips.

"Stop," Rohan demanded. "I can't unsee that."

Edi laughed as Riley handed the rolling pin to Ryder. "Welcome to the Telford Family Ranch, Ryder. Thank you for your service to our country and I hope that you will make your home here and be very happy."

And then she hugged him—lots of strength for such a small woman.

"Thank you for keeping Ro safe for us," she whispered, her voice ragged, "and for being a good friend to him. Thank you. We are always in your debt."

She released him. Her eyes were shiny with tears, and for a moment Ryder couldn't speak. He'd not been expecting such an emotional speech. He opened his mouth, but no words came out, and then he felt Edi's hand slip into his oiled, floured hand. Her fingers laced through his, and she lightly squeezed three times. It felt right and centered him.

"Rohan is my brother," he said simply. That didn't stop just because he was no longer on active duty and because he was trying to figure out civilian life. "I'd do anything for him." He didn't bother to censor words he meant.

"Right back at you, Cowboy," Rohan said quietly before he and Gin made space next to him and Edi and began to assemble pizzas to go into the pizza oven that was so hot it looked like it was taking only a couple of minutes to cook the three or four pies that a crew was feeding into the blazing-hot oven using a large flat wooden paddle.

Wood. Boone had a woodworking workshop. Ryder wondered if he had scraps of wood or plywood pieces that the clients could decorate, paint maybe. Something simple but colorful. That long beige hallway could be something—an art gallery or something. Maybe the clients could make things in that dark woodshop. Maybe Boone could teach him to make a few things, and Ryder could volunteer sometimes. Give back like Jace had intended to do. Or maybe school kids could display their art or locals. Have a show. Bring people in to share. Talk.

While his brain spun with novel concepts, Gin and Edi chatted. Edi bumped against his body a few times, and each touch felt like a jolt of life.

She dangled some green stuff in front of him. "How brave are you feeling tonight, Cowboy?"

"I'm up for anything," he promised. There were different types of courage, and he had no intentions of living his life in the shadows.

Ryder angled his truck up her uncleared driveway. The snow had fallen softly the whole way home from the Telford Ranch, cocooning them in an ethereal world.

"I'm still not used to the snow," she admitted. "I grew up in California and lived in Seattle for fourteen years, and just saw maybe a few inches a year if that, and I never drove in it."

"I grew up in small towns in Nebraska and Colorado so snow was always part of my life. I didn't realize how much I missed it until tonight driving you and your gran home."

"Thanks for inviting us. You were right. She enjoyed herself. It was a wonderful outing."

She'd spoken to Taryn Telford and his two sons who ran the ranch with him about a potential field trip to the ranch for the residents at the May Bell but also a day trip for the day clients, who would be able to safely attend. They were surprisingly amenable, full of ideas, and they'd promised to further discuss an itinerary of options. Edi would check with the center's director and coordinate with whoever was hired to be the new director of activities.

"I'm glad you both came." Ryder's words were formal. Even so her heart pounded. Though she continued to tell herself they were just colleagues, maybe friends, she was starting to slip into the hopeful zone where she wasn't sure she was ready to be. "Felt good to have you both there."

His stiffness was so uncharacteristic that for a second she wondered if he was nervous. Ryder? Why would he ever be nervous, especially with her? He oozed confidence and an easy attitude with all that life might offer or throw.

"Felt good to be there," she said sincerely.

He'd turned off the truck, and the engine clicked a little as it started to cool, and she couldn't seem to order her body to move—open the truck door, hop out into the freezing night and run to the small, quiet bungalow still crammed with her gran's life and very little of her own. She felt like a visitor and not a particularly welcome one.

"Ummmm, okay, Ryder." She reached out to touch his cheek but pulled her hand back. What was she doing? They weren't dating—despite her gran's dating tips—but sitting in the cab of his very clean truck felt intimate. She could feel his energy. Smell his fresh scent and pine and something with a hint of spice or tang that drew her in, and she had to get a grip on herself before she creeped him out.

She was older than him and should slam the lid on her jump-started libido and wildly wobbling heart.

But her gran's house is empty. And it's early, not yet nine.

What was she thinking?

"I'll see you tomorrow afternoon," she said brightly. "We can discuss taking a small group of clients to the ranch if I get the okay from Holly," she said brightly enough to blind herself.

How could she still at thirty-six be such a social dork with a man she wasn't even trying to attract?

But maybe she could.

No!

She couldn't bear the humiliation if he turned her down and hurried back to his truck because she'd still have to see him at the center. Or worse, he'd ask Holly to complete his hours elsewhere and she was beginning to count on his upbeat, can-do silliness that helped her find a little bit of her spark that had been doused for so long. She'd have to explain to the clients that he'd left, and they'd know she'd chased him away.

And then she couldn't take any clients to the ranch to see the bulls or broncs practice bucking or see a foal or calf be born, and it would be because she'd made Ryder uncomfortable—like she was probably doing right now by sitting here, frozen and freaking out. He deserved a younger woman with less baggage—like Riley, his best friend's sister. She was beautiful, young, sweet, and unencumbered—without an aging, declining gran, broken heart and a looming debt.

Her mind spiraled at the disaster if she made a flirty move.

"So good night." She flung open the door and hopped out before he could throw her out, which he would never do.

I am too old to be acting this ridiculous.

She'd not even rounded the truck's headlights before Ryder was there.

"What are you doing?"

"Walking you to the door," he said quietly like her clumsy behavior was normal. With his Stetson on he looked like some old-school cowboy, and her body had no right to turn liquid. She'd never even seen a real cowboy until she'd moved to Montana, and now she was hot for one?

She should think of him like a brother, which she'd never had.

"You don't need to."

"Yes, I do."

Okay then. They walked the short path to her door. Invite him in? Should she? Had she left the house clean? Did he want to come in? Was she ready for this? Did he want her to?

The questions bombarded her brain until she couldn't hear anything but her own ratcheting anxiety. Had she been this much of an internal blathering idiot with Derek? Unlikely. Their romance had been a long, slow, friends to dating to lovers slog over years.

She wasn't a hookup type of woman. Besides she'd sworn off sex. She wasn't even on the pill anymore and hadn't been for a few years.

Don't invite him in.

"Do you want to come in for a coffee?"

Yikes. It was too late for coffee, and she was not ready for anything else, except her pounding heart, breathy voice and the moist heat gathering at the apex of her thighs spoke of a body far more ahead of her stupid, terrified brain.

"Yes," he said. "But no."

"Of course." She turned away from him, fumbling for

her key in her purse. Why hadn't she had it ready?

She found the keys buried in the bottom of her purse. Of course they were. She yanked at them, and a pack of gum and a tampon flipped out with the keys, and she was so horrified that she dropped the keys.

She bent to pick them up, and bonked heads with him.

"Oh my God, I was smoother in middle school, and I was a disaster then."

He laughed at her mortified confession. Handed her the gum, the tampon and then unlocked and opened her door.

"Edi." His voice was quiet, and as she'd stepped through the door, she thought she imagined that he'd spoken. She held on to the doorjamb with one hand and turned around to face him.

"Yes."

"You don't have to be smooth," he said. "You're perfect."

She could barely swallow. He was sweet, and she was so far from perfect she couldn't see it anywhere on her horizon.

They were even in height now with her in the house, and he leaned forward to kiss her cheek, but Edi turned so their lips met.

HER LIPS WERE sweet, soft, warm in a world that was icy white with air so cold it stole his breath and thoughts. Edi was spring. He'd thought about kissing her. Of course he had. More than once. He was a guy. But he hadn't imagined this—the tentative exploration of her lips, and how her tongue would feel as she traced the seam of his lips, dipped inside his mouth and languidly licked along his tongue and inner lip. Her breathy sigh and swallowed moan had him at full attention and aching to pull her against his body. She was so naturally sensuous and swayed into him. He craved the contact although winter sucked as a sexy season. Way too many clothes. And he wanted to remedy that and take this inside.

But something held him back.

Maybe the way her hands, still in her gloves covered his—her touch light, barely there. Or perhaps how her heart pounded like she'd dashed up ten flights of stairs. Or the way her body brushed his and then shied away when she could feel his way too obvious erection through his jeans, even though he was doing his best not to grind on her. It had been too long.

Maybe it was his need that held him back.

He trembled with it.

"Edi," he moaned, imagining, rather than feeling the soft press of her breasts against his barn coat. She was so sweet, but so vulnerable, and he didn't want to hurt her. And he would. He was trying for a job that would keep him on the road for many days a month. Spring through early fall.

"Sorry," she whispered against his lips, and kissed him again, the touch too brief. Then her teeth lightly caught his lower lip, and her tongue touched where her teeth had been. "Not sorry."

He laughed a little.

"I should be."

"No." He held her then. "Don't be sorry. I'm not."

"I'm usually in better control." Her gaze was laced with regret and shone with honesty. "I know better. My life isn't…it doesn't feel like mine, but that's just weakness. I have to claim it back, right? The good with the bad. I'm an adult. I have to cope."

She seemed to be talking to herself. But he knew what she meant. If he could have chosen from a deck of cards—cards from someone else's hand, not the ones he'd been dealt—he would have made few if any of the choices he'd made in life. But life was what it was, and he learned to deal without looking back much or stewing in regrets.

He touched her lower lip with his thumb. Thought about saying "F-it," and kissing her like he wanted to—plunder those delicate lips, touch each freckle with his lips, his tongue, his finger. Breathe in the scent of her skin. Explore her long, pale, maybe freckled body. Count each freckle and leave no part of her untouched.

Except her heart. And that was the problem.

Just as he jammed his hands in his pocket to keep from pulling her into him and stepping way over the line, Edi, reached up, touched his rather wild hair that he'd yet to schedule a cut for, and smiled ruefully.

"Thank you."

"For what?"

"For being you."

His astonishment must have shone because very few people in his life had ever approved of who he was—Mom, her boyfriends, his sisters, teachers.

"For reminding me that honey works better than vinegar with my clients."

He laughed and the horrible tension that dragged at him eased a little.

"For tonight. For sharing your ideas and your time. And…" She reached out and touched his gloved hand before pulling back. She was tactile. He loved that. Craved that. Even as he told himself not to. "For the kiss. For not letting me push us over the line. It's been a long time for me, and I'm…I'm not ready. I don't know if I ever will be ready and you deserve someone whole," she whispered, her voice broken. Then she kissed his cheek and slipped inside the door and lightly closed it. He stood on the porch, heard the snick of the dead bolt and wondered what the heck she meant.

Not whole?

Did she know who she was talking to? He was about as broken as a man could get. She had a family who was struggling, but they loved each other. She was smart, young, healthy, pretty, had a good job and a home. He was starting over. Again. Alone.

And he'd do it over and over until he built the life he wanted, a life he was proud of.

But Edi felt broken?

It seemed astonishing, and yet perhaps that was why they were so comfortable together. He stepped off her porch to go back to his truck when he felt something hard in his pocket. He pulled it out. Stared.

The chain with the strange charm on it. Calhoun had asked him to hold on to it for safe keeping until he mustered out. Ryder climbed in his truck, started it, heater blaring, and looked at the tarnished silver disk. It looked like a cattle brand or a coin. It looked masculine even though there was an unusual stone embedded in the metal along with a bumpy piece of turquoise. It looked handmade—not particularly well crafted. Or maybe the rustic feel of it was the point. It looked old but somehow not valuable. The chain was tarnished silver, rectangular links.

Ryder had forgotten about the charm. He didn't want to lose it, so he looped the chain over his rearview mirror, watched it glint in the glow of the streetlight. The chain was long enough that it didn't block his view, but Ryder made a note he should probably find a safer place to keep it. He didn't want to get pulled over for some petty infraction. He had too much to do and couldn't afford a ticket.

As he drove back to the Telford Ranch, he wondered why Jace had the necklace, and what Calhoun was supposed to do with it—find the owner? For a moment, his mind drifted to his three buddies—Cross, Huck and Rohan. They'd found love fulfilling their vow to Jace. Maybe Calhoun would reunite lovers or...

"Not my mystery," he murmured, smiling before he turned on the radio to quiet his mind. His days of searching out targets, finding people and places that were carefully hidden were finished. He wanted them to stay that way.

Chapter Nine

IT HAD BEEN a week, Edi marveled, since Ryder had entered her life. A week. And she'd never enjoyed her job more. Or tried and failed to think about a kiss less.

She was starting to get in a rhythm that felt comfortable—arriving an hour early so she could check in on her gran, clean up anything in her apartment, start her laundry and ensure her gran ate something for breakfast and took her meds. Then she'd work with her individual clients, have a short lunch with her gran, and plan out dinner, and then try to persuade her gran to join any group exercise or activity later in the day.

And the whole time she tried not to think about Ryder's arrival, the energy, unexpected twists and humor he brought. And that kiss.

Edi felt a little like a high school student again when she'd had it bad for Brent Houghton and would linger near his locker in between classes and during break just to catch a glimpse of him. She'd feel sick with nerves and anticipation just hoping he'd appear. At least with Ryder, she was working, not loitering and mooning. But still.

"You are ridiculous," she told herself in the mirror, needlessly adjusting her sleek, low messy bun and sticking out her tongue. She was more dissatisfied with her appearance than she should be. Yes, she had mousy-colored hair, but it was thick and wavy. And she had freckles. So what? Not like everybody didn't notice them immediately. Growing up, her mom had tried to keep her out of the sun like she was a vampire. And she'd dragged her from one high-end dermatologist to another searching for a 'cure.'

And while she had a supermodel's height, she'd never had the waif-like body or small, perky breasts. Her mother, who maintained her extreme thinness for her acting career, had put her on one diet after another because 'once you hit puberty, it's over if you're not thin.'

By the time Edi was twelve, mercifully, her mother and father had finally split, and Edi had mostly moved in with her grandmother as her mom had given up, and she didn't want her fans to know that she was old enough to have a teenage daughter, especially a 'homely' one. Edi had been athletic in middle school and high school and had loved biking and running along the Burke-Gilman Trail in Seattle and kayaking in Lake Union and Lake Washington.

She might not be vivid or beautiful like her mother, but her body had served her well, and there was no need to cast shade now just because Ryder was unusually attractive. There were other men, if she were so inclined, but she wasn't and had no plans to hit Marietta's bar scene and flirt with any cowboys soon. But she would enjoy listening to the music she'd heard about at FlintWorks. Maybe even try one of their microbrews. She was so focused on her gran that she hadn't tried to make friends, but maybe Ryder...

No.

But that kiss.

She stuck her tongue out again as the always present image of Ryder interrupted her musings. She wasn't a daydreamy teen anymore.

Grow up.

He'd be done with his community service in a few months. He had to be—there would be cattle and horses to wrangle and move to summer pastures, calves to brand and vaccinate and who knew what else happened on a working ranch.

Just the memory of watching Ryder stand on top of the chute with his long, leanly muscular legs...

She cut off that thought. She needed to follow her own advice and stop thinking about him. She turned away from the mirror to see Ryder, lounging, arms crossed, ankles crossed, broad shoulders taking up a chunk of real estate in the doorway. His slow smile nearly knocked her sideways.

"Ahhh good morning...afternoon," she stammered feeling her face heat. How long had he been standing there watching her stare at herself in the mirror like a narcissistic ninny while fantasizing about him?

"Good afternoon to you too," he rumbled. His beautiful blue eyes twinkled like he had an LED light bulb behind his corneas.

She should say something. But what? She couldn't remember her own name, much less the exercise class she had planned.

"Holly wants to see us."

"Huh?" She frowned at her own ineloquence and glanced at her watch. Ryder was early. Very early. Early enough to grab a coffee and share a slice of coffee cake that she'd made with her gran this morning when she'd found her gran muddled and frustrated in the middle of a baking project going messily wrong. Edi had calmly rescued the baking project, trying not to cry when she remembered all the things she and her gran used to bake and cook together.

"What about?"

"Didn't say. She caught me on my way in. She did look harassed."

Not good. Edi racked her memory—had anything unexpected happened yesterday or this morning?

"Let's grab a coffee from the staff lounge," she said needing something to do with her hands, so she didn't accidentally, subconsciously on purpose touch Ryder. Plus the warmth of the rich roast would help settle her nerves. "Gran and I made coffee cake for the staff. There might be a piece left."

"There better be." He straightened from his sexy pose and stepped aside so she could leave the room.

She liked that he always let her go first, opened doors for

her. She shouldn't. She knew there was probably some feminist manifesto online that would rail against her girly urge to sigh over his 'gentleman' moves and swoon over his smile.

Edi walked quickly as if she could outrun from her thoughts. Ryder paced silently beside her, and she tried not to notice the fluid and stealthy way he moved—probably why he was still alive, she thought sickly, reminded of what his job had been before he became a cowboy again. They detoured by the staff lounge and each poured out a coffee, and Ryder cut himself a generous slice of the coffee cake, but Edi was too keyed up to eat.

"Hey." Edi rapped lightly on the doorjamb of Holly's perennially open door. "You wanted to see me? Us," she belatedly remembered and then cringed because she felt like she was trying to connect herself to Ryder but hadn't he said that Holly wanted to see both of them?

Nothing like getting tangled up in her same insecurities from high school half her life later.

"Yes." Holly looked both frustrated and apologetic, and Edi's anxiety ratcheted up. "I'm sorry. I'm in a bind, Edi. I've posted the job for an activities director on several online sites, and I've had some nibbles, but no one really suitable until this morning."

"That's good." Edi relaxed.

"Yes and no," Holly said ruefully. "The director is still a student, finishing her degree in Oregon at the end of March, and wouldn't be able to start until early April."

"Two months," Edi mused. "That's not so bad." She tried to put a positive spin on it.

"We lost our last activities director before Christmas, and while we managed to barely scrape through, two more months is a hardship on the residents and the day program staff."

"It seems like the assistants are doing their best," Edi said encouragingly, still not sure why she'd been called in, but Ryder reminded her of a hunting dog waiting for a command. She wished she could absorb some of his energy and ready-for-anything attitude.

"You thought of the visit to the ranch to watch them train the bucking bulls and the wood-burning pizza oven," Holly wheedled.

"Oh." Dismay washed through Edi. "That was Ryder."

She hadn't known anything about bull riding or bulls or local ranches with do-gooder cowboys.

"I think if we all work together, we can figure out a few activities a week for the residents in the assisted living wing," Holly said. "I'm meeting with the caregivers in the day program to see if we can expand some of those programs to suit, but it's important that we have activities for our residents to keep them active, and also to show families that if they choose the May Bell Center, their loved ones will have enrichment and social opportunities."

Holly looked every inch the director, and Edi felt like

she'd just flipped on a giant spotlight, and there was nowhere for the once again inadequate Edi to run.

But I'm a physical therapist.

In a small town, at a small facility, that was trying to grow to keep up with the community's needs.

"I…we'll ahhh…" She tried to grab some words out of her kaleidoscope of a brain. "We'll think about it…I mean we'll discuss it," Edi amended. She needed this job, and she'd always been a team player.

"What about reaching out to the community?" Ryder suggested.

Both Holly and Edi pierced him with stares.

"There are people with talents out there, I imagine. Maybe you could have guests come in—musicians, artists, teachers." He shrugged like it was a no-brainer.

"How about a Valentine's Day activity?" Holly asked brightly, seeming proud of her cleverness. "That's a nice easy start, and it's in a little less than two weeks."

"Valentine's Day," Edi whispered faintly. Even when she and Derek had been a couple, he hadn't made any effort, and the one time she had planned something special—bought a present, cooked a special dinner and planned a sexy evening, he'd texted that he'd taken a friend colleague's overnight call at the hospital, leaving her alone, again.

"There's a gallery in town and a music store, and Harry's House has a lot of community support. Maybe start there to see if you can drum up any community interest. Try the rec center." Holly's voice was breezy and firm. She'd dumped her problem on them, and she was done.

"We'll be good little drummers." Ryder pulled two drumsticks out of his back pocket and beat a catchy tattoo on the doorframe. "We got our marching orders." His smile dazzled, and Holly actually relaxed deeper in her chair, smiling back.

Edi had a childish urge to kick Ryder's shins. She'd never been a party planner, or social butterfly even when her life was on track.

"A fantastic Valentine's activity and party coming up." Ryder drummed in time with his commentary and then winked at her. "Follow me."

"What's with the drumsticks?"

Edi kept pace with him, her tight little ass tucked in and her shoulders back like she was about to fight. And the way her eyes had flared in alarm and her mouth had pursed when Holly had mentioned Valentine's Day, had made him mental.

Weren't women supposed to *love* that stuff?

What idiot had hurt Edi to the point that Valentine's Day was what the army shrinks would call a trigger? Or was it trauma? Jace would have known. He was Mr. Mental Health, always checking in with his team.

Whatever. He wanted to pound the idiot—whoever he was—so deep into the snow so he wouldn't be found until May.

"We're planning a Valentine Day's activity, and you want to know what's in my back pocket?"

"Ugh. Don't say that word. No V-words today."

"Valentine's. Victorious. Vivid. Vampy."

Edi scowled. "I am a physical therapist, not a party planner."

"Valor. Vague. Vital."

Edi's frown was adorable.

"Vacant. Variant. Vaccine. Vacuum."

"Vacay. Stop." Edi made a time-out sign.

"I did not picture you using a word like vacay," Ryder said conversationally.

"Well, I need one after Holly's bomb. How are we supposed to come up with an idea for a Valentine's activity? Just the thought gives me hives."

"Why?" Ryder stopped walking, finally accepting that Edi was really upset about this.

Edi swished her hand through the air and looked mutinous. "The reasons are many and obvious."

"Not to me." Ryder thought far back to elementary school. He remembered the class party—one or two, maybe. Candy and the store-bought Valentine's cards he received, but couldn't buy any for his classmates, so he'd asked his teacher for paper, markers, scissors and glue to make cards.

"Bad boyfriend? Burger King instead of wine and candles in a fancy restaurant?"

The varied expressions that chased across Edi's face were fascinating. He had no idea what she was going to say, and his breath seemed trapped in his throat.

"It's complicated," she finally muttered. Her expression briefly tragic before settling back into the lines of calm, stoic professional.

"Doesn't have to be." Ryder wasn't sure why he was so dogged about them planning a party, but he suspected it was more about his nana and not letting Holly down, which would in turn let Jace down, than the actual party.

"It's a party," he said, shrugging his shoulders. "It can't be that hard."

Tears welling in Edi's beautiful eyes and spilling down her freckled cheeks, like a leaky faucet, was not what he expected and had him feeling all kinds of mean and helpless.

"I'm sure it's just a party to you," she accused. "I didn't see you as a hearts and flowers kind of guy. But to so many of the new residents, Valentine's Day might remind them of all they've lost—their dance partner, companion, their best friend who remembers them when they were younger and strong. No more shared memories or jokes or dinners out, or walks after dinner or champagne."

Not a heart and flowers type of guy.

She had that right, but the more the tears trickled down her face, the more inadequate he felt. And when he'd been younger, those feelings had caused him to strike out. But he'd matured and learned to channel his feelings to action. Or deflect them with a joke. But seeing Edi cry wasn't something even he could dismiss.

"Edi, I'm sorry." He shoved his hands in his pockets because if he didn't, he was going to pull her into his arms and hug her. He shook with the desire to comfort her. To feel her body against his. He wished he could be the man who could comfort Edi. Make her feel whole and loved and…

Whoa, not your role.

He'd only brought irritation and disappointment to everyone, including himself, until the army. Now he felt like he was walking through a mine field all over again, just not literally this time.

"I agreed because Holly said it needed doing, and I think the clients deserve to have something special. But I shouldn't have dragged you into it."

He opened his mouth to tell her he'd plan everything on his own.

"I'm sorry I dragged up sad memories."

"No, Ryder. I'm sorry." Edi wrapped her long arms around her body, and tucked her chin to her chest. "I'm sorry," she choked out. "I'm overreacting and just seeing the negatives, and I don't want to be this person anymore. And you're not alone in the Valentine's Save," she said staunchly.

"The event has a name, does it?" He was touched by her determination to rally.

"That will be our private name until we have...I don't know...a theme or a plan." She briefly balled her fists and then shimmied her body like a dog shaking off water.

"Sorry for being such a killjoy."

He gave up on holding himself apart and pulled her into his arms because she looked so alone and so vulnerable, and though he was probably the last man anyone would turn to for comfort, he was the man here.

"You're not a killjoy," he reassured her. "You're dealing with a lot and bringing your best each day."

"I want to be better." She looked up at him, and it took everything in him to smile, but not kiss her.

"Growing up, I always wanted to be better," he confessed. "I'd watch teachers, coaches, co-workers, army brothers, to learn the secret to being a good man."

"I'd say you nailed that," Edi said.

He opened his mouth to deny it but paused. Wasn't he trying to reassure her that she just needed to try each day? If she wanted to change, she just needed to put in the effort each day—one positive action at a time.

Her ash-colored hair tickled his chin, and he rubbed against it a little, memorizing the silky softness. He inhaled her herby lemon scent that washed over him, leaving him feeling oddly content and yet bereft and longing at the same time.

He could feel her heart calm against his chest.

"I'm sorry to fall apart," she whispered.

"You're strong, Edi. I'm sorry you're hurting," he said. "But I'm not sorry that I met you or that I can be your cheerleader when you need one."

"Maybe when you're at the dollar store on your top-secret mission, you can pick up some pom-poms," she said quietly, and he settled at the hint of mischief in her voice.

"Don't think I won't, Dr. Martin."

"Edi."

EDI DRAINED HER bubble bath and lotioned her skin and belted her lavender chenille robe loosely around her waist. She was ready for bed embarrassingly early, but her gran had been tired after the drum class—and who knew her gran knew any of the words to a Twisted Sister song or White Snake music, so she'd made her a sandwich and tucked her in bed and headed home alone. Again.

Always.

And that should not burn. She was lucky to have a home and a job and her health and her gran. Ryder seemed alone in the world, and yet he was always cheerful, ready to lend a hand or an ear or…

"Friends," she muttered.

Which was better than last week. She'd had no friends then. Most of her Seattle friends and colleagues had avoided her when she'd shared the news that her baby daughter, Aria, would be born 'incompatible with life.' And when she'd taken a leave of absence and curled into a ball of grief, no one had come near, including Derek.

She still couldn't believe she'd been struck such a devastating blow, and yet that was arrogant. Why should she be spared over someone else? Life was random, and you did the best you could. A smile touched her lips. She sounded like Ryder. He wasn't letting the hurts of yesterday rob him of the joys of today. He'd lost a best friend recently, and yet he was honoring him and his life, not hiding away.

She looked around her gran's bedroom—almost everything was the same as when she'd left it except Edi had bought a new bed. She was not seriously contemplating getting into bed before eight was she?

A rat-a-tat-tat on her front door answered her, and her heart leapt.

No, she chided her imagination. Ryder had said friends. She had to be satisfied with that. She was lucky to have that. She just had drums on the brain since Ryder had run the drum exercise class after purchasing baskets from the dollar store where he'd placed the large yoga balls. He'd given each seated client the stationary ball and two drumsticks and then he'd cranked the music and proceeded to rock out with ten seniors following him rather devotedly.

Edi clutched her robe when the sound came again. Maybe it wasn't Ryder. Maybe it was someone breaking in.

"I have Mace," she called out, trying to cover the tremor

in her voice.

"That sounds painful, Edi. Can we skip the attack-Ryder part and head straight to dinner?"

Dinner?

She stared at the door like it would swing open on its own.

"We don't have dinner plans."

"We could. I'm hungry. My treat."

"I'm not dressed." Why had she told him that?

"And the evening just got more interesting." She heard Ryder's voice drop an octave, and she shivered in response.

"Friends," she whispered.

"Edi, it's freezing out here. Let me take you to dinner. I gotta eat. You gotta eat. We can talk. Open up."

"You're pushy," she said, nervously shifting from one foot to the other.

She found she wanted to go to dinner, but she was loath to open the door when she was in a chenille robe that was more like a cozy blanket than a come-hither outfit.

Wait, did she *want* him to see her in something sexy?

Not that she had anything remotely sexy anymore, and that was more depressing than it should be. She sounded ninety-six, not thirty-six, and probably most of her clients still clung on to a favorite piece of lingerie for the memories. Her gran definitely did.

But he said they were friends.

"Friends go to dinner," she muttered, and for some reason, she loosened the belt on her robe.

He beat a tattoo on the door again, and she flung it open, not wanting the neighbors to complain.

Ryder leaned against the doorjamb, two lavender drumsticks in his hand, and his barn coat open, and his Stetson tilted slightly down on his face. His smile stole her breath. It widened as his blue gaze drifted over her warmly and lingered on the V.

"Your gran does know her colors," he said softly. "Lydia said your favorite color is lavender, and I painted these for you."

Edi caught her breath that Ryder had even thought to ask. She took the drumsticks, too choked up to say anything.

"She also said you think guacamole is its own food group, and I googled…" his warm gaze never left hers "…and there's a restaurant in town, Rosita's, that has tableside guac."

She opened the door wider. He looked like every romance fantasy hero she'd ever dreamed of. "I'll get dressed," she said breathlessly.

IN THE SUMMER *we could walk to the restaurant.*

He mentally kicked himself. In the summer, he'd be on the road, not taking Edi to dinner. And she wouldn't want to date him anyway. A doctor at the local hospital would be more to her liking but having her in his truck where her scent teased and whispered and wrapped him up was madness.

"What is your scent?" He couldn't hold back the question any longer.

"My what?" She pulled her coat around her body more tightly even though the heater was working so well, he felt like shedding clothes.

But being around Edi often had him feeling like that. He wouldn't have pegged her as his type, but now she appealed so much that he was becoming obsessed with her long, strong athletic body, ash-colored hair that she seemed determined to tame, beautiful, emotive eyes that changed color with her moods and intelligence and vulnerability seemed like his type now. And why not? He was a different man in a different world.

"I like it," he said, hoping that didn't sound pervy, and wishing he were nimble enough to think of a lie like he thought it would be a good present for…but that was the rub, right? He had no woman to buy a scent for. And he never had. His sisters had sneered at his childish attempts to make them birthday or Christmas cards and presents. His mom had rightly accused him of stealing whatever he'd brought home. And with his nana they'd both been trying to survive.

"Lemon verbena." Edi spoke into the smoldering silence. "It's from L'Occitane. Is it…is it too strong?"

"It makes me hungry," he admitted.

"Whaaaa...?" Edi's eyes were huge, and her gaze clung to him like Saran Wrap.

He parked close to Rosita's, but left the truck running for a moment, wanting to choose his words carefully.

He was tired of dancing around the tension. The only thing holding him back had at first been honor—he could smell her vulnerability and tender heart, and he didn't want to hurt her. Then it was fear—laughable as was his arrogance, because he hadn't thought she'd turn him down. But he was rightly worried that if they hooked up once or twice it would make working together awkward for her, and he was determined to finish Jace's hours. He didn't want to have to go back to the judge, Stetson in hand, and ask for a new volunteer spot because he'd F'ed it up, literally.

"I think we both feel it," he said. The shock in her expression, reflected in the dash lights, was practically cartoonish. But why? Edi must have idiot men hitting on her all the time, but maybe she didn't get out much since her gran's diagnosis, and he wanted to kick the happy hop of his heart out of his truck's window.

He should want Edi to have a lot of choices for a partner, because he sure wasn't one of them, not for long anyway. There were so many better men than him. Men from stable families and with an education. Men who wouldn't be hitting the road for weeks or months at a time—he wasn't exactly sure how it worked. He could hardly expect Edi to sit around and wait for him to come home to change stock before heading out again on the off chance he'd have a night off.

"You feel *it*?" she breathed.

"Like a hammer to my head and other, more delicate parts of my anatomy." He huffed out an impatient laugh, turned off his truck, pocketed his keys and jumped out and rounded the truck to help Edi out in case it was icy, although she wore snow boots.

That's my Edi. Practical to her core.

Not yours. The thought startled him. Dumb. Why would she want anything with him anyway? He'd be a novelty—a man she thought would be more earthy in bed, maybe. He sure as hell felt primal right about now.

She watched him, a little wary, but wonder was on her face, and a pulse kicked up in her long, elegant neck that she'd thankfully forgotten to bundle up behind a gator or garishly festive scarf. Seriously how did anyone get laid in winter?

"Really? You are having…sexual thoughts?"

He had the urge to laugh and show her how she affected him, but he'd avoided arrest his whole life, and didn't want to get picked up for lewd public displays now. Who knew the rules in small-town Montana where he'd spotted several churches on his way through town?

"Just hearing you say sexual gives me a charge, and I'm trying to keep it G-rated, Edi. You could help me out," he said. "I'd planned to brainstorm ideas for the clients' Valentine's event since you said you are on board."

Her gaze searched his, and he wondered what she was looking for. "So not a date." Edi slid out of the truck, careful not to take his hand.

How to answer that? He just kept stepping in it with her. He crowded her against the truck a little with his body. "It can be whatever we want it to be," he said recklessly. "We're two consenting adults. Unattached. Free to temporarily indulge."

"I'm thirty-six."

As an objection it fell flat with him. "Not doing math here, Edi. I'm lucky to be alive and intend to enjoy it." He smiled lazily when he really wanted to curse because he was feeling desperate, and his balls were probably going to permanently ascend into his body if they didn't take this discussion inside the festive-looking restaurant that at a little past seven thirty was already winding down for the night. Rancher's hours.

"I can benefit from your experience," he teased.

Wrong thing to say by the flare in her eyes. "Good luck with that." She pushed past him and headed for the door. "Why not google tips? Your education seems to be comprised entirely of Google searches."

Direct hit. He absorbed it. He should be used to this by now.

"You're not wrong."

"Damn." Edi flung her arms around him and squeezed him tightly. Then she looked up at him, palming his chilled cheeks in her mittened hands. "Ryder I'm sorry. I don't know why I said that. It was ugly. Unfair." Her freckles stood out on her pale complexion like accusations. "You unsettle me."

He unsettled her? She filleted him wide open.

"But it's true," he said. "A recruiter had to help me pass my GED. I didn't make it past my freshman year because I had to work full-time and extra."

"I'm sorry," she repeated, her eyes glistening. "You're smart, Ryder. You're driven. You do what it takes, and I'm a coward, hiding behind my degree."

She gulped in a breath and didn't let go of his face, and he felt trapped in a melodrama, and yet, he had no intention of moving, of not hearing what she was so passionately going to say next.

"I sometimes strike out and get mean when I'm insecure and feeling stupid. My mother was mean," she admitted, as if coming to a realization mid confession. "And I don't want to be like her, ever. I've tried to not be like her, to not listen to her voice in my head, but sometimes I still hear her, and I hate that. I hate what I just said to you, and I was mean before, and yet you have been so warm and wonderful and—" she broke off and waved one hand out helplessly "—respectful toward me, Holly, my gran, the clients. You always think of others, and I've been trapped thinking about myself." She squeezed her eyes shut. "And I hate that. Hate it. It's like a ride I'm stuck on, and I want to get off."

Her words rung out in the night, and his responses stumbled over each other in his head.

"Why would you ever feel insecure or stupid?" He was utterly baffled.

"I...why wouldn't I?" She straightened her spine even though she had marvelous posture and rolled her shoulders back like she was taking on a really unpleasant, but necessary task.

"I was awkward growing up," she said like she was confessing some great sin. "I got tall fast, was super skinny though you wouldn't know it now."

His mouth dropped open. She looked strong and athletic to him. Was this one of those weird things women did to themselves, thinking that men wanted to take broomsticks with fake boobs to bed, although, he thought guiltily he'd done plenty of that in off-base bars.

"And I had a million freckles, and my mom is super beautiful and was once an actress in the one daytime soap that was filmed in LA, and she always looked at me like she couldn't believe I'd come out of her body. She and my dad separated when I was six, and I switched houses back and forth depending on when they were doing a location shoot, but mostly I was raised by nannies or my gran. As I got older my mom felt like I would age her, so I saw less of her."

Ryder blew air out of his nose. "Let's take this inside."

"Great, all I need is an audience to make my shame complete. And a hair shirt." She reached out for the door, but Ryder was there before her.

"What the hell is a hair shirt?"

"Historical reference. People wore them for penitence. And I'm going to shut up now."

A smiling server approached them, grabbed two menus and seated them in a booth by the window that had a pretty view of Main Street and the snow swirling down.

"I don't like to talk about my family or childhood. I just wish I could forget it, and some days I think I have and then, slam. And I'm sorry, Ryder, and let's leave it at that because I don't want to talk about high school although because I was with my gran, it was better than it would have been, so I owe her everything for that."

A server deposited a basket of warm tortilla chips and several salsas on their table.

"Tableside guac?" the server asked as if unaware of the tension.

"Yes," Ryder choked out the one word, when he had so many he wanted to say.

"Coming right up."

"It's expensive," Edi murmured.

"Your gran said guac was your favorite."

"You're not still playing that game with dating tips are you?" Edi asked, one chip in her hand.

"Why not?" he challenged. "I need all the help I can get."

"Make that two of us." Edi crunched down hard on her chip.

Chapter Ten

"SO IF THIS were a date..." Edi posited, just to see if Ryder really would play along.

"I definitely wouldn't talk about my past," Ryder said firmly, dipping a chip in one of the salsas. "But since you started it, and you say this isn't a date, let me keep cracking the ice and say that we got a bit of the boohoo childhood, sucky parents in common."

He plucked another still-warm chip out of the basket, but paused, and Edi had the unaccustomed feeling that Ryder was feeling more than he wanted her to know.

"My mom went through men like lunch sacks. She said she wasn't quite sure who my father was, and that she only kept me because by the time she realized she was pregnant, it was too late for an abortion, and she didn't have the money to see if she could get someone to do it illegally."

Edi gasped. Ryder crunched the chip, his expression shuttered.

"Ryder." Edi covered his hand with hers just as a young man arrived with all the fixing for tableside guac, and the timing couldn't be worse.

Her heart wept for him, and she could barely hear the

questions the young man asked about the spice level and everything else as he made a dramatic showing of creating their guac.

Edi couldn't imagine a mother telling her child something like that. She'd wanted her child so badly—even with all of her baby's health issues and even though she'd only had a few hours with Aria, she'd cherished each second.

"Enjoy." The server smiled at them both, and Edi couldn't remember feeling more awkward in a long while.

Ryder thanked him and slipped the man some money.

He was so effortlessly kind, and she ached to think of him as a hurt little boy, but Ryder seemed so strong and self-assured that it was hard to imagine him as anything other than the confident, kind, competent ex-soldier and cowboy.

"I've never told anyone this. Not even Jace. But I also had two sisters. They both had the same father and were eight and ten years older than me and looked like my mom, and they were a pretty tight group for a while until my mom took off shortly after the youngest graduated high school. My sisters dropped me off at my nana's when I was about eleven."

His casual delivery—the words between dips of guac and bites of the chip—didn't hide the tension and repressed pain behind the words. Edi could barely breathe thinking about how much that must have hurt, and yet, the same thing had happened to her.

"We do have that in common," she said. "Except living

with my gran was a relief. She listened to me. Didn't berate me about everything and was supportive and interested in what I was doing."

"My nana was for me too. It was the first structure—getting to school on time and regularly. School supplies I needed. Regular meals. Lunch. After-school sports. No more dodging fists of whatever man my mom dragged home from the bar. No more trying to navigate domestic mine fields, trying to keep the peace or anticipate what someone wanted or needed."

Ryder chewed thoughtfully, and she tried not to stare at his strong jaw and sensuous mouth and the way his hands looked as he scooped up the guacamole. It was one of her favorite things to eat, but her stomach felt in knots from her thoughtless comment and Ryder's rehashing of his past. And she was choking on her libido. This man was not only physically appealing and masculine perfection, but he was kind. Respectful. Goal-oriented. Loyal. Honest.

She, with all her insecurities and occasional swipes, did not deserve him.

"My nana started declining when I was fourteen, so I worked in the stables at a huge dude ranch to support us," he continued, his voice cranking tighter. He sucked in a deep breath, leaned back in the booth and ran a hand through his springy chestnut hair that looked even more sexily shaggy. "And I don't regret it. I joined the military to get some knowledge and skills." His mouth twisted as if mocking himself. "I loved the hands-on learning, but also the classes, the training manuals we read, the coursework, the drills, the in-the-field training simulations. I soaked it all up and thrived, but the skills where I excelled aren't so useful in civilian life. Thought I'd go to college after, and I still might online, but working with Jace and the other Coyote Cowboys..." He shook his head and smiled. "We were called that by some other teams as a friendly insult, but I loved it. Coyotes are scrappy, can survive in most any environment and are pack animals."

Edi listened, fascinated. She hadn't seen this Ryder yet. Serious, thoughtful.

"But working with Jace, he always talked about his family's ranch and wanting to get back home, heal the wounds in his family and in his land, make it thrive again, and I thought if I could get ranch work, come to Marietta with Jace, I'd be part of a team and belong somewhere."

Her heart hurt for him. But also for herself.

"Two lost souls stumbling home," she murmured.

"We're not lost," Ryder said. "And we're not stumbling. But some days maybe I'll trip or you will. Getting back up is the key."

"God, I'm still so sorry for what popped out of my mouth," she admitted.

He shrugged it off. "I've heard worse. Probably will again. Maybe even later tonight."

She shook her head. "Not from me."

"We're all products of our childhoods," he said. "The good and the painful, but we're adults now. The fact that you apologized shows that you're not like your mom. You're self-aware and making an effort every day to be the person you want to be. It's a choice." His voice was firm; his eyes looked lit from within. "The past should stay there, but now you know mine."

But he didn't know all of hers. Should she tell him about Derek? Aria? She still felt like Aria was with her—her shining spirit flying around her most days, comforting, curious, company. She thought about her every day. She opened her mouth to speak, but then closed it. Did she really want to talk about something so sacred and precious over a basket of chips?

"You have beautiful eyes." His voice sounded raw and his other hand snuck up to cover hers that still curled around his.

She was shocked. "They're muddy."

He reached out and traced a finger over her brow, down her cheek and cupped her chin. "They are like mossy pebbles in a mountain stream catching the light and the clouds," he said stunning her to silence. "Your eyes are fascinating. They are green, light brown with gray and black specks and always changing with your light, mood and environment. Your eyes are the chameleon that matches your soul so don't argue with me."

"Ryder…"

"Don't argue." He held a finger in front of her mouth—a mock threat.

"My eyes are nothing special. My mom's eyes are this amazing green that…"

"Don't care about your mom or her eyes. Yours are the most beautiful I've ever seen. They are; hazel is the rarest iris color on earth. The most unusual. I know." He smirked. "I googled."

"YOU SURE YOU want to walk?"

"Yeah. The Graff is only a few blocks away." Edi tipped her head back. "After a margarita and the fajita salad, I need to clear my head and get my digestion going. Wow. Look at the stars. I never saw them like that in Seattle or LA. But LA has beautiful daylight."

Ryder shoved his hands in his pockets to keep from holding Edi's hand or wrapping an arm around her waist. He'd always been a tactile person—probably why he got in so many fights when he was a kid—seeking contact in what he considered was a macho and socially appropriate way. He noticed she still had her drumsticks in the pocket of her jacket.

"So a drum circle." She slanted him a look. "I shudder to think what's next. Sunrise yoga with the new calfs or foals in a barn? Street art murals on the side of the library? Two-stepping ourselves to the courthouse for our vandalism trial?"

"I did not know you were so creative." Ryder was amused. "You've been holding back when I tried to get you to discuss the Valentine's Save."

"Ugh. Not the V-word."

Ryder made a heart shape with his hands like he was a BTS fan. "Oh, girl. The Valentine's Save is happening and a party will most definitely be involved, and dress-up, I think."

"I know." Edi sounded resigned, and yet he saw a glimmer in her eyes, and a smile teased at the corner of her mouth. "I agreed to head to the Graff with you to see if Miranda stocks arts and crafts supplies in her boutique. And we can talk to Shane about possibly visiting the May Bell Center to teach a cocktail or mocktail class, or maybe she'd teach it at the hotel before the bar opens on an afternoon." Edi ticked off her fingers. "She also sells bitters and essential oils at the farmer's market in the summer and fall so maybe she could teach a class on making lotions or soaps or witch's brew."

"Witch's what?"

"Just seeing if you were paying attention," Edi mused. "I don't want to let you down, leaving you to save the day that shan't be named alone."

"You won't let me down." And even though they'd had a rough start, he felt that sentiment, that trust to his bones.

They turned the corner and the Graff rose up in all its lit-up, historical and elegant beauty.

"It's weird," Edi admitted, also pausing perhaps to take in the splendor of the hotel. "I was dreading this assignment—trying to think of activities, especially a…themed party, but you make it fun."

He was going to tease her about not being able to say Valentine's, but her words touched him so deeply he stayed quiet. They climbed the stairs in silence, and Edi tucked her hand into his, and Ryder felt her touch to his toes.

He held open the door for her even as the doorman tried to swing it wide.

"Welcome to the Graff," Ryder intoned along with the doorman.

"Thank you, kind sirs," Edi said as if trying out a character from the past.

Ryder had seen the hotel boutique the first night he'd arrived and they headed there together. "We are about to conquer the color beige," he promised.

"What is your gripe with beige?"

"It's too indeterminate," Ryder said. "Institutional. The hallways of the May Bell need life, color, vividness to stimulate the residents. To show personality. To offer ways to engage, and it will be more cheerful, more homey." He remembered how his nana would put his schoolwork or artistic endeavors on her fridge.

"I feel sort of beige," Edi said, self-consciously touching her hair.

He groaned and stopped walking. "I was talking about

walls, not a woman," Ryder said. "But, while we're at it, and sorry, not sorry for overstepping, but I've been obsessing about seeing your hair down. It's so intriguing. Mysterious."

And while she gaped at him, which totally made him smile, he reached over, plucked her tan beanie with the silly pom-pom on top off her head, and tucked it in his pocket. Going for broke, he gently smoothed a palm over her bun, found the four butterfly clips and elastic and gently eased them out.

Her hair tumbled down to the middle of her back in loose waves that framed her serious face. He inhaled her lemon verbena fragrance and finger-combed her tresses.

"If this had been a date…" he stepped back so that he wouldn't do something totally over the line "…this is how you would wear your hair." His breath escaped in a long hiss. "Wow, Edi, beautiful."

HOW CAN MY life change in the lobby of a hotel?

Edi stared at him mutely. Never once had anyone used the B-word with her. Not even her gran. Not that she'd ever tried to fancy and feminine herself more than mascara and a swipe of lip gloss. And she was beige. She even chose colorless scrubs as if trying to fade into the background.

But Ryder saw her.

"Are you mad?"

She shook her head, and felt her body tremble as if it was going to crack open, and she was happy and scared at the same time.

"I understand the hair, and the scrubs at work," Ryder said. "But life isn't only work, Edi."

She nodded. "I know," she whispered, feeling a little flushed and hot.

"Let me help." Ryder helped her out of her parka and gloves and hung them up on the coat-tree along with his. His breath tickled her ear and cheek and a million butterflies took flight at the look in his beautiful eyes.

"I see Shane at the bar and luckily the gift shop is still open," Ryder said, as Edi tried to pull herself together. She felt utterly undone, and yet as if she were finally in the shape she was meant to take.

"What do you think—divide and conquer or team up?"

The old Edi would have been practical. Deferential. Divide and not so much conquer, but Ryder inspired her to be the change she wanted.

"Team up." Edi matched her words to her action, and slipped her hand in Ryder's—his palms were rough against hers and heat curled low in her tummy—and headed toward Lost and Found Objects.

"HI, EDI AND Ryder." Gin Lane, Rohan's fiancée they'd

both met the other night, greeted them both with a hug, and Edi's toes curled with happiness. Maybe she could build a life in Marietta—now and in the future with friends and…" Her gaze helplessly swung to Ryder.

She couldn't pin her hopes on him. He too was rebuilding his life and needed time and space.

As do you.

"Good to see you two again. How can I help you? I only help Miranda out a couple of evenings a week and one weekend day while she's on maternity leave—twins." Gin smiled.

"Twins. That's double the love," Edi said.

"Double the trouble too." Gin laughed, and she waited expectantly, and Edi, who'd paused to gather her thoughts and watch two young teens—Petal, Edi remembered and another girl—were cleaning and organizing the art supplies while Gin's son Lucas sprayed glass cleaner and scrubbed until the glass panels sparkled.

"Ryder's been volunteering at the May Bell Center for Jace." At least Gin would have context for this, and immediately her expression creased with sympathy and she lightly touched Ryder's hand. "I'm a physical therapist there, and we are down a few staff members and an activities director so Ryder and I have been tasked to come up with an idea for…some activities," she bravely plunged on feeling herself heat with self-consciousness, "for the clients—both the adult day care clients and also the new residents of the assisted living wing, and we were hoping—" she talked faster, feeling like she was going to start stammering "—that with you being a teacher and on the board of Harry's House and the Annex and a long-time Marietta resident that you might have some suggestions for a direction or people we can tap or…" She trailed off, hoping her ask wasn't too big.

"I have a list of board members and volunteers and am happy to do an all hands on deck email to see if anyone has the time or suggestions, but hold on. Girls, let Ms. Martin run something by you. This is Petal, Miranda's daughter and Arlo, Shane, the bartender's daughter."

Ryder did a double take, and Arlo, with her short-cropped hair and an ugly dog in a front pack on her chest, laughed at him.

"I've seen pictures of you and heard some stories," Arlo said. "It must be weird that Cross was like this broody single guy when you last saw him, and now he's married with a teenage kid. It's like a parallel universe."

Both the girls fist-bumped and made an exploding sound and wiggled their fingers.

"We're both adopted," they chimed together. "Only Petal was adopted by her cousin, and I was adopted by my stand-in godfather."

"I'm getting adopted by my new dad." Lucas looked up at them, made his pronouncement and returned to his cleaning.

"That's…" She paused, not sure what to say.

"Awesome sauce and a dash of congrats on the side," Ryder slotted in.

"Yeah, that." Edi laughed. Ryder made everything so easy.

"The May Bell Center," Gin broke in briskly. "You two will be in high school next year and will need to start accruing service hours with at least two different organizations," she added as both girls opened their mouths at the same time.

It was kind of eerie.

Ryder seemed fascinated by the girls and their energy.

"Working with seniors would give you a different perspective than when you work with the younger kids at Harry's House," Gin mused. "Ryder and Edi are trying to kick-start an activities program for the adult seniors with some physical and health challenges."

"Oh, we know all about activities," Arlo said. "We volunteer one afternoon after school at Harry's House. We tutor and then do games and art projects."

"We could do that with seniors. Do some research. Maybe get released early," Petal enthused. "Lucas, do you want to work with seniors?"

"Why?" He finally stopped cleaning.

"You're in," Arlo said, and Lucas wrinkled his nose and went back to his cleaning. "I bet a lot of them will have technology issues. Lucas can deal with that. Lucas, you can do workshops for the seniors."

"Why can't you girls do the tech workshops?" Ryder asked.

"We're the student coordinators," Arlo decided and she and Petal fist-high-fived again.

Ryder grinned. "Cross is in trouble."

Then he explained about the Valentine's Save and beige halls, and the next thing Edi knew, the three girls had dragged Lucas away from his cleaning, and they were dictating into one of their phones and listing possible ideas for the party, Valentine's-themed activities but also ways to get other local organizations and kids groups to engage with the May Bell Center.

"I feel superfluous," Edi murmured. "And old and tired."

"That's what you get for trying to get in bed before eight at night," Ryder teased.

Edi shushed him, and Gin laughed.

"I feel like that a lot of nights," she confessed. "But kids will keep you young."

Edi felt as if all the warmth of the room was sucked away. Ryder put his arm around her shoulders.

"While the kids form a Marietta UN spanning the generations in town, why don't we pick up some art supplies?"

Thirty minutes later they exited the Graff after a second cup of hot chocolate with the young teens who were still brimming with ideas including creating a group of May Bell Center volunteers at the high school when they started next fall.

"I feel flattened," Edi admitted. "And yet inspired. Remind me why I suggested the Graff. We practically bought out all their arts and crafts inventory."

Ryder carried three bags of supplies, Edi one.

"At least the girls have it in hand," he said cheerfully, all but whistling in the dark.

"What gives you that idea?" Edi demanded. "They wanted the seniors to paint the background colors of their heart canvases with their feet," Edi reminded him, shuddering at the thought of all the feet they'd have to clean.

"It was for the sensory experience," Ryder said seriously.

Edi dissolved into laugher so hard she couldn't walk. "Oh, God, was I ever that young and enthusiastic about anything?"

"You are now, Edi Martin."

The way he said her name made her feel like she was caught up in a river of heated honey.

"That was fun," she whispered as they neared his truck. "You're fun, Ryder Lea."

"I can be a lot of fun, Edi Martin."

She felt he was saying so much more than the words, and she was so tired of herself, of playing it safe, of listening to her clamoring inner critics.

"I'll drive you home?"

"Mind reader."

Ryder helped her up even though she didn't need it. His hands lingered on her waist, and her breath fractured.

As Ryder navigated the now snowy roads, she thought of all the reasons she should jump out of his truck the minute he pulled into the narrow driveway, but as each reason popped, she batted it away.

"What's this?" she asked lightly touching the charm dangling from his rearview mirror. It didn't seem like an adornment Ryder would have—but she didn't know that much about him.

But you could learn.

"I don't know really," Ryder said.

He held her hand as they drove, and she was conscious that neither of them had put their gloves back on. "I told you I was doing something for my former team leader, Jace McBride, who died on a mission a couple of weeks before he was due home." Ryder's face winced in pain, and Edi lightly squeezed his hand and brought it briefly to her lips. "There are five of us who are carrying out Jace's last wishes. I'm number four. Otis Calhoun Miller gave me this to hold on to. It was part of what Jace needs him to do, but we were sworn to secrecy until our task is done."

Edi was turned toward him, listening, and in the dark of the cab, the heater starting to warm up, she found herself relaxing, belonging.

"All five of us had to come to Marietta for Jace. Cross, Huck and Rohan are staying. That just leaves me and Calhoun."

"Aren't you staying?" Edi's voice was a little sharper.

"I've never really had a home for a long time," Ryder admitted. "Hoping to make one here. I'm hoping to make one. Learn to stay."

The rest of her tension eased.

"But it's a long-term goal. Not close yet," he said. "I've put most of the money I earned in college plans for my nieces and nephew. I want them to have the shot that my sisters and I didn't have."

"That's generous," Edi marveled. "I got the feeling you were estranged."

"We are. I left a note with the investment advisor to contact each of them during their senior year of high school. I want them to have the chances I never did."

"Oh, Ryder." Edi leaned into him. "That is so sweet, but it's not too late for you either."

He paused for a moment. Something flashed in his eyes, but then was gone. "No," he said. "I'm good on a ranch. That was what I dreamed about when I did think about mustering out."

"So there's one more of you coming to Marietta?" She wanted to erase the shadows from his eyes after he talked about his family.

"Calhoun, but you may not be so happy to see him. He asked me for a solid. His service dog Duke was injured and has been rehabbing and retraining with a former soldier who rescues military dogs that don't seem like they are going to be able to reintegrate into civvy. He's out in Texas. If he finishes training before Calhoun comes home or Calhoun doesn't…make it…" his voice dropped to a harsh whisper "…I promised to take Duke. He knows me best. I was always good with animals when I was working at the dude ranch, and Calhoun and I were pretty tight so Duke will feel safe with me."

Ryder might look tough, but his smile, the light in his eyes hinted that he was warm.

But his actions, oh his actions sang of a man who was kind and connected.

He turned into her driveway, put his truck in park and cut the engine.

He turned in the seat to face her. His face was in shadow.

"Edi," he said softly. "I want you, but I can't promise…"

She'd been promised forever and in sickness and in health before, but the words had proved as empty as Derek's heart and her womb. She was no longer looking for promises.

"Yes," she said.

Chapter Eleven

Edi unlocked the door of her gran's bungalow. Her nerves danced with excitement. She was so conscious of Ryder standing closely behind her, his body brushing her alert one. She pushed inside, hesitating for a moment as she automatically reached for the lights.

Was she really doing this?

She wanted to.

She needed to feel alive.

She should get candles. Wine. Music. Wear something other than her scrubs.

"Edi." Ryder's voice was a warm whisper against her ear. "It's okay to change your mind. It's okay to not be ready. It's okay to say no."

"Yes." She spun around and plastered herself against him, dropping her backpack and kicking off her Dansko clogs at the same time. "Yes." She looped her arms around his neck and buried her hands in his dark honey hair that had gold streaks that looked like fire lighting up short winter days when the sun shone just right. "Yes, yes, yes."

His hair was thick and glorious and springy, and she'd wanted to touch it since she'd first seen him. But she also wanted to touch him everywhere all at once and never let go. She peppered his face with kisses—the high cheekbones. The jaw that jutted like an old-time western star's. And then she kissed his lips.

They parted, and then he kissed her back. She cupped his face, and her fingers traced the shape of him before she tugged off his fleece-lined barn jacket.

"Unless you changed your mind." She still held his jacket but managed to drag out the words as her last caution flag waved limply.

"Hell no, never."

Even as he spoke, he took a few steps into the house, nudging her body forward.

Wanting a deeper connection, Edi stepped back into Ryder, pressing him against the door, which slammed shut. The noise echoed competing with their harsh, frenetic breathing.

Jacket gone, she grabbed his vest next, which joined the pile on the floor. Ryder toed off his boots while Edi fumbled with his shirt's buttons.

"Snaps."

Her brain hiccupped. Then kicked in and she pulled the shirt apart.

"Snaps," she breathed reverently. "I love snaps. But why are you wearing a T-shirt?" she demanded, when she encountered cotton instead of warm, hard flesh.

He laughed and caught her hands and kissed them. "We gotta slow down a bit," he said breathing heavy. "It's been a while, and I don't want to rush."

"It's been over three years for me," she blurted.

He blinked. And then his eyes practically seared her. "You got me beat, baby. That is way too long, and I intend to do several somethings about that. You deserve to be worshipped."

Edi had never once felt worshipped in her life. She'd always enjoyed the idea of sex so much more than the actual act. All the kissing and touching would get her so wound up and then the energy would immediately change when Derek and before that Sean would plunge inside her a few times, and it was over before she felt it had begun.

"I…I…" Was she really going to confess this to him? "I don't know what being worshipped feels like," she shared, "but your body definitely deserves an altar. Candles. Flowers."

He smiled and reeled her in tightly, just holding her for a moment, nuzzling her neck. She liked that he was taller than her, but wished he weren't so much younger. But she shoved that worry aside for another day.

When he breathed in her scent instead of kissing her, she fretted she'd done something to break the mood. Maybe he was already regretting his impulse and wondering how to let her down nicely.

Stop.

She didn't want to be ruled by her insecurities.

Not tonight.

Never again.

"I don't know if I want to risk candles considering what I've been fantasizing about doing with you." Ryder continued to nuzzle her neck with his lips. "But maybe we could turn on the gas fire? I want to see your glory."

"Glory is not the word I'd use," she said nervously.

Derek had always preferred the dark, or the room lit with the ambient light from the cityscape in their Belltown penthouse condo.

"It's the word I'd choose." He speared his fingers through her hair. "And unless you've been dating blind men, you've been with idiots. Men are visual animals, baby, and I want to see all of you under those scrubs that I've been fantasizing about peeling off of you since day one."

"You have? I thought I was the only pervert."

He laughed. "I'm right there with you."

"I'll turn on the fire," she said shyly, watching the flames spring to life, and wondering if she should take him to the bedroom, or the couch or...

"Come here," his voice invited. "It's hot as hell that you're such an intelligent woman, but sometimes you gotta turn off your big brain and just feel, Dr. Martin."

HIS BRAIN SHOUTED to slow down, but his Southern brain had a different idea. He'd fantasized about being with Edi for over a week, and it had confused, aroused and intrigued him. He'd never before wondered about a woman's life before he met them or considered their feelings other than desire and pleasure. He'd never let a friendship or trust build with a woman before taking her to bed. All his encounters with women had been totally professional at work or random hookups where they'd blow off some steam horizontal and naked.

This—touching Edi, being touched, hearing the catch in her breath, feeling her heart kick when he touched her—was magic. He was out of his depth, but he wanted to dive deeper and keep swimming.

He nibbled Edi's lips, and down her neck and his hands shaped her breasts under the stiff fabric of the scrubs. He hated these things. How could she stand such unforgiving fabric against her sensitive skin?

"Can I take these off?"

"Mmmmm. Yes please." She'd already pulled his shirt over his head, and her eyes widened, and that jacked him up hotter. "I didn't even know this was possible," she breathed. "If I saw you in a magazine, I'd think you were airbrushed," she whispered both hands on his chest, fingers exploring.

He smiled, accustomed to women's awe, but from Edi it felt more personal.

"All hard-earned," he said softly. "No photoshopping."

She nipped at his nipple and tongued around the mark. "You're beautiful, Ryder." She looked up at him. "I feel like I want a spotlight so I can see everything," she said, her fingers lightly tracing the large tattoo of the Colorado Rockies and a coyote howling at the moon in the foreground that wrapped around his left side.

Her fingers explored the lines of the mountains as did her mouth, and as she explored his torso, she found a few of his scars—some from childhood, and more from his years in the service. She hissed in a breath, her medical knowledge probably indicating awareness of how close he'd come once to not making it home. He braced himself for an intrusive question, but Edi made a happy humming sound that went straight to his cock, and then one hand dipped below the waist of his Wranglers to touch him while she slid his belt out with her other hand. He felt himself relax under her awed explorations.

He didn't want to talk or think, just feel, and Edi seemed on board with that.

He pulled off her top, and tossed it across the room, wishing he could burn it in the fire. Edi should only be soft fabrics—bamboo or silk or, even better, nothing.

His jeans slid down, and he kicked out of them while Edi shimmied off his briefs leaving him only in his socks. She backed him toward the couch that had some kind of knitted blanket tossed across part of it.

"Sit."

He looked up at her. She was even more spectacular than he'd imagined. Her waist was tucked in, and her hips flared, rounded, perfect for gripping, when he went down on her, and he wanted to, so much. His mouth watered for a taste. Her freed hair was thick and wavy around her narrow face and fell forward to skim her breasts. Edi wore a pale bra and red panties. Those were unexpected.

"You going to boss me in bed?" He'd had sex with more women than he could count. Enjoyable but none of the encounters especially memorable.

"You're on a couch."

He slid a finger along the elastic of her panties that had lace inserts and a tiny bow—much more playful than he'd imagined, and he wondered if she'd planned ahead. But women who planned ahead usually had matching lingerie. Edi's had a touch of playful, but it was mostly functional.

"You can boss me all you like on a couch," he propositioned her, "and I'll take over and boss you in bed."

"I didn't say that," her voice husked, and her eyes widened, as he cupped her breasts in the simple bra. He kept his eyes on hers, judging her level of shyness, wanting her comfortable and aroused, not anxious.

"It's only fair." He unhooked her bra, and his thumbs traced her pretty, pink nipples that hardened under his touch. "You're spectacular." He drew her closer to him, marveling at the constellations of freckles that splattered across her chest and arrayed her teardrop-shaped breasts that he wanted to fondle and kiss all night.

He peeled off her panties first with his teeth—her ragged

breathing was musical—and then he finally gripped her flared hips and indulged himself in a long sensuous lick of her slick mound.

She jerked and held on to his shoulders. With one foot he eased her legs wider and tasted her again, varying his strokes and speed as he played with her clit.

"Ryder," she gasped. "I thought I was the boss."

"You are." He pulled back slightly so he could gauge her reaction. Her lovely pale nipples looked as swollen as her lips, and the firelight played over her creamy skin, and he vowed that he would count each freckle, even if it took years, and he was so far gone into her body that the thought of more nights with Edi, when the most he'd had with a woman was a few nights of leave, didn't faze him.

"You tell me how deep you want my tongue or my fingers. How fast you want me to stroke you. How many times you want to come."

She made a sound between a laugh and a choke. "But I thought you'd want me to…you know."

"Suck me?" he tested her. She seemed shy, uncertain, yet she'd been frantic to undress him, and she kissed like fire.

"Um…yeah."

"Later." He resumed his feast. Edi's short nails dug into his shoulders, and he hoped she made a mark so he would feel it tomorrow when he was working. Her tension cranked, and her mews and moans became faster. Her legs shook, and he sucked her clit hard between his lips and bit down lightly.

Edi screamed his name as she came. The hottest part was they'd never stopped looking into each other's eyes. Usually, women closed their eyes when they came, turned their heads, pulled on his hair. But he'd always had his eyes closed too—focusing on the sensations he was feeling, and the sounds of pleasure his partner made.

This moment felt more intimate than anything ever had in his life, and he felt like something hot, yet edged with cold, bloomed in his chest.

"Ryder you're amazing," Edi panted, still staring directly at him like he was the only thing in the room. "So amazing."

She swiped her finger over his slick lips and then tasted herself, her multicolored eyes looked dark gray in the firelight. She was still flushed pink, her breathing elevated, and then she smiled and stroked her fingers through his hair.

"I've never…no one ever…Derek didn't…"

"It's only us here tonight, Edi."

He definitely didn't want to hear about an ex, especially one who didn't like the taste of his woman, but his competitive nature did rear up, take the reins. He didn't ever want future Edi to compare him as lacking when stacked up against another man.

She jerked a nod, and then leaned down and kissed him so sweetly. She stood up again so that her sex was once against even with his mouth.

"Time to switch," she said, kneeling in front of him. "My turn."

"You're the boss," he groaned as she sucked him into her mouth, and Ryder gripped the back of the ugly floral-print sofa to keep himself centered and not take over Edi's sensuous, exploratory rhythm and thrust into her mouth.

He clung to control as long as he could, and then he pulled back, although it was torture. What he wouldn't give to come in her mouth, but he wasn't sure how she felt about that, and he ached to be inside her.

"I want to be inside you," he said.

"Okay." Edi immediately straddled him, but he caught those gorgeous hips in his hands, and excitement flared as he thought about controlling his thrusts into the tempting haven of her body.

"I'm clean," he said. "But we should still use a condom. Are you on birth control?"

She paused. "Sorry." She ducked her head and then looked directly at him. "It's been so long. I didn't even think. I haven't been on the pill for a few years," she whispered as if it were some moral lapse.

"No worries." He kissed her. "I got us covered." He set her on his thighs, loving the warm wetness of her.

He toed over his jeans, reached into his pocket for his wallet and pulled out a row of three condoms.

"That's ambitious." She choked out a laugh.

"Baby, that's just for the couch. I got more for when we finally make it to the bed, and I get my turn to boss you."

She lifted her body, so that her slick heat rubbed against

his painfully aroused cock.

"Hurry."

He opened the wrapper with his teeth, but she took the condom from him, angled it over the tip, and as she slowly impaled herself, he felt her fingers stroke on the condom all the way to his hilt.

"Someone's got mad skills."

She nipped his ear. The biting was a bigger turn-on than he would have imagined. Then she kissed his earlobe, and her laughter was soft and inviting.

"Not yet, but I intend to develop some tonight."

"You're still the boss," he reminded her.

Edi set the rhythm, using his shoulder for leverage. At first it was languid while she got the feel of him, of them together. He used that time to explore her small, pear-shaped breasts, taste her nipples, bathe in her arousal.

"You're amazing. This is perfect," she breathed, catching his cheeks between her palms. "You are so perfect."

She meant that. And Ryder, who'd never heard the adjectives 'amazing' or 'perfect' once ever lobbed in his direction felt as if she'd cracked open his sternum and something dark and fetid hissed out, and even though his eyes burned with some emotion he didn't dare name, he didn't hide his face in her neck, or kiss her yet, because Edi's face glowed as she rode him. Her eyes shone like twin North Stars guiding him into her soul, and she never once looked away from him, and if she were that brave, he wanted to be too.

He let her keep control even though every atom in his body urged him to crush her to him, kiss her breathless and pump hard into her body. He held himself back as long as he could and then some, as he watched Edi begin to crest again to her peak.

"Ryder," she whispered in wonder, and he caught his name with a brush of his lips against hers.

As Edi's muscles clenched him, and her body worked his with subtle shifts, Ryder learned the difference between sex and making love.

And as she tipped over the crest, still staring into his eyes, Ryder finally dropped his rigid control and orgasmed along with her.

THEY DID MAKE it to the bed. Edi hadn't planned on taking Ryder this far because she was afraid she'd never get his scent or his touch out of her memory, and a man like him wasn't sticking around with a woman like her. But there was something so delicious about lying with a man, totally sated, while he stroked her and kissed her as if she meant something to him other than a moment of pleasure.

You got what you wanted. Don't get greedy.

His hands stroked her breasts, her ribs, and then lower. He traced her C-section scar, and she stiffened. He was already up on one elbow so she could see the angles of his face and feel his long body, chest to hips to legs touching hers.

"What happened?" he asked, kissing the scar as she had kissed the scars she'd found on him.

Edi had never intended to talk to anyone about this. Her gran knew, but maybe she didn't remember anymore.

"I had a baby," she whispered. "Aria. She didn't develop properly. She was incompatible with life." She used the word the maternal fetal medicine specialist had used. "No kidneys. Her esophagus wasn't connected. And…" Edi couldn't seem to stop talking, yet Ryder listened and continued to stroke her body, whereas Derek had turned away when she'd had to share the news.

"I'd had a midwife. I wanted low medical interventions. Be more organic and natural so I didn't know until later in the pregnancy that something was wrong because there was a problem with my amniotic fluid. I had to get saline injections to help Aria's lungs develop, but it was clear there were more problems, and several ultrasounds revealed the extent of the problems. She lived less than a day."

"Edi." Ryder whispered her name and pulled her close into his body, spooning her. His arms wrapped around her, sure and strong, and he kissed her nape. "That's so heartbreaking to lose your baby."

It had been. She'd been broken, and she hadn't wanted to be put back together again. Not for a long time.

"I had the C-section because she wouldn't have survived

the birth, and there were more complications for me and for Aria."

No need to go into those.

"I'd been with Derek for five years, and when we found out we were going to have a baby we got married. Courthouse. He didn't believe in marriage, but he knew I did, and he wanted to do the right thing. But when we found out that Ari wasn't normal or healthy, he didn't want to deal with it or me."

Ryder's whole body stiffened, and she winced, wondering what he thought. Then he kissed his way down her spine.

"It's weird," she said. "Derek was a pediatric orthopedic surgeon. He worked with children and their parents all the time. He was a specialist and had many challenging patients. He was skilled and in demand, and yet when he found out his own child had severe birth defects, he didn't go to any of the medical appointments," Edi said, needing to get all the hurt out, hopefully where it would stay—a painful memory, but not crippling.

"He wasn't there when she was born or when she died," Edi whispered.

Ryder continued to hold her, but she could feel his energy in waves.

"I got to hold her, sing to her, read to her, name her." Edi was quiet for a while, exhausted and yet strangely at peace. "I gave her my last name. Aria Martin."

Ryder now knew her worst secret, but why should she

keep her daughter a secret? She was forever a part of her life. Edi kept the ashes with her. She still thought about her, even spoke to her sometimes when she saw something beautiful or funny. When she saw certain dresses in toddler sizes she wondered if she would have bought the dress and what Aria would have spilled on it.

"That's a beautiful name, Edi."

"We had bought a home in Kirkland near Lake Washington to raise our child in but hadn't closed on it. I never went there after. I never went home to our condo in Seattle that we were selling. Derek filed for divorce, and I signed everything over to him just wanting to get free as quickly as possible. I didn't ask for anything, just moved into an apartment in Ravena in Seattle and zombie-walked through the next couple of years."

She didn't tell him she'd curled up on a huge beanbag called a Furlicious from the Pottery Barn that she'd still had from college every night for the first six months.

"Even with counseling I couldn't seem to break out of the grief cycle, and working with children when I'd lost mine was torture. I saw that my gran was having health and memory issues, so I packed up a few things. Sold most everything else and left Seattle, figuring at least my gran needed me."

"He still breathing?"

"What?" She turned to look at him. Instead of the sensuous cowboy she'd made love to on the couch and twice on the bed, a harder man looked at her now, a soldier, all business. "Of course he is. And he's going to stay breathing. I hope you're joking." She searched his expression, waiting for the laugh creases.

"I know a guy," Ryder said innocently.

"Great."

"We could just scare him a little, maybe when he's on a date."

"He remarried within six months."

That had stung.

"And he's still breathing?"

"I'm better off without him," Edi said, and for the first time, she believed it. Not that she'd ever mourned Derek. She hadn't. His betrayal of Aria had been soul-deep. She couldn't respect a man like that, much less love him.

"You deserve better, Edi. The best." He choked on the word a little, and she wondered if he was thinking of his own demons again.

"Really." She turned in to him and ran a hand down his spine, feeling oddly buoyant after such a heavy conversational share. "How much better?" she asked and was amazed to feel him harden against her.

"I can show you."

She smiled. Traced his coyote and the moon and the peak of the mountains inked on his skin. "Let's see what you got, Cowboy."

Chapter Twelve

"I STILL THINK Ryder's idea to paint with feet would have slayed," a young voice gushed.

Edi, rinsing off another set of paint-laden brushes—in *cold* water the four young teen volunteers for the first day of the Valentine's art project, had repeatedly reminded her, turned around.

"Why?" she asked, looking at the tall kid, Parker, whose mouth never seemed to stop moving.

His ideas popped like popcorn, and the girls practically freestyled suggestions right back at him. How did Gin teach this age group? They were so energized and so different from the clients she had once served, but then she'd never worked with groups of children—all her therapy had been individualized.

"Let me guess, you don't like cleaning."

"Ahhhh." He held his head, rocked back and forth and made an exaggerated face. "All I do is clean. Clean. Clean. Clean. When I get up in the morning, I help my aunt Tucker clean out the horses' stalls. Then I take a shower for school. Then after breakfast, I have to help my mom or dad clean off the dining room table and kitchen because I have a three-year-old brother who's a class-five hurricane when he eats—we don't even try to dress him for preschool until after breakfast, and then I have to clean his room after he gets dressed because he can 'do it himself.'" He pouted and scowled and spoke in a babyish voice. Clothes all over his room every time like he's a supermodel and late after his last outfit change to walk the runway for Gucci."

Parker scrubbed the table as he spoke. "After school I have to clean out my mom's car because she's a vet and travels all over the county, and she's pregnant with my sister so my dad is all about making things easy for her and then on Fridays after I volunteer at Harry's House, I clean up whatever project or game we were running."

"You could start a janitorial service," Edi suggested with a straight face, surprised at how much she had enjoyed the afternoon she'd dreaded. The May Bell clients had found Parker to be 'a hoot.'

"That's a thought. If I had my own business, I'd get paid." He paused, snapped his fingers, and then held his cleaning cloth aloft. "Or I could do a TikTok series: 'Pitching in with Parker.' No wait. How about…"

"Might I suggest 'Rockin' it with Ryder.'" Ryder beaned Parker on the head with a small, soft ball that they had been using in some of the group exercise classes and individual therapy sessions and games.

"Oh, it's on, old man." Parker headbutted the ball back to Ryder and they played…Edi didn't even know what to call it, but she's stopped trying to interfere with all the youthful masculine energy since the kids had started coming in on Sunday afternoon for a couple of hours for the past couple weeks.

Today had been painting the background colors of the canvases, and next Sunday they would paint the hearts and have a small party with sparkling cider and decorated cookies shaped like hearts that Edi had volunteered to make with the kids at Shane's house.

Old man. As if. Ryder was just hitting his prime. He had so much ahead. She'd been feeling used up, still grieving Aria, then struggling to adjust to the move, her gran's decline and new job. That was all PR. Pre Ryder.

Careful. He's temporary.

But maybe not. He was staying in Marietta. His geography and schedule were compatible with hers. And the nights they spent together. He'd even taken her out to the Telfords' ranch, and they'd explored on a snowmobile.

She laid the brushes out to dry and then turned and watched Ryder and Parker help a few more of the clients to sit in the circle with the stretchy bands around their ankles so they could play with rolling the ball back and forth and calling out a word that fit whatever topic Ryder or Parker came up with. Lucas and Petal were doing the up-high, down-low, high-five exercise with a couple of seniors, working on stretching their muscles and practicing their visual acuity and reaction times that she'd showed them when they'd first started volunteering two weeks ago.

Had it only been two weeks?

What a radical change. The room was full of energy. And all the assisted living clients were here engaged in something, even her gran.

Arlo had brought her odd-looking dog, named Beast. Edi had been unsure of the dog—it wasn't an official therapy dog, but Beast loved cuddles. He was so ugly, he was cute, and he'd spent the art class on Edi's gran's lap. Gran stroked the dog and instructed Arlo how to finger knit. Gran got flustered on some of the simple steps, and called Arlo 'Edi' sometimes, but Arlo was patient. When she'd retraced the knitting steps to get her gran back on track, Edi had realized that Arlo already knew how to knit.

So sweet.

They talked softly, and Edi wondered what they were discussing, and her heart swelled with gratitude. Ryder had helped her to find this new balance in her job and to reframe her life, and her clients were definitely benefitting. She wondered if he was too?

Edi kept a close eye on her gran along with the other clients, but it was hard not to stare at Ryder.

He was beautiful.

He would laugh at that adjective. But she'd seen him naked—almost every night, although he'd usually leave some time around midnight, and then she'd sit, clutching her phone, waiting for his text that he'd arrived safely home, even though she knew her worry must amuse him. Still, he humored her, not pointing out that he'd survived extreme danger over the past twelve years and a fifteen-to-twenty-minute drive in a four-wheel drive truck with snow tires was not all that perilous.

She observed the activities, noting mood, mobility, engagement and charted them on her iPad and created goals for future skills to work on. The kids definitely brought the light, but so did Ryder. He seemed a natural at everything.

He'd be a wonderful father.

She knew she was way overthinking. They were casual. They'd never once discussed their relationship. And when they'd brought their first group of clients out to the ranch to observe some cowboy skills demonstration and the bucking broncs, he'd kept his distance and had definitely seemed part of the staff—not a May Bell volunteer.

After the exercise session, she and Ryder walked their clients back to their apartments, ensuring they were safely settled in and then walking the four teen volunteers to the lobby where Gin was waiting to drive Lucas and Petal home and Cross waited for Parker and Arlo. Cross had asked to speak to Ryder and without waiting for an answer pulled him aside and around the corner of the building.

Edi watched them both stalk off—total masculine energy and swagger—and her tummy flipped and heated.

Gin had laughed. "You got it bad, girl, not that I blame you. I resisted Rohan when he burst back into my life for all of a minute and a half, and that's being generous."

"Oh. We...ah...Ryder's doing community service for Jace, and he...I'm older than him by almost six years."

Gin laughed. "Don't waste time. Life's short. Why don't you both come to a family dinner tonight?"

"But we're not..."

"Are you kidding? Rohan and Ryder are tight. They all are. They might not be blood, but they are definitely family. Think about it. Dinner's at six, but you can come anytime. Door's always open."

Gin had climbed back into her SUV and headed out just as Remy Cross and Ryder returned, looking serious.

"Think about it," Remy said, in an eerie imitation of Gin, and then he texted someone—probably Arlo who had stayed with Edi's gran along with her scraggly mixed-breed dog with a profound underbite. Arlo shot out of the sliding door, Beast in her arms, red winter parka dragging behind her, and she jumped into the massive black truck with the Wilder Dreams ranch logo on the side and scooted next to Parker.

Edi and Ryder walked companionably back to the activity and therapy rooms to make sure everything was put away for the next time. Her heart thumped a little unevenly and her tummy heated thinking about the fact that they were both done for the day. Maybe. She and Ryder hadn't made plans, exactly.

"You seemed thoughtful today," Ryder said.

Edi sucked in a deep breath. Jump off the bridge? Open the discussion about what they were or weren't to each other?

"I am," she admitted. "I was surprised how much I enjoyed the day, seeing everyone working together."

Ryder smiled—his full smile that creased his cheeks. "On the V-word Save that shall not be named?"

"I was being melodramatic," she admitted. "I was holding on to childhood hurts and the last few years have been stark. Hard. Lonely. I let myself wallow."

"Grieving means you loved. It's part of healing." He walked toward her with that rolling walk of his, and with his blue eyes intent, but she held her palm out because if he didn't stop, she'd have a hard time keeping a G rating.

"I know we're not… dating," she stumbled over the word. "But Gin asked if we wanted to go to dinner at her house, well, at Rohan's family's ranch house, I think is what she meant."

"We're not dating," he repeated in a very different tone from hers as if testing the words. "What would dating look like?"

Edi didn't know how to answer that. They worked together for a few hours in the afternoon, then she spent an hour or two with her gran while Ryder went back to the ranch to do his evening chores, and then he'd meet her at her house, and they'd strip off their clothes. And she'd usually have a stew or soup or chili in the Crock-Pot to feed him.

Was that dating?

"Do you want to date me?"

Yes.

She didn't know what to say. Panic squeezed shut her throat.

"I don't know what we're doing, Edi." He ran a lean hand through his honeyed hair. "I've never dated other than meeting a woman in a bar and buying her a few drinks, talking, maybe dancing before…" He broke off, looking sheepish. "Maybe dinner a few times, but you're…you're a whole different kettle of fish as my nana would say."

Edi laughed. "My gran used to say that too."

"I get the feeling you're slumming with me to find your footing again."

She stared at him, shocked by his take. But didn't she think he was just biding his time with her before he found someone younger, hotter, with less baggage?

"You've taught me things I never even imagined were possible," she said striving to sound playful and not desperate. "In and out of bed so maybe…" Her fingers skimmed one of the buttons on his open blue plaid western shirt. The navy shirt underneath did dynamite things to his eyes. "You're slumming with me."

She thought he'd laugh. Instead he muttered a curse and turned away.

"Hey." She had her hand on his shoulder and the other at his waist. "What did I say wrong?"

"Nothing wrong," he said. "But the truth, Edi, is that you're a cut above me. Make that two cuts."

"What? W-why would you say that?"

He turned back. Took her hands in his and looked at them.

"You help people with these hands. Heal. I've killed. More than once," he said rawly.

The truth of that hit her full frontal even as she opened her mouth to defend him.

"You were married to a doctor."

She rolled her eyes at that dubious accomplishment, which had flamed out in disaster.

"You have an education. Not just college but the whole enchilada with a side of rice and beans and tamales. Grad school. Doctorate. I went to high school for a year then dropped out to work full-time and nobody noticed. Nobody cared. Nobody checked up on me—not the school. Not social services or the cops. Not my employer. I joined the army after my nana passed because I thought I could do something with my life. Do good. And I don't know if I did."

"You have," she whispered, no longer able to contain all of this energy inside her. She wrapped her arms around him like she was an octopus, and he was her last meal. "You absolutely have. You've done so much good."

"You don't know the bad I've done," he whispered tightly.

"I know whatever it is—and you can tell me when you're ready if you ever want to—but I know that your good far exceeds the bad."

"You act like I'm a prize, Edi." He ran an agitated hand through his hair. "I'm not. My mom walked out on me. My dad didn't even stick around to meet me. My sisters got rid of me and never looked back. They didn't even come to help with our nana's funeral."

His voice was raw, and Edi blinked back tears. She ached for him, and in that ache, she let go of some of her own so that she could help to carry some of his burden, even if only for a little while.

"I got you," she whispered, still holding him tight in the May Bell foyer where anyone could see them.

"I don't know what you see, but I'm not the man you think I am."

Edi turned him around and held his face between her palms.

"What your mother did, what your sisters did is on them. Their flaws, not yours. Their broken souls not yours. You served your country. And when you came home, you are serving one of the last wishes of one of your fallen friends. I've seen your kindness and intelligence and warm spirit in everything you do at the May Bell and at the ranch. Everything," she repeated, stomping her foot and pressing her hands against his cheeks so hard she could feel the cut of his cheekbones.

"You try to make people's lives easier, warmer. You googled exercises for seniors, games, ways to make it fun. I was just going through the motions. I was stuck. Feeling sorry for myself. I'd lost my daughter and walked away from a job I loved because I couldn't handle working with kids. I couldn't handle anything familiar. I couldn't cope and I gave up," she said fiercely, stroking his cheek.

"You, Ryder Lea, never give up." She gulped in a deep breath and careened on. "You, Ryder Lea, have helped me to find meaning in my life again. You've upped my game as a physical therapist and granddaughter."

He stared at her in wonder, like he'd never seen her before.

"You have the most beautiful heart," she said, poking his chest. "You inspire and terrify me."

They stared at each other, the silence fraught as if the words that still needed to be said were gathering strength like a summer storm building up over the Gallatins.

"Boo," he whispered.

She laughed and cried and threw her arms around him, again, not caring if Holly walked out of her office or the front desk receptionist returned from her break. Edi was tired of hiding. Tired of squeezing the reins on her heart.

"You also lost your husband, Edi. You're still grieving that."

She shook her head. "I feel betrayed by him. Let down. Stunned that he could walk away from his child who was struggling for each breath and not offer comfort, but I was relieved the marriage was over. It never felt like a marriage," she said testing the words for the first time. "It felt like an afterthought."

They stared at each other, faces inches away.

Edi felt like she was standing on a cliff, but instead of fearing the fall, she felt like she just might fly.

"Should we go home?" she asked wryly, because her gran's house still didn't feel like hers, so maybe she should sell it, or redecorate.

"You mentioned we had a dinner invite."

She nodded, feeling a stab of disappointment that he didn't feel like being alone with her, but she also wanted to go to dinner. Build community.

"What time?" His voice held all the sexual innuendo she'd been trying to bank.

"Six. We have a couple of hours," she invited.

"That'll do for an appetizer."

EDI LOOKED LOVED up. Her long, lean body was relaxed in the passenger seat of his truck, and a smile teased her sweet lips as she scrolled through his playlists for some music.

They'd barely made it to her bed, tearing off each other clothes, and then after they'd taken a shower together, where she'd soaped him with body wash that advertised smelling like the ocean and sea salt. He didn't know about that. He'd never had a chance to visit the ocean on either coast. Even during his missions abroad he'd never had a chance to lounge on a beach, so he'd never taken a sniff of any body of water.

He'd washed her hair, and they'd made love in the shower, which had required dexterity and flexibility that had had Edi laughing about offering a yoga class for them at her work. He'd wanted to distract her. Spend the time together instead of at Rohan's.

The conversation earlier with Cross about a business opportunity for all of them had put him on edge. It was another slap in the face about how other he was. It had thrust him back into the uncertainty of his childhood—he was going to let his friends down.

But Edi wanted to go to dinner at the ranch. Gin would be a good friend for her to have. The Telfords were his bosses so he should show. He'd figured no one could tell if anything was bothering him, but when they they'd stopped by Edi's gran to check to see if she'd eaten any dinner, she'd been in one of her piercing moods.

She'd sat up in bed, TV blaring, a piece of peanut butter and jam toast half nibbled on a plate on her lap and glared at him. "'Bout time you dropped your mask."

Edi had waited until they were in the truck and the silence continued to unravel.

"What's bothering you?" Edi slipped her hand in his that

rested in his lap. He looked down at her hand in his and then at her, before returning his long gaze to the slightly snowy ribbon of road.

He opened his mouth to say 'nothing.' He thought about who he'd been. Who he was. Who he wanted to be. And then something Jace had said regurgitated in his brain. 'No one defines you but you.' A smile touched his lips. Jace had had a lot more to say on that topic, but at that time, just as he was warming up for one of his impassioned speeches, the shooting had started and all the words except terse directions stopped.

"I thought you'd want to have dinner with your army buddy," Edi ventured, searching his features, but he was good at keeping his thoughts locked down. "Is it because he's your boss, now?"

"Just feels strange. Me at a family dinner. I didn't have family dinners growing up."

"Me either," Edi said wistfully. "My parents were always separated, off on one shoot or the other, or fighting. I think the reason their marriage only lasted for ten years was because one or both of them was always away working." She looked at their linked hands. "Huh."

"Huh?"

"Mini epiphany of sorts. I chose a partner kind of like that. Derek was often gone—working long hours, on call, traveling to present a research paper."

"And you want a man who sticks around."

"Doesn't everyone?" Her smile was luminous in the lights of his dash. "Well, I can't speak for men," she said quietly, "but I bet a healthy portion of women want partners who stick around."

Her expression invited him to smile so he did. The one he'd practiced as a kid so no one would know when he was hurt or scared or hungry.

"What's bothering you?" She touched his cheek, her fingers long, slim, gentle. "Gran picked up on something. Interesting that she can be so astute sometimes and yet scattered at other times." Edi's voice was sad.

He shifted in his seat. She knew him a little. Wanted to know more. He wasn't sure how he felt about that.

"Ryder, we don't have to go. You can text Rohan and tell him whatever you want, make an excuse. If you'd rather be alone…"

"I don't," he said quickly. Not sure what he wanted but alone with his head like this wasn't good. "It's a lot," he finally said. "Being back. It sometimes hits me."

She waited for more.

He couldn't believe he'd said that much.

"Can I help?" she asked in a whisper as if she wasn't sure she should make the offer.

"Being with you soothes me," he admitted, and the way her eyes shone felt like a gut punch. He was going to hurt this woman. He felt it in his bones. He'd disappoint her.

But maybe he could learn to change. Maybe Jace had

been right. Only he could define himself.

"I'm stewing," he admitted, and once he did that, the words kept coming. "More than usual." He winced at that admission. "Got some things to figure out."

He wasn't sure if he was ready to tell her about Cross's ask, and why he couldn't participate. And how pathetic for her to know that he'd created college funds for his nieces and nephew who he'd never get a chance to meet.

No. He was better on his own.

"I'm a good listener, Ryder. You can bounce ideas off me," she said. "You've certainly been free with ones about exercises and activities for the May Bell clients."

She smiled, inviting him to share their common experience, but he was trapped in his head.

The silence felt snarled. Awkward. He had no idea how to bridge it. Usually this part was easy. He was the good-time cowboy. The charmer.

That was all.

Edi played with the charm dangling from his rearview mirror.

"This feels like special—handcrafted. I think it has a meaning, perhaps a family charm," Edi mused, holding it in her palm. "There's etching on the back like it was made for someone and has a message, not just an unusual medallion with a charm sold in a jewelry store."

Her words made him feel itchy. "It's Calhoun's mystery. Not mine. That was the deal. We each got a task and carried it out. No sharing. No switching. And Calhoun's somewhere out there. He'll come when he can, but he was worried enough about making it back that he asked me to cover."

One more person he couldn't let down.

"It must be awful not knowing," she whispered.

He turned off at the now familiar country road that led to the ranch's entrance.

"It is, though I should be used to it." He ran an unsteady hand through his hair. It trembled and he shoved it back into Edi's hand and squeezed. "Still need a haircut."

"I don't know." She'd angled her body toward his and smiled up at him, running her fingers through his hair. "I like it shaggy. Very sexy. I love how silky it feels when I'm naked and you're kissing me."

His foot spasmed off the accelerator, and the truck rolled to a stop. Edi's peal of laughter made a crack in the gloom that had enveloped him since Cross's proposition.

"That was a little too easy, Cowboy."

That's right. He was a cowboy now. With their linked hands, she brushed against his growing erection.

"Pretty predictable." He laughed ruefully.

"I like that," she said happily. "I love that you're so sexual. I've denied that part of myself for a long time."

Edi drew her knees up to her chest. "I was never comfortable with my body. Even when I got into exercise and physical therapy, I thought of my body more as a tool, not for pleasure."

He listened, weighed her words. They both had family issues that weighed them down, and for once he didn't feel quite so alone.

"You've made me look at myself, look at sex…at making love…" she tasted each word "…differently."

"I'm glad," he said in the biggest anticlimactic statement this winter. He navigated the last turn onto the ranch. He'd plowed all the way down to the road this morning early, but the wind had picked up creating some drifts. "Our team leader, Jace, the soldier who died, he said that no one can define you but yourself. He really believed that. He believed that you could be whoever you wanted to be. It just took courage and determination."

This was the tricky part of the road—not exactly hairpin turns, but there was some serious elevation on the part of the ranch where the main house was as it was in the foothills of Copper Mountain.

"Do you believe it?"

"He did."

"Maybe that's the first step: believing," she mused.

He crested the last turn and instead of parking his truck down by the first set of bunkhouses, where he was, he pulled into a spot by the front door of the sprawling house. Cut the engine. It felt weird to take up a family parking spot, but he didn't want Edi to have to walk a quarter of a mile in the breath-stealing snowy night.

"Takes more than that." He fiddled with his key chain—

a copper coyote that Rohan had had a local artist make for all of them. She'd even made one for Jace, and they were going to put it on his grave marker when they were all together in May and their tasks completed, God willing.

"But belief is the first step," Edi said firmly. "Then the action plan. I bet you're good at that."

"Not good enough. I...I should get you inside."

"We have a moment before we Popsicle."

He looked into her eyes. God, they were beautiful. Charcoal now, but full of stars. Each moment with her felt brand new.

"Not as good as I need to be." His palm closed over the coyote charm.

"Yes, you are," Edi said. "You are a man who will always do his best to rise up and bring his best."

"Some days my best isn't good enough," he admitted. "I was supposed to be with Jace on the mission, the one where he died. I got benched because I...well I...I was on a different base, reporting on something I can't tell you and helping on a project I can't tell you about."

He expected her to make a joke or say something light, but she faced him, expression serene, gaze steady on him, listening.

"I met a woman at a Mexican restaurant a short distance from base. Hot. Definitely up for some fun. It was one night. I didn't know who she was, and I didn't ask."

He saw Edi smile, but she might as well know the man

he'd been.

"Sex was always casual and fun with me. I didn't ask a lot of questions, and I made it clear I wouldn't be around in the morning. It was how I lived. What worked with who I was."

"I think it was more that it worked with your lifestyle then," Edi said slowly as if thinking it through. Of course she did. She was smart. "Quick, anonymous hookups were practical, easy for a soldier who traveled, but now you're making a home, creating a career as a ranch hand."

He opened his mouth to correct her. He was going to be a stock contractor, travel a lot, but she likely wouldn't know what that was, and he didn't want to explain now. He wasn't ready to let her go. Not. Yet. She filled a hole in him, hell, holes he didn't admit to having, and she felt essential to just taking his next breath.

"Who was she?"

"Base commander's daughter-in-law. His son's wife, and I didn't know she was married. She came on strong, and I didn't object. Bought her a margarita, talked outside on the patio for a bit. She asked if I had a hotel room, and next morning she was gone, and I was getting hauled up, threatened, lots of testosterone and posturing, but I had a lot of witnesses in my favor so I was just sidelined, then sent out on a shit assignment to teach me to keep it in my pants. When I got back, Jace was gone."

Edi stroked his arm as the engine popped and clicked as it cooled.

"I know it's not my fault, technically," he said—he'd had to talk to the army shrink about the incident, and he'd hated that humiliation, but he'd done it because Jace would have.

"Survivor's guilt is pervasive and persuasive," she said thoughtfully. "There are so many little inconsequential pieces that can make up a tragedy, and so many are out of our control, but then our ego takes over, makes us larger than life."

He wondered if she blamed herself for something going wrong with her daughter's development. Probably. And here he was selfishly focused on himself and his own shortcomings.

He kissed her lips quickly and pulled back. "Let's get some dinner."

He got out of the truck and rounded it even as she slid out and caught his hand.

"Was that what was bothering you on the drive up after you spoke with your friend Remy, survivor's guilt?"

"Yes, and no," he admitted, pausing before he grabbed the large metal T that served as a door knocker.

"That's conclusive," Edi said briskly, and even he had to smile.

"Cross wanted to talk to me about an investment opportunity. He and Rohan and Huck. Rohan has some rugged forested land that's part of his ranch property And there's more that's adjoining that's going up for auction at some point. He and Cross and Huck have been talking about turning it into some kind of a survivalist course for bored high-tech and business guys with a lot of money and attitude but little sense. Thinks it could be a high-end, badass weekend retreat winter and summer."

She stared at him in awe. "Wow. That sounds amazing. That sounds like it could take off since you'd want the area to remain rough. There are some high-end resorts and vacation packages in Montana, and I heard there's a zip-line and ropes course somewhere in the mountains on the way to Bozeman, but nothing like that. What's wrong? You don't like the idea?"

"No that's what's wrong. I love it."

Edi frowned, not understanding, but before she could hit him with another question, the front door swung open. Rohan stood there, open beer in hand that he shoved at Ryder. "You do realize we got a Ring camera, and we were all waiting for you to knock but no knock, you were just staring into each other's eyes like newborn calves, and we were all waiting for the show to begin."

Ryder flipped Rohan off, made a monster face at the Ring camera, and handed the beer back to Rohan. He took Edi's hand and pulled her inside what felt like a lion's den.

Chapter Thirteen

EDI ROLLED OUT a ball of dough using a vintage rolling pin, which had until a minute ago been hanging on a buttery-yellow wall in a charmingly rustic kitchen that she thought would be considered farmhouse rustic chic. She, Gin, matriarch Sarah Telford and Petal rolled the dough on a floured massive butcher-block kitchen while Ryder and Rohan washed dishes, pots and pans and his sister, Riley, put them away. Rohan's dad and brother Boone went outside to do one final check of the livestock and ensure that the horses in the barn were tucked in for the night.

Ryder had offered to do it—apparently it was part of his usual duties, but Taryn had waved him off with a smile, saying he needed the quiet of the barn after the boisterous family dinner. By his smile and sparkling eyes, and the way his wife, Sarah, pinned him with a look, Edi suspected he was joking.

She'd never been at a dinner like this one. A large, extended family, clearly close, and enjoying each other. Everyone pitched in without being asked. The eldest son, Witt, was a surgeon at the hospital, and he'd been called in for an emergency case. His toddler son had clung to him like a monkey, while he'd been shoving into his boots and coat to leave, and Rohan had scooped the kid up into spy airplane mode to go upstairs and watch Daddy leave from 'the big spy window.'

Aria would have been the little boy's age, but instead of feeling the devastating heaviness that had made acting normal around babies and then toddlers painful, Edi had been able to enjoy the moment of a little man missing his daddy, and an uncle stepping in to comfort him.

The conversation at the table was lively. She'd expected to sit next to Ryder and for both of them to be observers, but instead she'd sat next to a very chatty, and very pregnant with twins, Miranda, one of Rohan's two sisters-in-law who'd quizzed her about her job, thoughts on leaving Seattle and settling in Marietta and what type of supplies and activities and excursions she thought the residents of the May Bell would enjoy.

Riley had immediately offered to organize some regular musical performers and even offer musical classes—she'd loved the drumming on yoga balls story and had demanded to see pictures, which of course, Ryder, documenter of all, had. Then Riley had run downstairs to grab a yoga ball for Ryder to demonstrate. Then she'd pointed a fork with a slice of meat loaf at Ryder, who after finishing a drum solo, had sat across the table from her.

"You've been holding out on us." She'd narrowed her eyes. "We have quite the collection of yoga balls in the basement that's once again been converted into a playroom since we're all squeezed in the main house this winter. Family concert after dinner."

"After baking sugar cookies for the Valentine's party next weekend," Petal had reminded her, eyes shining.

And that had prompted a boisterous discussion of the events at Miranda's annual Valentine's open house at her boutique in the Graff Hotel.

"My last one as owner," Miranda had mused sadly, "but with four kids soon and a busy husband and Petal starting high school next year, I'll be plenty busy on the ranch and volunteering at the school."

"You can also volunteer at the May Bell with me, Lucas, Arlo and Parker. You can bring the twins. Old people will love holding the babies."

"Your babies can be human service dogs," Ryder said, and then his eyes widened as if he couldn't believe he'd said that, and Miranda had laughed so hard she jumped up from the table saying she had to pee.

"That's a great idea," Petal sang out. "Service dogs. We could train dogs from the shelter to be emotional support animals and take them with us to Harry's House and the May Bell Center when we volunteer. I need to text Arlo." She'd jumped up from the table. "She can get Beast certified. Lydia, Edi's gran, liked him."

"After dinner," Miranda said, and Petal sat back down.

And the rest of the meal had been just as rich in conversation, the topics flying fast and turning like a careening race car, and Petal didn't let go of the service dog idea, and had quizzed Ryder about military service dogs, and Ryder had told her about Duke, and how he too would be coming to Marietta after he healed and retrained. Rohan also shared a few stories about Duke's adventures as an officer, and Lucas and Petal's eyes had been huge with curiosity, and their mouths constantly in motion as they spit out question after question like it was a competition. And they wanted to know why Rohan hadn't had a K9 officer to bring home.

And now, making a mountain of sugar cookies that they were going to cut into heart shapes that they'd freeze before the party next weekend, Edi still felt buzzy with all the conversation.

"You look happy," Ryder said, as he stored a clean Crock-Pot on the open shelves under the island near her.

She shifted so that he could access the shelf, holding her breath, wondering if he would touch her, but no. He hadn't acted as if they were a couple, which was fine because they weren't officially, even though she felt like they were.

Maybe because he's at his boss's house.

That could be, but Edi felt she was reaching for straws and that she was in trouble.

"I am," she admitted. "I feel like I'm in an alternate universe, like this is how my life could have been maybe if I'd gone left instead of right or been born to someone else, or…" She broke off not wanting to get too serious. Plus she felt Riley's gaze on her now that she'd joined the cookie-making party.

"But yes, Ryder." She strove to sound breezy. "Thank you for inviting me. I've had a lovely evening."

He cocked his head as if he weren't quite sure she was telling the truth, but then he nodded, expression serious, and stalked off without another word.

"What was that about?" Riley whispered like it was a secret.

"No idea."

"Men," Riley said like that was an answer, and since Riley had three brothers and a father, perhaps it was.

RYDER COULDN'T REMEMBER feeling so extraneous and out of sorts—not since he'd been a kid. He always stepped up, made himself useful, but tonight at this family dinner, Rohan and his dad kept telling him to chill. Relax. What did that even *mean*?

He was an employee. He should be checking the animals. Not be cooped up in the main house with the women and kids. Okay, that sounded sexist. But he needed to do something. He felt useless. Extra. Unneeded.

"How long you been out?" Boone asked, grinding some beans for after-dinner coffee. Yeah, he hadn't even let Ryder do that.

The loud noise that he'd prepared himself for stopped.

"About three weeks now." He checked his watch like he didn't know the time, the date, the flipping longitude and latitude that he found his dumb ass at.

"Ro was the same way when he got out." Boone measured out the grounds into the filter. "Restless."

"You make Special Forces sound like prison." Riley hip-checked her brother out of her way. "Was all the super-secret stuff thrilling or scary or just tedious?" She smiled at Ryder, sympathetically. "Ro won't say much about his time in Special Forces, and he hasn't even told Gin much."

"That's what top secret is, squirt." Boone shook his head at his sister. "A vault."

Ryder noticed Gin and Edi watching them while trying to look like they were not paying attention to the conversation.

"You're still making it sound like prison."

"Boone, Reid's ready for her bath and story time with Daddy." Boone's wife, Piper, poked her head around the corner of the stairs. "Actually, you have Reid and Cannon tonight because Miranda and I want to gossip and eat cookies."

"Got it," Boone said good-naturedly. "No interrogating the guests."

"I'm an employee," Ryder griped.

"And a guest tonight and fast becoming a friend, so you don't have to constantly anticipate everything that might need doing." Boone smiled as he said it, but Ryder still felt the delicious dinner harden to sludge in his stomach.

The job had been a pity hire. Take care of son Rohan's teammate, give him a job, place to stay, keep him off the ledge.

"My getting mash potatoes out of hair skills are required." Boone squeezed his shoulder as he walked past. "Hang out for a bit. Dad and I want to discuss something with you. See if you're ready."

"Of course," he said, heart kicking up in anticipation.

"You may be packing up one of your duffels a month earlier than we anticipated."

Ryder nodded, rejoicing and conflicted at the same time. They needed him. He might be hitting the road before late March or early April. He'd be busy. Needed. On the American road.

But he'd be away from Edi. And his volunteer hours would be put on hold.

Edi stared at him wide-eyed. Maybe he should have told her about putting in to become a stock contractor. It hadn't been relevant before, but now he felt he'd just blown by some imaginary line.

"How's dough rolling? You going to make enough of those cookies for me to taste-test?" he teased, feeling more energized with the sense of purpose, but also heavier because he didn't like the thought of leaving Edi. And potentially missing the Valentine's Save event careened dismay through him.

She slow-blinked and then turned away. "I...I'm not sure."

"THANK YOU FOR taking me to dinner at the Telfords," Edi said formally. It was like they were back to square one, and she was reeling with questions and doubt.

"You sure?" Ryder asked, sneaking a quick look at her as he exited to downtown Marietta. "You've gone quiet."

Again. She felt like she was on a roller coaster with him. Up. Down. Fast. Jerking to a stop. Unexpected twist that left her stomach at the last turn. Edi kept thinking about Ryder's job—Piper and Riley had explained what working with the rodeo stock meant when Ryder had joined Mr. Telford, Boone and Rohan later in the barn while she'd rolled out dough.

Sheesh it had been like a blast back in time, and yet she'd felt sick with nerves.

Handling the bulls and broncs could be dangerous.

And Ryder would be away for long stretches of time.

What would that mean for them?

Was there even a them?

The question squeezed her heart and made her feel a little sick. She primly held the large Tupperware of sugar cookies for the May Bell event next weekend.

"You've been quiet too," she accused. Had he been planning to tell her he was taking a job that was on the road?

He's said no promises.

But she still hurt.

"It's a lot," he said. "I haven't been in family situations like that. It was…" He broke off searching for an adjective.

Now her heart pinched in guilt. He was still adjusting to civilian life, and she was angry because he was going away. He'd never once indicated a future for them, and even though she'd told herself day-by-day was fine, she'd long ago emotionally jumped into a relationship with Ryder. She was in love with Ryder.

Love.

The word exploded through her like a bomb.

No. No. No.

But how could she not love him?

"Surely you and your team would socialize together," she asked a little desperately to distract herself from the revelation. When she messed up, she really jumped all in.

"Yes." He chewed on his lower lip and turned onto her gran's street. It still didn't feel like hers. She wouldn't have picked this house or any of that furniture. She also hadn't loved the penthouse condo she and Derek had bought though insisted was perfect because of the light and large balcony and views of Mount Baker and Rainier and Elliott Bay. The house in Kirkland she'd loved because it had been built and designed by a young family.

But that too was in her past.

Have I been living in the past? Sleepwalking through my own life?

No more. She had to stay present. Go for what she wanted. But what did she want?

Ryder.

But she'd have to tell him. Fight for him. But how? Edi realized she'd never fought for what she wanted. She just accepted what happened and soldiered on. Bruised but still standing.

Ryder pulled into the driveway, and her brain and body seethed with conflicting signals and desires. She wanted to be alone to process, but she didn't want to be alone. What if this were one of their last nights together?

"It's late," he said, the truck still running.

He hadn't done that before, and her heart lurched.

"Do you need time to be alone?" she asked, taking the jump.

"I thought you might. You seem…"

"Distant. So do you."

"Lots to think about."

Edi covered his hand that rested on his thigh. "I don't want to think, and I don't want to waste any time that we might have together."

Ryder turned off the truck.

"I know it's late, and you're tired, and you have an early start." She brought his hand to her lips, and kissed the tip of each of his fingers, gaze holding his before she planted a soft, lingering kiss in the center of his palm. "But I don't want to be alone."

Was she being too cringy?

"I want to hold you," she said, exposing her vulnerability and clumsiness at seduction when Ryder was so dang good at it all. "I want to be held."

It was the first time she'd asked him for anything. The first time she'd ever asked a man for something.

His gaze searched hers as if trying to divine some cosmic meaning when her need was just so basic. "Sure?"

Her soul felt naked. She nodded.

Ryder leaned across the console and kissed her sweetly. "I'm yours."

RYDER LAY ON the hard mattress, with his arms wrapped around Edi, his lips at her nape and feeling her breathe beside him.

It was heaven.

And hell.

He could feel her moving away from him, and that was as it should be, what he'd expected. What he hadn't expected was how much it would hurt. He'd known he should have kept his distance. He'd known he was reaching for the stars even as he told himself that Edi was a woman who could handle herself and her heart. She'd been clear she was only looking for fun.

I was clear too. Look where that got me.

It was time he should head back to the bunkhouse, catch some zzzzzs before he got up for his morning chores. But he just wanted to savor this moment in case it was his last. Part of him argued that Edi hadn't said anything about breaking up—as if they were a couple who could break up. He sounded like he was a teen in school mooning over the popular girl. But he'd hone his instincts to read a room and dodge or defuse trouble.

The look Edi had given him tonight when Boone had told him to hang out for a bit as he and his dad wanted to talk to him—that was a look of fear. Speculation and if not one foot out the door, it was definitely a pivot.

"You never fall asleep with me," Edi said softly.

Her breathing and the tension in her body hadn't changed. Had she been awake the whole time he'd been memorizing her body?

"I don't sleep well," he said. "Never did."

Even before years of having to be alert on one mission or another.

"You cover it up well—better than I do." Her voice was soft, warm with wonder, affection, and his heart left with hope and then doom.

"Cover what?"

"You seem so well adjusted, easygoing, and yet you are a Walla Walla sweet onion. The layers keep coming."

"No one's called me sweet." He pressed his lips to her neck, closed his eyes and breathed her in. "I'm just an onion."

He rolled over and stood up, but she caught his hand and sat up, the comforter pooled around her waist, and he couldn't help looking at her pretty, creamy, freckled breasts that he'd obsessed over for the past couple of weeks they'd been together. Had he kissed each freckle yet? He might never have the opportunity now.

"You're sweet, Ryder. Why do you run from that?"

"I'm a man," he said, not really an answer, but it should be. His brain cast wildly about for an explanation or a joke because this was goodbye. She was going to do it. Or he should, but he wanted her to have the closure so she could move on healthy and healed from her divorce after their romp of a rebound.

Her questioning gaze drifted south to his erect again dick that never seemed to accept the message the party was over.

"Duh," she said, getting up on her knees and kissing the circle of his Coyote Cowboy tattoo. All of his team had one—different places, different sizes. His was large and wrapped around his left rib cage—Copper Mountain rose up behind the coyote, and above and slightly behind, the full moon. He'd had the moon colored reddish after Jace had died. A Strawberry Moon because Jace had died at the end of strawberry season, and the fruit had been his favorite flavor of anything. Two large ocotillo cactus stood sentry on either side of the coyote. His teammates had laughed at that. Ocotillo grew in the southwest, not Montana where they'd all talked about heading.

"They're hearty, but not that hearty," Jace, Rohan and Cross—the three Montana coyotes—had teased him, but Ryder hadn't cared. He'd always loved ocotillo. The shape of them. The spines. The resilience. How they could be used to protect and to fight off predators. He'd had a hummingbird added to the top of one swooping ocotillo arm for Jace.

Her tongue traced along the branches of the ocotillo. First one and then the other cactus tat. It was not the first time she had done this, but it always made him feel weak, exposed, but he let her do it again and again.

And he waited for her to snip their invisible thread.

"Why didn't you tell me your job was going to involved so much traveling?"

They hadn't made any promises. "It didn't seem important."

She pulled away. "Not important?" She echoed his words in a whole different tone that chilled him, and even though he'd expected to be tossed out tonight. Part of him wanted to fight. Persuade. He could. But he'd be lying, right? He wasn't a man like Rohan who could offer a woman a home, family, stability. He'd come from nothing. He had nothing. No one.

Edi stood up and reached for a kimono wrap she had that was silky and deep blue and had white dandelion seeds flying across it. He'd loved to peel that wrap off her when they'd come out of the shower.

She belted the kimono tightly. Clear message. He began to dress.

"Shouldn't we talk about this?" Her voice was uncertain.

"Talk." He zipped up his jeans.

"Ummm, Ryder." The break in her voice had him pausing and he pulled on his second sock. Sucking in a breath he pulled on his long-sleeve cotton T.

"How long will you be gone? How often?"

"Does it matter?"

Yeah, he sounded like a belligerent kid when charm had always worked better. But he didn't want to play Edi. He was just so tired of trying and fighting.

I want it all.

What the hell was all?

"I took the job at the Telford Ranch to be a stock handler."

"I'm not totally clear what that is. Riley explained a little."

Of course not. She was from Los Angeles. Seattle.

"I will travel with a team during spring, summer and early fall bringing livestock to rodeos, caring for them. Helping during the rodeo. Buckin' broncs or bulls. You saw me training."

"I didn't…understand that that's what you were doing on top of that chute thingy."

"Looks like I made the bull team this season. It's good money. I can see the country." He was proud of that, but he felt empty. But he'd achieved his goal. "But don't worry. I'll finish Jace's hours. I'll coordinate with Holly." He pushed the words out with a cold finality.

Edi stepped back. Her eyes flashed with pain and shimmered with unshed tears in the golden light cast by a bridge lamp in the corner.

"That sounds like goodbye," she whispered. Her eyes searched his. "Is that what you want?"

No.

But what else could he have? He couldn't leave Edi hanging for weeks at a time. They couldn't build anything with him working and living on the road, and her here alone, taking care of Lydia, and doing her job and trying to build a social life for herself. Loneliness would consume him. And so would worry and guilt. And he'd make a mistake and get himself or someone else or an animal injured through lack of attention.

No. It was better to be alone.

Even as his soul howled like a lone coyote in protest.

He looked at her and let her see who he really was. How empty he was. And selfish like his mom accused him of. He ruined lives. Derailed plans. He was a man who should stick to picking up women in bars, charming them for a night, and promising nothing but a fun romp in bed.

His chest filled with the loathing.

"Everything I want," he said flatly, ripping the thread connecting them.

"I don't believe you," she said shakily. "You want more."

"I want to have space. Freedom. A job that matters." His voice rang out. "I want to travel and see this country without being shot at." Somehow the words sounded sarcastic even though he'd said them over and over to his teammates, to the Telfords.

"But what about…?"

"Us. Come on, Edi, we're not kids. There wasn't an us. Not like Rohan and Gin or Boone and Piper or Cross and Shane. I know Huck's married and expecting a child, but, look at me." He spread his arms wide. "Look. Nothing about me screams family. Nothing."

She notched up her chin. "Liar."

"What?" He reeled under that accusation.

"You're lying to yourself and who said I wanted a family anyway?"

"You did," he said. "With every touch. With every look. Every action. You did. You're not the hookup kind. That's all I am."

He should say he was sorry, but he didn't regret a moment with her. But he hated hurting her, and he'd known he would.

She squared her shoulders. Her beautiful eyes glittered.

"You don't know everything about me, Ryder. You don't even know yourself, but you keep on running. It's great exercise and will keep you in tip-top shape so you can dazzle the next babe in the bar looking for a quick hookup. Look for a tan line where her ring should be next time."

And as she spoke, she propelled him toward her front door, which she opened, then she shoved him outside and slammed the door. He stood freezing and stunned on the small front porch, no boots, no coat, no keys. The door opened and Edi tossed his coat at him. Keys and gloves in the pocket.

"Edi." He felt compelled to what, argue, when he'd just been a dick so she'd throw him out because he didn't have the balls to walk away on his own?

She lined up his boots in front of him. "I'll tell the clients you send your Valentine wishes from the road."

"I'm not leaving until next week."

Why the hell had he said that? He'd set this car crash in motion. But it was happening so fast, and he felt dizzy, disoriented and sick like the first time he'd jumped out of a plane.

"Fine. You can tell them goodbye then. You're good at that."

She slammed the door, and he heard the dead bolt slide into place.

Mission accomplished.

Only Ryder felt like he'd never failed more epically.

Chapter Fourteen

THE WEEK SUCKED. Edi wasn't sure what she could have done differently or even if she should have tried, but seeing Ryder around the May Bell Center—helping with routine maintenance, helping out in the kitchen when a line cook called in sick and helping her with the residents with the group exercise classes or playing games with them in the activity room—was bittersweet.

He was the same. Charming, gorgeous and quick to smile. He gently teased the clients, encouraging them, but his quiet, respectful manner around her made her want to hit him.

And scream and sob.

"It's your fault," her gran said. "You let him get away."

"He left. He took a job that involves a lot of travel for months out of the year. He wants to travel. To work with animals. He only volunteers here as part of a promise to one of his fallen brothers."

"And you pushed him away," her gran insisted, "and he respected your wishes."

Of course it was her fault, Edi thought with a spurt of deep resentment. She was so tired of holding in her feelings or biting her tongue.

"I didn't push him away," she said with dignity. "I tried to hold on."

"He's afraid."

Her gran seemed to switch arguments midsentence.

"Ryder's not afraid of anything."

"Sure he is. We all are." Her gran picked at the napkin on her lap, her hand trembling. "All of us, Edi."

"Oh, Gran." Edi sank to her haunches, covered her gran's hands and next thing she knew she had her head in her gran's lap and her gran stroked the crown of her head.

"I'm afraid of being a burden," her gran said. "I am a burden."

"You aren't a burden," Edi said fiercely looking up into her gran's face.

"I am."

"No," Edi denied, her tears flowed freely now. "I want to spend time with you. Take care of you. You took care of me when I came to live with you, and you made me feel loved, accepted, not a burden."

"I know it's not my fault that my mind is failing."

"Oh, Gran," Edi hugged her. "Of course it's not your fault."

Just like it wasn't Edi's fault that she hadn't been petite or blonde or charismatic as a child, endlessly disappointing her mother, who'd wanted a mini-me Barbie.

"It's awful and scary, but we're in it together."

"But I want you to have a partner, someone to love." Her gran's voice shook. "You have so much love to give, Edi."

She did. She swelled with it, wept with it. Ached to share her heart.

She'd thought she'd never love again. But Ryder had stormed her defenses, and she knew she didn't want to build them up again. She wanted to rebuild her life. Have friends. Hobbies. Be a part of the community even if Ryder wasn't by her side. She'd already made progress. She'd met Gin and Shane for a glass of wine one night. They'd assumed she and Ryder were together, and she hadn't bothered to set the record straight.

That news would be obvious soon when he left for months on end and didn't contact her.

"When's he coming back?" Her gran interrupted her train of thought.

"He hasn't left yet," Edi reminded her gran tiredly. It would have been easier if he had after she'd pushed him out into the snow.

"Then there's still hope. He's running scared."

Edi swallowed her sigh. "Gran, we want different things from life. He wants to travel. Have freedom. No ties. He sees me as home and hearth and a drag on his freedom."

"Nonsense." Her gran took her hand and Edi sat back on her haunches and looked up into her gran's still-sparkling eyes. "That boy wants a family. He needs a family."

Edi thought of a few snarky comebacks but of course she

didn't say them.

"I do too," she whispered.

She washed her face in the kitchenette sink.

"Ready to paint your heart? It's time. What color are you going to choose?"

"I only get one color?"

"Maybe two if you behave."

"There's no fun in that. I'll do as many colors as I want." Her gran was back to being spunky and they walked together down to the activity room, knocking on doors as they went and gathering up a small parade of residents.

"Travel schmavel," her gran muttered. "So what? Let him travel. Welcome him back. Don't be so black and white. Who wants a man around all the time anyway?"

"I do."

"Nonsense. That spineless traitor you married was rarely around. Never heard you complain. You had weekends away with friends. Read books. Went to concerts and lectures all without that cold fish stewing by your side."

They were nearly to the activity room, and Edi could already hear some festive big-band music with Ella Fitzgerald belting something out. Another female voice joined in, and then Edi heard the click-click of drumsticks.

Ryder was here. Edi's heart leapt, but she schooled her features into what she hoped was calm as she and her gran entered the activity room. Petal and Arlo and another girl Edi had never seen before set out jars of paint, bowls of water and paintbrushes. Parker was the one playing the yoga ball drum, and her heart sank, and for a minute she thought she'd burst into tears.

She chastised herself. Everything glorious required work, and she shouldn't give up so easily. And who knew? Maybe after a few seasons of traveling the west with bucking bulls, and probably a lot of what Riley called buckle bunnies, Ryder would be ready to try to build a family.

She hoped so. She wanted him to feel loved and happy. He deserved that.

And she did too, but it was up to her to build her dreams, alone or with friends, and maybe someday a man.

FRIDAY, LATE AFTERNOON, Ryder slid home the bolt on the last pen. They'd delivered ten bulls to the exhibition rodeo in Las Vegas. Ten broncs.

"This is a big one." Rohan rubbed his hands together, looking at the line of Telford bulls happily munching, and ignoring their cowboy handlers.

Rohan had flown in joining him and Garrett Hayes. Ryder wondered how long Rohan intended to stay—the whole weekend?

"Still not sure why you're here," Ryder said. "You and your dad don't think I'm ready?" He kept his voice light, not wanting to reveal how much power the answer had.

"You're beyond ready. My dad? Not so much. That man is hands-on," Rohan said affectionately. "He and another ranch—the Wild Wind have been building up their joint bucking-bronc and bucking-bull breeding business the last six or seven years, and there's a lot of money and a lot of animals on the line."

Ryder blew out a breath. "I am aware," he said solemnly. He planned to sleep in the trailer, which he'd parked on the fairgrounds near the livestock buildings even though the fairgrounds and rodeo had security. "It's my word and future on the line as well, Ro."

Rohan nodded, slid his booted foot up a couple of fence rungs, his pose deceptively relaxed. Ryder stiffened, knowing that here it came—the real reason why he'd come along this weekend instead of staying home and celebrating his first Valentine's weekend back with his sweetheart fiancée.

He wondered how Gin had taken it. Edi had frozen him out when she learned about how much he'd be traveling, but he'd definitely put himself in the freezer and dared her to crank it up high. He'd done the right thing, but it burned more than it should. Tomorrow she and the other volunteers would be celebrating Valentine's Day and hanging up their painted hearts.

Edi had texted him a few pictures of the clients painting their hearts. They were also attaching little wooden doors on the hearts—Boone had made them. The doors were locked with a copper clasp that a local artist had made, and some of the clients were writing messages of hope.

Hope.

A four-letter word that he'd kicked to the curb in order to cut Edi loose so she could find a more worthy man.

"You're not on trial or probation with us, Ryder."

He jerked his head in a nod. He had to stop thinking of Edi. He'd done what he needed to do. Let her go like everything else in his life.

"And you're not on probation with Edi."

He sucked in a breath. "Not going to talk about it," he said through stiff, frozen lips.

"If you don't want to be honest with me, Ry, at least be honest with yourself. We take care of each other, true? We have each other's backs?"

Ryder didn't say anything, just waited to see where this would go.

"Always," Rohan answered his own question.

Belligerence looked up from his feed, side-eyed the two cowboys and snorted loudly.

"Same to you." Ryder stared down the bull, then he reached forward and scratched the bull's head, and Belligerence leaned into the touch.

"Bull charmer can be added to your long list of skills," Rohan said, and Ryder tried his best to ignore him, not look pleased by the praise.

"We probably do look stupid," Rohan speculated. "Two cowboys, having trouble letting go of being soldiers, trying to communicate. Gin and Edi would have handed out all the committee assignments and gotten the emergency phone tree in place already."

"You could try spitting it out," Ryder suggested, irritated that Rohan knew what scab to pick.

"Why don't you want to go in on the survivalist camp? You don't like the idea? You don't want to work with us? Is it the money?" Rohan's voice was laced with doubt.

No wonder. Of all them, he'd lived the leanest, although they'd only been brothers a little over three years. Still the Coyote Cowboys had been the first place where he'd felt home. Accepted.

So be honest.

"I love the idea," he said. "But I can't."

"You don't want to build a business with us? A legacy to Jace? We're naming it after Jace. Camp McBride. Keep his name, his memory alive."

Ryder looked away toward the shaft of light at the end of the open door of the livestock-holding building. Vegas was colder than he'd imagined, but there was no snow on the ground. Was Jace looking down on them? Was his spirit on what was left of his family's land in Marietta? Or was the spirit able to move around? Follow them? What would Jace think of him turning his back on his brothers because he was too proud?

Every cell in his body screamed in protest.

"I don't have much money saved," he admitted, imagining Rohan's crinkled brow, disbelieving expression. "My nana was sick when I was growing up. Left medical bills. I've got those paid off. I have two sisters. Not part of my life, but they got kids. I wanted them to have the shot at college that I never had."

"So you put all your money over the past ten years into college savings accounts?"

"There were a lot of medical bills," Ryder said drily, remembering. "I don't know my dad, but my mom, my sisters, they weren't particularly responsible people. I didn't want to be like that, so I paid the bills. Created the college savings. I got a late start on it, but they have enough for a good start in life if they choose to take it. Haven't heard one way or the other."

His eldest niece was a high school senior. The investment broker he used should have sent her the letter about the money this fall.

He and Rohan were quiet. Now Rohan knew—not only that he came from a long line of deadbeats, but even that family had rejected him, that he'd sacrificed for them, and they still didn't care.

"Dumbass."

Ryder stiffened. It was the last thing Ryder expected from Rohan. He'd always been quiet, thoughtful, respectful.

"The only reason you are *not* building the survivalist training course with us is if you don't want to."

"Of course I want to," Ryder burst out in frustration. "I

can't. I know y'all have money saved. Your brother Boone has an economics degree and he helped you invest, and you shared the info with the others, and they followed his advice."

"You always said you had your own advisor."

"I did. It was the college plan in Colorado where they lived. I dumped most everything I had in that and paying the medical bills. I knew if I survived, I'd be able to work. Do something when I got out. Live light. No idea what my sisters' kids were up against. None of them treated me well."

"You're still a dumbass. A blind dumbass."

"Thank you."

Rohan laughed and then pulled him in for a hug. "Idiot," he said in his ear, and then pushed him away. "There are so many ways to invest—sweat equity, brain power, time. You're in. In fact, you're in whether you want to be or not because you're our brother, and we're not leaving you behind. You are inside the circle whether you want to be or not."

Rohan's green eyes flared bright and determined.

"You're in. You're home. You're family."

TUESDAY AFTERNOON, RYDER arrived slightly late at the May Bell Center after driving much of the night to get the Telford bucking bulls tucked back in their pens on the ranch. He'd settled them in, caught a couple of hours of sleep before he was back on the job doing his chores even though Boone and Rohan insisted he take the morning off. But Ryder was too determined to be a man of his word to slack off and so he'd worked, had a quick chat with Boone to know he was interested in investment advice now that he had a full-time income, and had contributed his last payments into the college plans.

He pulled into the center's parking lot, seething with an equal amount of anticipation and dread. He wanted to see Edi. He'd missed her. He'd thought about her all weekend, but he'd also tried to self-talk himself out of thinking about her.

Epic fail.

He wondered how the Valentine's art party had been and anticipated seeing the colorful hearts lined up and down the beige hallway. A pop of color in a stark world. He looked down at his own offering that he'd worked on over the past few nights on the road. Rohan had brought him one of the wooden boxes that Boone had made along with one of the copper clasps the artist Sky Wilder had donated.

He had a rolled-up message and a small present. Hopefully it would be enough to get him back in the game with Edi where, this time, he'd play to win if she'd give him a shot. He was finished letting his past and fears dominate him.

His steps hastened as he rounded the corner, and then he

stopped. Stared. Nothing. The walls were still blank. He heard some music kick on and feeling rather off-balance, he walked toward the activity room. A chill stabbed his heart when he heard Edi's brisk voice call out a pattern followed by the first thump on a yoga ball. More thumps followed and the music continued along with the drumming. She'd kept the drumming exercise class.

Pleasure filtered through him, but still he hesitated.

She had this. Of course she did. Edi was trained. She was adjusting. Moving on. Without him. Would she want him to talk to Holly to see about fulfilling his hours elsewhere on the facility? Everything inside him rebelled at that idea. But the previous week had been hell volunteering with her, when they'd both been scrupulously polite. He couldn't imagine never laughing with her again, cooking dinner with her, making love if she wouldn't give him another change.

Yeah, love. Not sex. The L word had lodged deep.

"Why are you standing in the middle of the hallway?" a querulous voice demanded. "You think you're Copper Mountain?"

Ryder felt something hard hit his heels. "Move, young man."

He turned around and saw Mrs. Johanson and Edi's gran, glaring at him.

"Are you finally here to dig up the body?" Mrs. Johanson demanded, hitting him with her walker again. "A body should rest in peace, but the kin should know."

"Ahhhh." Ryder wondered why they were back to this. Maybe he was in a time loop, and he could get things right this time.

"You missed the party," Lydia accused.

"I was working."

"You broke my Edi's heart," Lydia stated. "What do you intend to do about that?"

The music and the drumming and the questions beat through his head.

"I...we..." He paused as the two women looked even fiercer.

"You broke it. You fix it. What's that you're holding?" Lydia asked suspiciously.

"It's for Edi."

"Let us see," Lydia said.

"Edi gets to see it first."

Not that he'd be enrolling in an art class anytime soon, but he'd always heard beauty was in the eye of the beholder and that the message mattered more than the execution. Time to put those theories to the test.

Mrs. Johanson banged on his ankles again.

"Ouch," he said, and she smiled. "Wish me luck," he said and walked the activity room, the two women following and muttering behind him. It was a weird parade, and before he could lose his nerve and get bruised again, he ducked inside the activity room. Edi looked up, and her beautiful eyes brightened to a gray green. Everyone stopped drumming but the music—'Here Comes the Sun,' not exactly ideal for drumming—played on.

"Are you joining us?"

"I am," he said, determination filling him. He'd been a soldier who hunted people down. And now he was a cowboy who got things done. He solved problems and cared for animals and the land. Surely, he could find the courage to hold on to Edi's heart and hand her his.

"We saved a place for you," she said softly. She pointed one drumstick toward the other end of the drum circle and there it was. A chair, a yellow ball balanced in a basket and two drumsticks. Stickers of various coyotes covered the drumsticks.

"You did." His heart warmed. "But we need two more," he said, springing into action, but Lydia and Mrs. Johanson stood outside the room looking in.

"No, you don't," Mrs. Johanson said. "Too much racket in here. Lydia and I are going to the knitting circle to knit some newborn caps."

"Gran." Edi rose up. "Are you sure? Ryder can…"

"Stop fussing. Start…living."

Edi sank back into her chair.

"You're not the boss of me yet. Not until I lose my…what are those things? The round ones? Eggs. No…"

"Marbles," Mrs. Johanson filled in. "Between us, we still have a few."

Edi choked on a laugh, and her eyes shone with tears.

Ryder tucked his personal drumsticks—Valentine's present? He'd never received one before—and crouched down by Edi.

"I missed you," he said.

"I missed you too," she whispered. Her tear-filled gaze met his.

He was conscious of the ten pairs of watchful eyes, but he didn't care. The song played on.

"I'll leave sometimes, but I'll always come back."

She nodded. "That will make the times we have together even more special," she whispered, and he searched her face, seeing that she meant it, and everything in him tunneled, settled. The music played on, and he thought he could crouch in front of this woman and look into her beautiful eyes where her thoughts and emotions shone unfiltered every day for the rest of his life.

"Aren't you going to kiss her?" someone asked.

"I am," Ryder said. "I definitely am."

He did.

"I HAVE SOMETHING for you," Ryder whispered.

"I suspected you'd been holding out on me," Edi said, her voice playful. She'd been eyeing the canvas that Ryder had put face down against the wall during the drumming class. She was not the only one waiting for the big reveal, but Edi didn't push.

She did let hope soar in her heart. And she'd done her own painting—a blue heart—the color of Ryder's eyes against a brilliant bright red background, with the sun poking over at the top, and the moon rising on the bottom. Passion. Love. Tides. Earth spinning. Life.

Quite a few of the clients and their families had arrived later in the afternoon to watch the art unveiling. Fifteen hearts now lined the hallway. Ryder had taken polaroid pictures of each artist with a device he'd found online that interfaced with his phone and printed out the pictures. The clients had loved seeing their pictures and quotes on the wall.

"What are we doing next month?" Mrs. Johanson demanded around a gingerbread cookie that Ryder had brought from the Copper Mountain Dessert Company.

"You'll just have to show up and see," Ryder teased.

"That means he's got nothing planned," Mrs. Johanson announced much to her daughter and grandson's embarrassment.

"Oh, I got something," Ryder said and winked. He tapped his head.

"What about your heart?" Mrs. Johanson challenged. "Too afraid to put it up on the wall."

"Not scared. Just waiting for a more romantic moment. Timing is everything. Lydia's dating tip number six, I think we are up to."

Edi's gran preened a little. "You're getting it, finally," she said. "But you still have more to learn."

"You can share them with me the next games night at the Graff," he dared her.

"I just might."

Two blonde teen girls walked down the hallway and looked startled to see what amounted to a party in the hallway.

"Hi." Petal handed each of the girls a punch and Arlo handed them a gingerbread cookie and a napkin.

"Which grandma or grandpa is yours?" Petal asked as if she were the hostess of the party, and Edi was so grateful that the teens were really enjoying their volunteering and were already signing other students up for shifts to play games or just talk or do a craft or take a walk once the weather warmed. They'd also met with a high school advisor to get the student volunteer club approved.

Ryder had done this. She looked at him, and he smiled at her, and the rest of the hall and the people faded as she lost herself in his warm gaze and beautiful blue eyes. He was definitely worth fighting for. Definitely worth any risk. He was the keeper of her heart, and she intended to keep and cherish his.

Ryder, oblivious to her swelling emotions, picked up the last picture, nailed the hook onto the wall and carefully attached the canvas and artist's picture and statement.

"Taaaadaaa. What do you think?" he asked no one in particular, as he eyeballed the art collection. There was a smattering of applause, but most of the clients and their families were focused on each other and their pictures.

"Excuse me," one of the blonde newcomers spoke during the lull in conversation. "I'm Jessa Lea, and this is my sister Melanie, and we're um looking for my ummmm uncle. We heard he volunteers here during the afternoons."

"Lea?" Petal sounded puzzled. "That's Ryder." She pointed, just as Ryder tucked the hammer in his back pocket and turned around.

Edi, stunned, slipped her hand through Ryder's as he stared mutely at the two girls, his expression stunned.

"Ummmm… Hi, Uncle Ryder." She waved awkwardly and nudged her sister, who did a little wave too. "I'm Jess. This is Mel."

"Ryder."

He sounded like he'd swallowed rocks, and Edi tugged him a little to close the distance, just as Jess linked arms with her sister and walked to him.

They stared at each other and Edi felt a sob warring with a shout of happiness to escape.

"Hi," Ryder said, his smile a little awkward, but still warm. "You found me. I didn't think you would."

"My mom never said she had a brother. And then I got a letter in October from a lawyer saying that I had a college fund."

"Me too," Mel piped up and then ducked behind her sister, but peered out at Ryder, looking so young, and curious and hopeful that Edi's heart felt like she was bleeding out.

"I wanted to meet you and thank you." Jessa drew herself up even taller than she already was, and she stuck her jaw out in a way that reminded Edi of Ryder when he was doing something that had to be done. "I wanted you to know that your money hasn't been wasted. I got into the University of Colorado on a merit scholarship, and with the money you set aside for me, I won't have to take out any loans as long as I keep my GPA above a 3.0 and do work-study, which I will."

"That's great," he whispered. "Congratulations."

"I wasn't sure I was going to make it to college—well, I was determined to go, but it was going to take a lot of years and part-time study, but now I can go and really focus on my studies. I want to be a surgical nurse and then later a nurse anesthetist."

"I'm going to apply next year," Mel said quietly. "I want to help teens. I've been volunteering at a teen shelter, and I want to become a therapist or social worker."

"Wow," Ryder breathed. "That's awesome, you two. You look like Michelle," he said.

"Yeah. We hear that a lot," Jessa sighed. "I don't know what's up with my mom. She's weird about some things. She doesn't know we're here. We told her we were going on a camping trip, but we wanted to meet you and thank you and…" She paused as Mel whispered in her ear. "Yeah. We wanted to meet you and you know, see if we could, ummmm, maybe keep in touch. If you'd be down with that."

"I'd love that."

"The lawyer said you'd been in the army, and he didn't know when you got out so we've been googling your name trying to find you, and an article pinged finally in the *Marietta Courier* about a new volunteer program at an assisted living facility that linked teens and local businesspeople and artists with the residents here. You are the coordinator."

"I am?"

"That's us," Petal and Arlo sang out. "We wanted some press so we started a TikTok and other social media. We're applying for a grant for our high school club so we had to show community engagement, and you look hot playing the yoga drums."

"I what?" Ryder sounded off in disbelief while Arlo and Petal fist-high-fived each other and made the exploding sound and Parker rolled his eyes.

"Are you like an artist?" Jess asked.

"No," Ryder said. "I'm a cowboy. I work on a ranch and volunteer here."

"My boyfriend's on the junior rodeo circuit. He has a scholarship to University of Nevada," Mel said. "But I'm only applying to Colorado schools because I don't want to be in debt all the time like our mom so Cody and I will likely be…" She drew her finger across her neck.

Edi smiled at the melodrama. "You never know," she

said. "Distance and romance can still work if there's love and a willingness to work at it."

She felt Ryder's gaze on hers, and she squeezed his fingers. "All good things take time and effort and a willingness to compromise."

"We're going to the ranch tonight," Edi said.

"We are?" Ryder asked.

"Kick-off of the stock contracting and rodeo season, and I was invited," Edi teased, hoping to lighten the mood because Ryder was definitely struggling to absorb this moment. "Jess and Mel, we'd love for you to join us. There's always room, and we are bringing a group from the May Bell Center so it's going to be quite a party. Other teens will be there as well helping and enjoying the barbecue."

"We'd love to come," Jessa said. She still stared at Ryder. "So can we call you Uncle or do you prefer Ryder or…?"

"Whatever you want."

"What I'd like to know is why Mom is so weird she wouldn't tell us about you, but I supposed all the family drama will require years to unpack so it can be a story for another day," Jess said.

"Good thing I've been doing a running start so when I graduate and get to the University of Colorado, I'll already be a junior in college and will learn all about psychology so I can head-shrink Mom and anyone else, free of charge. Just wait 'til I get into my master's program."

"I'll sign up," Ryder joked, and then Mel, who'd clung

to her sister, launched herself at Ryder and hugged him and burst into tears.

His eyes rounded and he patted her back and whispered that it was fine, and even he too was tearing up.

"She's the drama queen," Jessa said, "just in case anyone was in doubt."

She took a bite of her cookie, wiped at her eyes a little and then Edi introduced herself.

"Are you my aunt?" Jessa asked.

"No," Edi said, quietly, wishing she could say 'not yet,' but it was too soon. She and Ryder hadn't begun to talk about a future.

Baby steps.

But life was short, and she knew her heart.

"Like never or like maybe someday?"

"Definitely someday," Ryder said, over Mel's head, his jaw angled out like it did when he was making a point.

"Good to know," Jessa said. She sized Edi up, looking at the scrubs. "Doctor? Nurse?"

"Physical therapist."

"I want to hear more about that."

"First we have to finish our art opening party," Ryder said. "And then a family dinner at the Telford Family Ranch."

"I THOUGHT I was never going to get you alone," Ryder complained sitting next to her on her bed.

Jessa and her sister were in the guest room, already crashed out from their long drive, dancing to the music at the ranch and trying repeatedly to ride the barrel on springs that Boone had set up in the arena with a bunch of mats underneath. Even Edi had tried it, and she'd managed to stay on all of four seconds.

"I want a rematch, when all my bones go back in correct alignment," she'd complained lying flat on her back until Ryder had helped her up.

"We're alone now." She stilled his hand as he started to get up. "I want to see your painting," she said. "I do. But I want to know how you are. Big day meeting your nieces, knowing that they want to keep in touch. The door's open."

"Yeah," he said. "It is. I don't want to go behind Michelle or Mia's backs but Jessa's eighteen. Mel will be eighteen end of the summer. They can make their own decisions then."

"We'll cross that bridge when we have to."

"I like that," Ryder said. "We. I've always been an I."

"Me too. Even when I should have been a we."

"I want it all with you, Edi." He traced her lips with a finger. "I want to be a family with you. I want it all. Marriage. Home. Kids. Either our own we can adopt like Rohan and Cross did, and if we are blessed with a baby and something happens, Edi…" he shifted to his knees "…I promise you, I will never leave you alone. I would never walk away from our child if they were sick or hurt. I would never not hold them or love them and be with you on any leg of the journey. Good or bad."

"I know," she said. "It's not in your nature to abandon anyone—not family, not your team, not your co-workers. You're a wonderful man, Ryder. The best. A keeper."

"So you're keeping me?" He smiled his special smile, but there was a hint of anxiety that she'd happily ease for the rest of her life.

"Forever," she promised.

They kissed. A sweet kiss at first, tender, emotional, and Ryder's heart soared, but before passion could interrupt, he pushed off the bed, and feeling hopeful as well as overexposed, he brought the canvas to Edi.

"Close your eyes."

She did.

He handed her the canvas. She opened her eyes. The heart was the same shape as the others, but the paint was thick, swirly, greens, browns, grays, a little black and then a hint of yellow. The background was gold with hints of warm orangish pink.

"Mud?" she teased and bit her lip to keep from crying and laughing at the same time. This man. Her man. So strong and sweet.

"I wanted to capture the color of your eyes. This is what I see when I look at you Edi. All the colors, and the sunrise every day."

She cried, and he showed her how to open the box in the heart.

She read the message.

"I want to be your forever family."

She nodded and threw herself in his arms and he held her, and she felt her heart beat against his and every painful thing that had happened to her—every loss, every rejection, every betrayal—settled just a little bit more, faded.

"There's more," he said. "I thought you'd run for Copper Mountain if I bought you a ring, but I wanted to give you something to remind you of me when I'm on the road."

"That's so like me to forget you." She laughed.

"Still." He brought the necklace with the two charms on it. One was a gold heart and the other was a small seated coyote, head back, mouth open.

"Ryder, it's so sweet. I love it."

He put the necklace on and closed the clasp. Her fingers lightly touched the charms.

"I have nothing for you."

"You've given me you," he said, his voice rough as he choked the words out around the emotion. "You're giving me a family. A home. A place to belong and a purpose. A new way of seeing the world. You, Edi Martin, are all I'll ever need."

Epilogue

"Kai." Ryder held Edi's scrubs up to the canine's nose. "Find."

He held the harness and Kai—short for Coyote, the name that Calhoun had chosen earlier for the former Duke while he'd been rehabbing and retraining in Texas—quickly walked down the hallway of the May Bell Center. They'd been playing 'find the person' for a week now with a few of the residents, but this was a tougher test as Edi's scent was all over this part of the center. Still Kai didn't hesitate. Instead he beelined down the stairs to the lobby where Edi crouched behind the front desk.

"You are so brilliant." She popped up and lavished the dog with affection and a jerky treat.

"What about me?" Ryder asked.

"Did you know where I was?" She laughed at him.

"You are not very creative at hiding," he teased.

"Just because I didn't want to crawl in an air vent like you did last week." Edi shrugged.

"It's a test. Not everyone who's lost is going to pop up like a Jack-in-the-box when they're found. You're supposed to wait for him to alert."

"I'm just excited," Edi bubbled. "And nervous."

"Just be excited," he said softly, unable to resist pulling her into his arms. Kai, finally alerted and looked at Ryder expectantly.

"Get your own, mate," Ryder said, but snuck him another treat.

"We could get a dog," Edi said as they walked outside into the May Day sunshine.

They'd talked about it. Ryder had picked up Kai two weeks ago. Ryder had taken time off to drive to Texas, work with Kai and the trainer for a week before Edi had flown to Austin and they'd driven back together.

"I put in our application to adopt," Ryder said. "The Telford Ranch has ranch dogs, but with the business that we are going to start, a few ex-military dogs would work well. The trainer liked the idea too. And Kai's been good on the ranch. He stays with me and doesn't bother the bulls or the working dogs."

They linked hands and walked down the street.

"You don't want to drive?"

"No, it's a beautiful day," she said. "And I thought walking would settle my nerves and Kai needs the exercise."

Since Kai ran with him every morning and then in the evening with him and Edi after work, Ryder felt neither he nor the dog were slacking off.

"When do you want to tell Lydia our news?"

He saw her swallow, and he could feel her tension return.

"Baby, whatever happens is going to happen." He pulled her into his arms and held her close. She buried her face in his neck. "We should let ourselves experience the joy whenever we can."

"I know. I'm just scared. What if…"

"Then we'll deal with it together."

"I know," she whispered, her arms wrapped around him.

"I'd never leave you or our children. Not ever."

She nodded, and even though he was aware of time passing, he just held her on the neighborhood street, letting the late afternoon filter down on them. Edi smelled like lemon verbena, and her abdomen had a slight softness to it that he savored.

"I think I'm going to be one of those men who obsessively touch their woman's stomach as you grow. Peanut will never get any peace."

"I never should have told you that the baby was the size of a peanut."

"She's a raspberry now, and next week she'll double in size, and she'll still have a tail. I'm going to call her tadpole and then frog."

"She, huh?" Edi straightened away from him, and went to wipe her eyes, but he was there first with his bandana, gently wiping away the tears.

"She feels like a girl. I can feel so much life in you, Edi."

"My cowboy." She laughed. "I'm so emotional lately," she admitted.

"Hormones heighten your emotions. That's a good sign, until you start throwing things if I don't bring you ice cream at three in the morning, which will be tricky without an all-night grocery store."

She slipped her hand in his and they started walking toward the medical center where she had her first OB-GYN appointment. Ryder felt like he'd made the right decision switching to working the Montana rodeo circuit. The money wasn't as good, but he was home for a few days most weeks.

"I'm sure you'd find a way," she said. "But last time I didn't crave weird food, but I was very heightened sexually."

"I can definitely handle that."

Edi laughed, and they walked the rest of the way to the appointment, Kai, with his service dog vest that was so much lighter than the Kevlar vest he'd had to wear on missions, on his six.

Edi stopped outside the office.

"I love you," she said. "Whatever happens."

"I love you too," he said. "And I'll love raspberry no matter what. Should we get married?"

It wasn't the first time he'd mentioned it. Seeing Rohan and Gin marry on the ranch during spring break had pushed marriage to the forefront of many of this thoughts, but before he'd thought of a romantic way to propose, Edi had had a 'vivid dream,' and she'd woken up in the middle of the night convinced she was pregnant and had paced the floor of her gran's house that they'd recently put on the market so they could rent something. They'd bank the proceeds for Lydia's future medical needs.

By the morning they knew for sure and Edi had alternated between sheer joy and terror. Ryder had bought a ring, and Edi had made a doctor's appointment.

"If we hear a heartbeat, we'll tell Lydia tonight at dinner," Edi said, twisting her fingers together.

"Okay," he said. The ring felt like it weighed a hundred pounds and was made from lava. He wanted to drop to one knee now and propose so she'd know that he loved her no matter what, baby or no baby.

But he could feel the baby's soul, and he wanted his daughter to know that she would always have a father, always be cherished and loved, and he didn't want to wait another second.

But Lydia would want to be a part of the proposal too. Not like she hadn't been dropping hints, and he'd snuck her out one afternoon to visit the jewelry store to help him choose.

Heart in his throat, he took both her hands in his.

"I love you," he said. "You make me feel totally loved and accepted and you've made my life complete, Dr. Edi Martin."

Out came the bandana again. "Pretty sure that means there's a heartbeat," he said softly, as they entered the office.

After ten agonizing minutes of waiting, Edi was lying down on a table and had gel smeared on her lower abdomen.

Ryder sat beside her, crawling out of his skin, and Kai rested his head on his thigh. Ryder had seen Kai do that with Calhoun when he needed comfort and with one hand in Edi's and the other stroking Kai's silky head, he held his breath as the doctor put the Doppler on Edi.

A swishing sound filled the room.

"Congratulations," the OB said.

Edi burst into tears and the doctor, because of Edi's history, used a portable ultrasound to 'give them some peace of mind.'

"You're at least ten weeks along. Your fetus looks…"

"Beautiful, and she's the size of a prune." Ryder couldn't contain his joy, and if Edi kept crying, he was going to fall apart and join her. "I know. I googled."

The End

If you enjoyed *The Cowboy Charm*,
you'll love the next books in...

The Coyote Cowboys of Montana series

Book 1: *The Cowboy's Word*

Book 2: *Marry Me Please, Cowboy*

Book 3: *The Cowboy's Christmas Homecoming*

Book 4: *The Cowboy Charm*

Available now at your favorite online retailer!

More Books by Sinclair Jayne

The Misguided Masala Matchmaker series
Book 1: *A Hard Yes*
Book 2: *Swipe Right for Marriage*
Book 3: *An Unsuitable Boy*
Book 4: *Stealing Mr. Right*

Bear Creek series
Book 1: *Lighting Up Christmas*
Book 2: The Christmas Blueprint

Montana Cowboy Rodeo Brides series
Book 1: *The Cowboy Says I Do*
Book 2: *The Cowboy's Challenge*
Book 3: *Breaking the Cowboy's Rules*

The Texas Wolf Brothers series
Book 1: *A Son for the Texas Cowboy*
Book 2: *A Bride for the Texas Cowboy*
Book 3: *A Baby for the Texas Cowboy*

Smoky Mountain Knights series

Book 1: *A Country Love Song*

Book 2: *The Christmas Sing Off*

The 79th Copper Mountain Rodeo series

Book 3: *Cowboy Come Home*

Holiday at the Graff series

Book 1: *Halloween at the Graff*

Book 4: *The Giving Hearts*

The Wilder Brothers series

Book 1: *Seducing the Bachelor*

Book 2: *Want Me, Cowboy*

Book 3: *The Christmas Challenge*

Book 4: *Cowboy Takes All*

Hot Aussie Knights series

Book 2: *Burning Both Ends*

Sons of San Clemente series

Book 1: *Crushed*

Book 2: *Wrecked*

Book 3: *Broken*

Available now at your favorite online retailer!

About the Author

Sinclair Sawhney is a former journalist and middle school teacher who holds a BA in Political Science and K-8 teaching certificate from the University of California, Irvine and a MS in Education with an emphasis in teaching writing from the University of Washington. She has worked as Senior Editor with Tule Publishing for over seven years.

Writing as Sinclair Jayne she's published fifteen short contemporary romances with Tule Publishing with another four books being released in 2021. Married for over twenty-four years, she has two children, and when she isn't writing or editing, she and her husband, Deepak, are hosting wine tastings of their pinot noir and pinot noir rose at their vineyard Roshni, which is a Hindi word for light-filled, located in Oregon's Willamette Valley. Shaandaar!

Thank you for reading

The Cowboy Charm

If you enjoyed this book, you can find more from all our great authors at TulePublishing.com, or from your favorite online retailer.